u/u

Black American

1st ed.

f u vg dj

35¹

367323592ℓ

25-d

THE MAN SAYS YES

Also by Dan McCall | THE EXAMPLE OF
RICHARD WRIGHT

The
Man
Says Yes

DAN McCALL

NEW YORK | THE VIKING PRESS

First published in 1969 by The Viking Press, Inc.
625 Madison Avenue, New York, N.Y. 10022

Published simultaneously in Canada by
The Macmillan Company of Canada Limited

Library of Congress catalog card number: 69-15656

Printed in U.S.A. by the Colonial Press Inc.

ACKNOWLEDGMENT

The New York Times: For "Hold Fast Your Dreams" by
Louise Driscoll. Copyright 1916 by The New York Times
Company. Reprinted by permission.

For Dorothy

BOOK LS

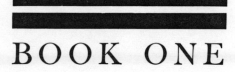

BOOK ONE

My Uncle's PR Man was laying for us in the Dallas airport. His domed straw hat sat very quietly on top of his big black head, and he had cultivated suggestions of a cool mandarin beard. As we followed him, poppidy-plop, his massive hindquarters boomlayed out from under his double-vented Madras tail like two squarish sofa pillows. Habitually pleasing the dignitaries, double-taking my wife's whiteness without a sound, Homer Brown put our matching bags in the back of a Chevy station wagon, bullet-green under its thick coat of dust. And we moved on out.

Through the colorful guts of Texas bugs splattered on the windshield, we gathered the landscape. More vegetation than I had expected, and the soil reddish. Enormous bare trees, bones of old giants, stood gray-gaunt and hacked up, planted with power towers in oil fields. But the important thing was the endlessness of God's sky.

We widely by-passed Dallas, shimmering in sunny fall-out, and after some easy chat about scotch—Homer's allergic to some brands—we lost our superhighway, the dotted center line fell away, and the pavement narrowed, split open and gravelly. Refrigerated, we hummed along prairies. Homer had asthma, wheat-harvest always brought it out, and in the fall his cheeks would balloon up; a doctor taught him to stick a needle for it in his thigh. Finally, on a plateau, after a traveling silence, Homer lifted his right hand from its tidy death-grip on the wheel and pointed over to the right. "There she is," he said in a high nasal whine.

We looked above a school decal on the buggy windshield, and there beyond a high silver water tower sharply reflecting the afternoon sun, there she stood in open country: a crowd of red brick buildings, my uncle's campus. Bundy (Colored Agricultural and Normal) University. Oh, Jesus.

"Now that biggest one is the auditorium. We had her put in in sixty-foah. We'll be payin' for that for some time. And beyond, there, that low-level buildin', she's the new Achille T. Washington Student Union Complex."

Ruthie said, "He's a fast worker."

"Ma'am?"

"He's got the student union named after him."

Homer Brown looked over. "Does that strike you peculiar, Mrs. Green?"

The Little One said nothing more, not having been struck peculiar.

Homer twitched his little mandarin beard, whined under his breath—pay no attention—and we drove down into a little gully and then up again, on campus. Perched by the road was a metal signpost; jutting out from it, white unlit neon tubes: BUNDY UNIVERSITY. Sign for a motel. Vacancy. Stretching out beyond, the long yellow lawns of the campus, rolling. The eyes of Texas are upon us.

And Homer pulled steadily onto Opportunity Drive. A

string of tidy brick cottages primly asserted community morality. "These are for senior faculty," he said. On the left was a large dark pond; some wind had come up to ripple the black-metal face of the water and blow slightly in the high water-grass. "That there is Freeman Hall."

That high nasal whine—Brother Homer is run by a little electric motor, and I am now checking the back of his neck for a plug.

Finally we seem to be coasting up to a large white house. In front, a long black Cadillac, its whitewalls snapped into the curb in a sharp salute. Caddy is a henchman. "This," Homer said, beginning to smile, "is the White House." His smile blossomed for our amusement. "President Washington lives in the White House."

It was large and square, one story high here at the front, with a big porch swing on the flat roof. The White House was fringed with sharp bushes, green, yellow, and one ice-blue tree at the corner; the yard dropped away so that the rear of the structure pulled herself up into two stories.

Homer Brown's mandarin beard went to twitching again, little crab claws scuttling at his lips. "Presydent wanted me to bring you by before taking you to your quarters."

Quarters? It was too much. The front door to the Texas White House opened, then the screen door. Homer said formally, "That is he."

President Achille T. Washington, smiling, radiant, came down the white walk set in the diamond-green sparkle of the lawn. Above five-nine, he looked like a halfback: extraordinarily well put together, wearing canvas shoes with high rubbery soles, black suit coat buttoned over a trim waist, shining white shirt and blue tie. His head was deep and very dark.

I opened the door of the school station wagon. "Uncle!"

"So—well—the Greens, Beaunorus and Ruth, welcome to the great state of Texas, welcome." His head buzzed with good will and administrative ease. He looked just like the last time, ten years ago. A little hearing-aid was lodged in his left ear, a cord running sharply down his neck. Squarish gold-rimmed glasses. He peered into our faces, slightly turning the hearing-aid toward me. "Well, Son, they grow them tall in California."

I stared into his big handsome white teeth, fine choppers. He was on to me and on to Ruth, my white woman. He's here, all here, power on the walk.

Homer Brown had stepped back slightly, looking at the ground in front of him. He wiggled his nose, his hands clasped in front of him below his belt. He is a huge black electric bunny-rabbit.

Archie raised his voice. "What say, Homer? You let me have an hour with these folks. Then you drop back by and take them to their apartment, y'hear?"

"Presydent, that's what I'll do."

Homer nodded at us and reversed himself clickity-clickity-blop into the station wagon.

"So." Uncle Archie was still curled around us in welcome. "We're so glad you two could come down from old New York and spend the summer with the Bundy family."

We stepped beside him on the walk. At the back of the White House there was a space down near the grass where the white boards looked black, ashy. There had been a fire.

Opening the door for us, he continued to smile. "I think you will learn something down here, you two, as well as teach."

I shuddered in the terrific dark cool of his White House. There were no air-conditioners gummed up at the windows, so apparently there was a central unit. Ruthie sneezed. When she sneezes, she does a nice dance movement. She should sneeze more. Now over here along the east wall you will notice the pleated sea-green drapes; President Washington imported them babies, pleat by pleat, from the old Bunkum movie house in Monticello. Perhaps you remember: Mr. Jefferson himself designed them and when the house lights dimmed, the curtain rose, picking up its huge pleats, and when the film was over, the curtain slowly dropped, the pleats going out, billowing cash.

"How was your plane trip?"

"Turbulence over Oklahoma," I said. "We didn't throw up."

"Good, good."

I looked at Ruth: she had, actually, puked delicately into a paper bag, and now looked at me.

"United," he said, "has given me a captain's card— nothing, really, it only means I have flown fifty thousand miles with them."

Ruthie said, "I suppose administrators have to do their penitential flying."

He moved, smiling at her, at me, at her, over to a light blue French Provincial chair. "Have some seats."

The mixed marriage glommed a low gold couch. Baby grand, black shiny wood, in the corner beside a wall shelf filled with books, gray carpet fluffy underfoot. On the shining cherrywood coffee table little glass pieces, feminine —glass slippers and glass candy dishes, delicate junk. I touched a little blown-glass rocking chair, lovely glass, poised in its dimensions, and it clicked and gently rocked under my fingers. I rocked it and watched it rock itself, te-dum, te-dum—

"So I have saved this time for you. May I offer you something to drink, kids? We have Sprite, iced tea, or perhaps something stronger. A highball?"

The word "highball" came oddly out of my uncle, second vowel dipthongized—a gentleman of parts. I said bourbon. For us both. He went out into the kitchen and I heard him cracking some ice cubes. Just beside the doorway into the family room was a massive console color TV. On the top was a little gold picture-light; it shot a white spray up into a large photograph-painting of Himself, full face in history. A color photograph that had been retouched in oils. His painted eyes stopped somewhere in front of our eyes; he had found something in the air between us to look at. Ruth was examining the absence of a hearing-aid in the portrait when the lord of the manor returned with a frosty silver ice-bucket.

"Your aunt," he said, "was so sorry she could not be here to meet you. She is in Austin at a state convention of her sorority. The sorors have elected her Texas State Treasurer."

"That's quite an honor."

He chuckled. "Oh, that woman's worth ten of me." He unlocked his liquor cabinet. "How do you all take your poison?"

"On the rocks."

"Both?"

"Both."

He bustled with close credit-card appurtenances. "I'll have some of this Sprite to take the edge off." He mixed, then came to us with the drinks in his hands—closing the distance easily between us—when there emerged from the family room a vast rumbling bag of fur. Now this was the largest cat in captivity, gray, with bright blue ice-cube eyes.

"Well, hello, Dixie."

I stepped back.

"Don't worry, son." He handed me the drink. "She's quite harmless—unless she sits on you."

In low gear the vast cat came slowly, with great tufts of dull hair jutting out like leaves. Tham-tham, paws on carpet. Holding its heavy tail low, it stalked over, crouched, and went under the piano. It had eaten on Saturday and wasn't hungry yet.

Archie leaned back in his chair. "Isn't that the grossest animal you ever saw?"

I sipped on the couch. Lovely bourbon.

"It's my wife's cat. Mrs. Washington does think highly of that animal."

Dixie was curious about the white body. Ruth was sitting there quite clearly, and finally the cat made up its mind: it came forward, softly, then sprang up beside her on the couch. Another moment of checking, and then Dixie stepped onto Ruthie's lap, took command, and two heavy forefeet fell heavily on the white woman's shoulders. The cat decided to stay and got down to the serious business of possessing her, yielding to her demandingly, like a child.

The men had kept silent, and now Archie said, "I declare."

I smiled at him. "This is only the beginning."

We watched it all for another minute and then Archie sipped his tall, diffused drink. "Our campus is empty today. But Sunday's Commencement, there'll be quite a crowd. Would you care to march in the procession?"

I indicated we would string along.

And he would find us robes.

"Then, Bo, you'll start into action on Wednesday, with summer-school registration. And"—turning to her "the Head Start kids on Thursday." He smiled. "No rest for the wicked."

We stared into our drinks. Dixie was snoring on Ruth. I was starting for the Kents on the coffee table when I looked up.

The boy was standing at the doorway into the family room, standing where Dixie had just come from. He was skinny and handsome, fine young features. But as he came to us I saw that on the right side his face had been burned; beside the ear a thin stripe of new plastic-colored skin, smooth rubber skin without pores.

I put my glass down on the coffee table. His eyes went out of focus for a second, from me to Ruth, and as he started to turn he seemed to be in pain. He was wearing a short-sleeved shirt and light blue slacks. He stood in black-stockinged feet.

"Abner," said President Washington, "come on in and say hello to these folks."

The boy turned and looked at his stockings. "Sorry," he said, "I didn't know we had company." He was very thin.

"Meet the pair I been tellin' you about. I want you to take Beaunorus's course, maybe learn something this summer."

Our boy was surly as he stepped forward. He stuck out his hand, eyes down. He stayed that way for a splitting moment and then his head turned, puppety, and he and Ruth were having a staring contest, hushed. While his hand remained in mine and Dixie the giant cat was asleep on her breast, its arms—child arms—on her neck, I glanced at my uncle: he was quite another man, rigid black in his chair, a Salem judge, no lips. A mile away in the faculty apartment, H. Brown had run down in midpassage, one foot off the floor, stopped with a needle in his thigh.

Ruthie cleared her throat and stroked the tabby back; the world began to move again.

Abner stayed only five minutes, listening, and then went back into the family room. My uncle and I talked easily; I filled him in on my mother's latest project at the Modesto Library, her finances—including the thanks for all his checks over all the years since Father died. He waved, absently. Then we talked about how Ruthie and I liked "the big city," and affectionately, distantly, he sized us up. Ruth was quiet like she is, and eventually the cat got tired of her and left to kill something it had forgotten.

Archie handed us to Homer—returning on the hour, like a station break—at the door. The Boss had requested dinner for "the three of us" over at the Student Union. We were to meet him there at six. Homer helped us with our Samsonites over to the new apartments "for junior faculty." Bouquets of livid plastic flowers bloomed on the formica blond coffee table and on top of the twelve-inch-screen TV. Honeymoon Haven: the living room opened up on the right into a kitchenette and on the left into two small bedrooms, where more hard plastic had thought its way into foliage. Homer was bustling like a bellhop and gladly took the white lady into the kitchen, where the range and fridge were brown all over.

Ruthie said, "Fine."

We showered together—just Ruthie and me—changed, and made it back up to the Student Union at six. A gold sign: ACHILLE T. WASHINGTON STUDENT UNION COMPLEX. Each letter was six inches high, bolted on its own into the red brick. The T. I wanted for my collection. In a little room just off the kitchen, Uncle was reading a Dallas newspaper. He stood up when I rattled the locked doorknob; through the top glass of the door he smiled. He motioned for us to sit down beside him at a table set for three.

Over the main course he offered us his *curriculum vitae:* high school in Houston; college here at Bundy, where he met his wife; then on up to the University of Michigan and a Ph.D. in sociology. "Always had my nose in a book," he said to Ruth, "the only one in the family. My brothers were always off fishing, and I was always under the house reading."

He had a way of immediately letting you know that the school was his life, and building contracts and Communications Arts and the discus champ buzzed throughout his arms, his chest, his head; his physical being was tuned to one station, buzzing to its signal. And he anticipated any questions about politics on the campus. Leaning back in his chair, he smiled at us. "Down here, children, Black Power means oil."

"That's Jasper there," he said, smiling up at one of the string of white faces in gold frames lining a wall of the faculty lounge. "Jasper is a real hard-drinkin' Christian." He said it with that clear sense of manipulation—Jasper's boozing might come in handy, some way, sometime—the way LBJ knows about a Southern Congressman who can get erections only on trains.

After presenting the bookstore and the snack shop, he unlocked the big recreation room. "Do you shoot pool, Beaunorus?"

I did, and we settled on nine-ball. I had a fine run of four in the second game, and after my third, a very soft shot oozing along the cushion at the foot of the table, he stood back and tapped his cue on the tile floor—applause. He took off his coat. In his white short-sleeved shirt he moved easily round the table, smiling with his big white teeth, squeaking his rubbery shoes. He saw that I could indeed play—and so he killed me. The administrative mask fell off and he was superb. After a fantastic bank-shot he said, "Lord, I'm glad I don't have to play against myself." And when the table was bare he turned to Ruthie. "Your po' hubby's just out of his league."

We hung up our cues and re-covered the table. As we left the chilly air of the Achille T. Washington Student Union Complex, I saw a sign on a little white building: COSMETOLOGY. Ruthie saw it too. And he saw us looking at it. "You see, folks, Bundy is undergoing a period of transition."

The Texas sun had gone somewhere now, and it was almost cool; we decided to walk off our dinners. He took us over to main buildings and into his office: big golden drapes on the windows and a deep walnut desk and thick carpet. All paid for. There were plaques sneezed up all over the walls, distinguished service, diplomas framed. There, in the place of honor, you will see himself in black and white shaking hands with Governor Connally; above them, presiding over life, a full-color post-office picture of old Honey Lips.

Archie turned over the folders and papers on his desk

and came up with something for us, mimeographed.

TO: *Faculty and Staff*

FROM: *Achille T. Washington, President*

SUBJECT: *Visiting Professors for the Summer Session*

I am pleased to announce that my nephew, Beaunorus Green, and his wife, Ruth, will share the summer experience with us. The Greens are married with no children, both educated at Stanford University and both members of Phi Beta Kappa. Beaunorus is presently at the Columbia School of Dramatic Arts in New York City. This summer at Bundy, Mr. Green will be in charge of our Basic Communication Program and his Mrs. will assist in Operation Head Start. I hope this material will be helpful to all of you and I know that each of us will do all we can to help in the adjustment and orientation of our distinguished colleagues.

Archie smiled. "Just wanted to make sure you had a welcome, and make it clear that you're only here for the summer." He turned to me. "Didn't want my regular liberal-arts people to think you might be gunning for their jobs."

"Not us, we're only distinguished colleagues."

He touched me on the shoulder. "Well, if at the end of the summer you two find you like it here—oh, we can talk about that later." He paused. "What you doin' up at that white school, anyway, boy? Your people need you."

"Well, as you say, we can talk about that later."

He turned to Ruth. "Now don't you let Beaunorus forget he's a colored man."

Absently she said to the floor, softly, as if she were thinking it, not saying it—the Little One smiled— "No, once you go black, you never go back."

It rocked the bejesus out of him. The Little One with the tongue of flame.

"Uhhunh," he said. He really couldn't believe the white girl had said that. Molecularly assaulted, he gazed, lost, around at his plaques and then stared at me. Grabbing grace, he snapped off his office lights.

The moment went with us as we walked across the campus and stood outside Freeman Hall and smoked.

"Well, folks, I'm proud of my university. In a few days I think you'll begin to fit things into place." He stepped on his cigarette, spraying red ashes with his toe, playing with them. "Breakfast at seven?"

I shrugged. "We'll have to get used to that."

He put his foot out gently on his pavement, to get the last piece of glowing ash. "Oh, I'm always up by five." He sighed and he was suddenly very close. "I invited you down here, I wanted to see how my brother's boy turned out. And to meet the little lady. But I tell you straight, children, you're going to meet folks here who don't like me."

"Oh?"

"You can't get through a summer down here without hearin' a lot of bad things about your poor old uncle."

"They true?"

He looked at me. Suddenly he laughed, a big one. He enjoyed it so much he repeated it to himself: "They true?" It seemed to fall into the same pigeonhole with Ruthie's remark. And to Ruthie he said, "I think I'm goin' to like you two. Yes, I think I am." He pointed across the highway to the lights in the new faculty apartments. "I hope you can find your way." He stuck out his hand. "Don't you fall in that pond now, y'hear?"

"Not tonight." We walked back in the empty Texas darkness, watching the little electric bursts of the fireflies in the long grasses of the frogpond.

Ruthie said, "They really *are*."

"Whoot?"

"*Fire*-flies."

We decided not to go straight to the crib, but roam. We talked about my uncle. The two of us, there in Texas, away from everything, taking the night air. At length we prowled around the pasture across the road, and all we could find was one black shaggy calf on the loose. It came out of air deepening into its own color and trotted down the lowland. I gave chase—"Here, boy"—and it ignored me. I haven't been good with animals since the Christmas holidays of '65, when Ruthie and I hopped for a quickie back to Europe and in Madrid I got hit by a goat. Brought in for Epiphany.

Meanwhile, sixty miles west of Louisiana, the black calf comes bouncing back with a palomino pony, me and Ruth giggly. The four of us stand around self-conscious. It reminds me of something, and as I look to her for help, she breaks out laughing. Her laughter skids around the empty acreage.

"Listen?" I say.

She listens for a long time. "Did you fart?"

"No." And we're off.

Approaching the corner of the gym, we heard stifled laughter and whispers. Like our echoes finally catching up with us. Peering around the brick, we saw two boys up on the metal ladder of the water tower. In the darkness I thought at first that it was a body they were struggling with, a body with a rope around its neck. But then it became a dummy: a straw man in an old black coat with a white sign across it. Three more people came out from behind a hedge, two girls and a boy. The boy called up to the two on the tower; there was a round of low, intense directions. The boys worked a minute more and it was done: the effigy went swinging out from the silver tower. The boys jumped down. After looking up for a moment, five figures beat it back into the night, through the bushes and trees. I waited, then went out and looked up the ten feet to the swinging effigy; printed on the sign, across the black breast: CHIPPIE CHASER. And below, a white penis— an enormously long peeled Texas banana coming out from the fly, bending majestically earthward.

Horatio Sanders, Agriculture, hands full of empty plastic wastebaskets, was laying for us on the stairs. He jumped when we came in and in the next hour, as we talked, frequently jumped. "Did I take that stencil? Yes, I did take that stencil, yes, I believe I did." (Jump.) "Was he from El Paso? Yes, he was from El Paso, yes, I believe he was." (Jump.) He had effaced his self for so long there just wasn't much self left to work with. "Did I cut off my hand in your electric saw? Yes, I do believe I cut off my hand in your electric saw. I sure hope I didn't rust your blade." (All jump.) Well, he went on up, early to bed with a Bible.

And so we unpacked. After I'd got my stuff fixed, I sat on the bed and watched her filling the dresser. Ruth, my wife, my Tigress Jewess. She'd seen me in the theater productions back there at Stanford, and she was in charge of make-up. (Little brunette head poking in the dressing-room door: "Hey, uh, do I make you up or not?") She has no talent for acting because she has an utterly clear sense of who she is.

She's not really American, and there aren't those laborious, extensively frenzied hang-ups, even though she is kind of white. In the house of her childhood there were plenty of passions, but love was not among them. Everything wonderful in her she made up on her own, on the

way. With and in between and through all the men she
slept with before me. I mean, she slept around with a lot
of men; even today they keep hanging around us, dropping
in of a midnight, insinuating claims, shared despairs and
happy hours. We got really serious, *la petite et moi,* over at
the Stanford campus in Tours, our junior year. (Just last
June in Paris a little detoothed concierge with many cats
on the rue Mouffetard told me to my face, "You don't
need to worry. We don't rent to Arabs." God*damn!*) When
we got home, Ruthie had me meet her family. Her father
wouldn't come out of the bathroom. Her big mother just
stood there looking at me; surrounded by furniture
brought over in '36 the tears slowly rolled down that Jewish lady's fat cheeks as her brain waded in my shitty color.

The problems preceded me. Making love was the Little One's way of knowing the world. Her parents told her
she was a whore and no man'd ever respect her. False, people. She never wanted to hurt anyone. Just touch them.
Just sit in soft light, saying the right things at the right
time, with an open mind and an open ear and an open
heart, and then, since everything else is open . . . well
. . . I suppose people took advantage of her lots of times,
but *she* didn't have to. Extraordinary woman, day-by-day;
eyes like enormous quantities of supernatural mornings.

I want to forget stuff, and there's a hell of a lot. What
can you do in this fucked-up country when on the street
we are Walking Miscegenation and the brothers ogle my
white meat and snowy matrons cluck and honky truck
drivers reach for steel bars? Our honeymoon, August '65.
In the motel room I flipped on the TV while she was in
the bathroom, and there was Watts flaming on our screen.

But how can it make sense? We get back from France,
and late at night on Broadway she huddles in a doorway
and I try to flag cabs in the street and the empty bastards

whizz on by me. And yet I am such a fool American. I love big cars and read *Playboy* in the Garden Supermarket while she grabs yogurt. Oh, I don't know. I just don't know. Too many times I have had to say to her, in too many places, "I do not claim emotional control."

She wanted me to store the empty suitcases.

So I got them together and fumbled off toward the storage closet in the front hallway of our quarters.

Out on the porch, on a folding chair, Zip Luper, a big man with a barrel chest. He was sitting without his shirt, sporting a pair of brightly striped Bermuda shorts. In the fall he was moving on to a college in Florida to be a football coach. "I got to take a cut in my salary," he said, "but all my life I had me a dream. 'Coach Zip.' I want to be a football coach." He punctuated his observations with a high whine, the first half of the word "shit," drawled out —"Sheeeeaaa"—you could never quite tell if Zip made it to the end of shit.

Ten o'clock I picked myself up off the porch and started back in. Zip said to me, "You goin' to cop a few Zs?"

"Yes," I said, "I plan to cop me a few."

Ruth was in bed, reading under the sheet. I heard through the window the approaching roar of a souped-up car engine and then a skidding and shooting of gravel. Zip, who was still whistling on the porch, growled. "How many times I got to tell you boys not to scatter my gravel?"

Then a car door slammed and a couple of low laughs and a brother's voice: "How you makin' it tonight, Zip?"

"Oh, purty good. These bugs like to eat me alive."

Another voice: "You know, Zip, Dr. Hamilton say if them skeeters go at you all the time that mean you got real high sexual power."

Zip, he laugh.

———————————————

A group of four faculty men stood around down by the neon Bundy sign. Homer Brown beckoned us over and introduced us around. I was invited to join them, driving little-bitty golf balls up and down the long yellow lawns. Jim Marshall, golf coach and Health Education, was a big man, even bigger than Zip Luper, honey-colored with black spots sprinkled across the bridge of his flat nose. Shoulders, a yard. He carefully helped me correct my swing and he laughed at my blunders, throwin' back his big head and showin' me his gold dental work.

We drove a good hour, us Golfers in the yellow stiff grass, and Ruthie without bra stood in her mini-dress, orange and purple, making friends with a kid she'd conjured. Back to the action here at Bundy Stadium, you just take Homer: he stand beside the ball, wiggling those sofa-pillow haunches, and he strikes down, chopping wood, and then he look high high up into the air, peering out, and that little ball it has not moved. Once, halfway down the range, I tried to chip up a little rise, and I topped it. Jim Marshall laughed at me and said privately, "Come on, Homer." I looked up at Jim and he was standing there with his mouth open like the treasure of Sierra Madre. "Come on, Homer."

We quit at six, and Jim asked us over for a drink. Ruthie bade her child good-by, and the boy went tearing off in linked parabolas over the yellow grass. Walking beside Jim, I said I had enjoyed the golf; he nodded his head and lazily swung his club. "Evra day, Bo. Evra day."

It was the second faculty cottage down from the White House. On the front step, a little white sign: THE MARSHALLS. Inside, the color TV was going full blast. Barbara Marshall requisitioned us for dinner. She was taking her time to gauge Ruth and me, but Jim just pulled out matched bottles, like six-shooters, bourbon and scotch; he placed them on the table before me, saying, "Pour your own troubles."

I did, and then in the middle of dinner the Marshalls' boy, Buddy, came in and sat down on a towel in his wet fluorescent pink and green swim suit. He had been diving for pearls in the frogpond. Jim demanded from him a mumbled little grace; the boy's pudgy fingers interlocked in a golf grip for a fast-driving prayer.

I was going to gather my woman and head home when Homer Brown rang the front doorbell. He was invited in for a drink. Jim looked back down at me. "What's the matter with you, Yankee brother? You *like* ice water?"

I stared into the used-up ice cube in my bourbon glass. I guess I will have another. Jim put Redd Foxx on the record-player, and the menfolks sat hee-hawing at the dirty jokes and looking at *Bonanza* pictures without sound on the television screen. The ladies are cleaning up, kitchenwise. Then, gathering spirits, Zip Luper and his wife dropped in with their twin ten-year-olds. Jim went out for more liquor; Barbara made sandwiches in the kitchen. The language teacher, Gladys, a skinny little divorcée, came in

and giggled at me and Ruth. Homer introduced us in his
gas-on-the-stomach way. It was the first time in fifteen minutes that he had said anything. Homer was stuck on the end
of the couch with Zip's wife, and he was having a hard time
staying awake; he sat there, his big eyes closed, his huge
mouth hanging like an open cave. Occasionally he would
shake himself and his eyes would fall open, thonk.

Jim came back in with bottles and Lucretia Strout. Mrs.
Strout had a permanent pinch, a nervous dean-of-women
pout on her face. She threw long whoops of Christian con-
spiracy at me, and I was most pleasantly profane. By nine-
thirty parents and children were running loose. The new
bottles were opened; the cowboy on television rode silently
over the Supremes on the phonograph.

Shortly after ten, Uncle Washington himself came
down. When he walked in and saw me talking with Jim, a
quick smile dropped onto his presidential lips. He stepped
back, slightly surprised, as he looked around at the
crowded, smoky room. He spied Ruthie in a corner with
Barbara, and he said, "Well now, I guess the Greens are
going to fit right in."

Jim said, "What you drinkin', Presydent?" He led Archie through the crowd and then I found myself alone
with the language teacher. She was a sweet little piece, a
miniature, in black stretch pants. Her skin was yellowish
white, and with those high Cherokee cheekbones she
looked vaguely Chinese.

Buddy and the Luper kids were tearing through the
crowd, squealing and horsing around our legs and butts. I
followed them into the back bedroom. It was very small,
with model airplanes and a ball glove and a golf bag
strewed around the bed and floor. Buddy had just put on a
pair of cordovan boxing gloves, and he was squaring
off with the taller of the Luper boys. When I bumpered

into the room, Buddy looked up at me and said officially, "This here is Beaunorus Green. From New York."

The Luper twins were silently unimpressed.

I said to Buddy, "Let me go a round with you, Muhammed."

Buddy laughed. "You're too big for me, Mr. Green."

"I'll get on my knees."

He giggled and got bashful. "I don't know. I don't kno-ow."

"Won't hurt you, Muhammed." I leaned over to the Luper boy, and he worked his hands out of the ripe purple boxing gloves. I got into them and eased myself down on my knees. "Okay, come get my ass."

I was sluggish on my kneebones. Buddy danced and poked; I held out my glove and caught his jabs—I had half a foot of reach on him. I was laughing, saying, "Kill, Bubba, kill," and Buddy was laughing and I cuffed him on the ear, and then Abou Ben Hernia let his guard drop slightly and that little sombitch clip me fine. Right on the nose, *funch!* I fell back and put one glove on the floor and felt warm liquid running on my lips.

"Buddy, what you did," said a Luper boy. He shot out of the room.

Buddy stared in disbelief.

My nose was flowing away. I cupped my hands and tried not to let any get on my shirt or their floor.

Barbara Marshall came rebounding into the room like a yo-yo, with the Luper boy wide-eyed at her skirts. Barbara shouted, "Buddy, what you done to Beaunorus Green?"

The boy cowered.

I said softly, "What he done to Beaunorus Green is—"

Barbara squinted. "Is you hurt? That Buddy, that boy of mine is always fighting."

I looked down at my red-splattered hands and tried again to be sufficiently clear. "What he done to Beaunorus Green is—"

She ran back to the bathroom and came in with her hands full of Kleenex. I swabbed around, then followed her into the bathroom; I put my head into the sink and stood dripping. Barbara hovered around me, went out for a moment, and returned with her husband.

Jim came in and said with his arms folded, "Bo, I was real sorry to hear what my boy done to you."

Bled out, I pulled myself together. I went back into the living room, where the language teacher was trying to teach Homer Brown how to do the Jerk. Poor Homer, I think we're phasing him out. Gladys had been into the liquor, and every inch of her little body was lithe, moving in reckless control. As I passed, she carefully measured me. Against my whitely wife.

Who, by this time, was up-sweet with Uncle. I watched them on the couch; his wide right hand was up at his hearing-aid. He smiled at me as I came round them, and he was saying, "I always call it the Bundy *family.* We *do* get together like a family." He patted her on the bare knee. "I hope you two will find this summer experience to be a profitable one."

When he said "you two" he was staring at her knees, and "you two" seemed to refer to them. While I was seeing that, Jim rushed up and took me by surprise. "Hey, Yankee brother, I got a little lady here wants to dance with you." Jim was laughing and he had the little language teacher struggling on his big left arm. "You come dance with Gladys, Bo."

Our record-player was now convulsed in Motown. I stared at Gladys and she was both sleek and sheepish and I wanted to make up for what Buddy had done to me. I threw myself at her. These boots are made for walkin', and we took over at the center of the floor, and she smiled. I threw her out and in, and I shimmied and then she shimmied, everything of her cutting loose. I turned, and Ruthie was watching with genuine pleasure. Mentally I said to her, "What do the Iceman do?" Mentally she responded, "He cometh, Bo-jangles, he cometh." Gladys did not hear that little conversation and she was beaming; she stuck up her chin and so we went on doing glad things to each other and when the record was finally over we fell laughing together, out of breath, wet with the room happy closed round us.

We went into the darkened kitchen. "Get me some of that Cutty Shark," she said. She pulled her hair delicately back. She was breathing little and hard. I poured a glass for her on the sink and then some for myself. Splosh. I handed her the glass and she took it and I looked down at her and she looked up at me and we looked over our rims at each other. Pretending it meant world-shit, we drank together. Then a little smile flitted across her face and she said, "You's some distinguished colleague, honey." She took my hand and cupped it on her flowered blouse and I felt the breast and the sharp beating of her heart.

Barbara Marshall came swooping, laughing, into the kitchen. When she saw us, Gladys and me, Barbara blinked for a minute and then said, "How's your nose, baby?"

"Fine, thanks, how's yours?"

Back in the livin' room-a-boom, Homer waddled forward. He touched my arm and took me to a Lady of Color. She was wearing a fur around her satin and lace dress, a fur in that heat. She was enormously wide with corky flesh, legs like tree trunks, breasts rising like balloons out from under her dress. And eying me surspiciously. Homer said, "Mr.

Green, I'd like you to meet Miss Ophelia Jones. She's chairman of our Home Economics Department."

Ophelia Jones, Madam Chairman, called her proud bosom to order, ba-*loom,* and continued to study my face. "So you're Presydent's nephew." It did not sound like a nice thing to be. Here was a hate-Archie faction. We stood awkwardly with the party swirling around in front of us. I was about ready to move that the minutes be approved without a readin' when she muttered, to no one in particular, "I heard about this little get-together."

I stood beside her for a minute, staring at some of her left boob. What time does the balloon go up? "Well, nice to meet you," I said and went over to where Archie was sitting, weaving slightly now, on the couch with Ruth.

Boss was deep in his cups. He nodded to me as I bumped into the curb. His head swayed, and after a few reflective seconds he murmured, "Do you know, Ruth, that fifteen thousand Negroes a year pass into the white community?"

She kept silent. It is her gift.

Archie pointed up to Gladys dancing solo, extravagantly, flaming in front of things. "Take that little high-yella gal. If she marries the right man, their children might be white." Archie turned to her, largely. "Your children might be white, my girl."

Ruthie nodded. I thought she was going to stick to her silence, and then she said softly, "And they might be black."

He was looking at her very carefully. "Does that frighten you?"

She nodded. "Of course it does."

The "of course" stayed there between them for a moment.

I started away, toward the door, my glass in hand. I took off my coat and laid it on top of the TV set—"Heeeeeere's

Johnny"—and I wove outside into the darkness. I swayed through the cars parked in the driveway, and the Texas stars up there are one fine audience: vast expectation. I addressed them, in a slight breeze, and spread myself a bit. I leaned back on the haunch of an older T-Bird.

So here I am. Beaunorus Green. Statistical fluctuation, house nigger, Stanford man. With the sounds of the black party in my ears I began to think about how I have lived as colorlessly as possible in this gross country. Father dead before I could know him, Mamma and I going on in Modesto. Hell, I grew up surrounded by white people.

I moved off the T-Bird and into the clear wide slope where I could see the White House. It was softly incandescent in the moonlight. I stared at it for some time, now and then bringing my drink to my mouth, holding it there so that the ice numbed my lips. I got to get my drama classes prepared. At Columbia we did Robert Lowell's "Benito Cereno"—and there Bo was, Babu. In the great shaving scene, when black slave me drools and cows and goos to Don Benito, Ba-BU with the straight razor eying the white flesh above the napkin-flag, a black brother in the audience found it a little too much to bear. He began to giggle hysterically. The whole theater was hushed except for me groveling SamBo on the stage with my razor and the soul buddy gasping with giggledom in the audience. After the show he came round to my dressing room and said, peeking in the door, "I'm sorry, man, but I just couldn't help it."

"So, Beaunorus, you taking some of our good Texas air."

I turned, and across the yard he stood up and out, sharp and clean, carved in the moonlight. "President." I raised my glass to the man.

He came forward, and his face was blank and not wanting to be fooled. He touched the plastic thing in the ear. He is with me in the moonlight and we hold our drinks chest-high. "Say," I said, "I don't know if Ruthie was entirely clear in there."

He looked at my face; his upper lip came up slightly from those handsome teeth.

"When," I went on, "she said about being afraid our children might be black. It's not that she doesn't want black babies. She just realizes the problems, you know, she—"

He waited until I had quite finished. "Oh, yes, it was clear," he said. He sighed and gently clicked and rolled the ice in his glass. "Do you remember much of my brother Bill, your father, Beaunorus?"

"A little."

"He was a very gentle man, your father."

"A Christian gentleman, I hear."

"Now don't you be ironical about him, boy." Archie slightly tottered. "He could forgive more than any man born."

"I don't remember he ever whipped me."

"Your father—" my uncle said, and he sighed again. "Your father." We stared at each other for a minute, and then he looked at the ground.

We are participating in a queer little silence.

He moved back toward the house. "Comin' in, son?"

"In a minute."

He went on. He whistled absently, a whistle that was mostly air, mainly a sigh.

I finished my drink and sat down on the grass beside the driveway and said the dogwood trees might sleep with themselves if they so desired. On cue with that thought, Ruthie was beside me. "Say," I said, "I'm goin' to take up permanent residence out here."

"Huh?"

"Such nice folks come out to call on me."

She sat down with me, and she'd been drinking too. I touched her breast, free and soft under the nice cloth. "How are you, Little One?"

"Okay."

"Sure?"

"Sure."

Behind us, inside, there was a whoop and a lot of laughter. Somebody'd spilled a drink or taken off his clothes. Sitting there on the grass with my gal, and the party close and far, I'm in the Village again, stoned in some attic, and a white kid cries out, "Hey, baby, where's it at?" Over there in a shadow you see a girl on a trip talking to her hand. She says to it, "Faster, faster, honey." She is not playing with herself, you understand, just lookin' at her hand in front of her face, and to its motionlessness she says, "Faster, faster, honey." It was an awful nice party, that one in the attic, and five men fell down a stairwell into the New School. "I think I'm falling asleep."

"Me too. It's the time difference."

"Huh?" We stretched out and counted stars, alternately balancing the books, and gave up and closed our eyes in each other's arms.

Apparently we did sleep. Awakening, I discovered a bloodthirsty chrome automobile bumper, tonnage moving over our heads. I shouted out, and the bumper stopped, jerked down toward my face, and then bounced back up again. I scrambled out from under, pulling the Little One with me, and she whimpered, always hard to awaken. It was the Luper's old T-Bird.

Zip leaned out the window. "Sheeaa—Greens?"

"Yes." I was shaking.

"Hell, this what you folks do in New York—sleep on the driveways?"

Mrs. Luper called out from her side. "You'll get chiggers, lyin' in the grass."

Ruthie tugged my sleeve. "What's chiggers?"

"What?"

She was desperate, still asleep. It seemed very important to her. "What's chiggers?"

Zip still had his foot on the brake: the old T-Bird's rear lights were deep purple. "Come on and get in. We'll take you back. Sheeeaa—you give me a start, you two, sleepin' on the road like that."

"I left my coat inside." I pushed my lady into the yawning car-door-body and stumbled myself back toward the little cottage. When I went in, the party was still thriving. I picked up my coat. Down the hall, the door to Buddy's bedroom was open. I started toward it, looking around for the Marshalls to thank them for the fine time, but then I stopped: Buddy was there, panicked, alone, his eyes bloated and fixed on something to his right. From that direction a woman's voice cried out, half laughter and half hurt. Right after the shriek there was a thud, a body heavily hitting the floor, and then a pair of naked male legs rolled into view. Powerful legs. Again the woman's voice from the bed—it did not sound like Barbara—called out, and I was starting in toward those tough-as-hell legs when Jim Marshall came hugely athletic and shoving past me. He stood for a second in his son's room, looking at the bed, and then he reached down toward the naked, muscular legs on the floor. "Easy—hey, now, let's take her the easy way." Jim slammed the bedroom door closed with his foot.

The parents arrived for Commencement; some of the back seats of the cars had been hacked off, a last surgical measure to make them into flat-bed farm vehicles. Now the fragments of families sat in the auditorium, sighing and hushing one another, destitute clans, a nose occasionally clearing itself, everybody just holding in, enduring this customary price for the swingin' picnic dance on the tennis courts. President Achille T. Washington—blue sash and gold trimming brilliant on his black robes—had come forth in utterance.

Uncle had quite a way about him. His whole body heaped itself up in trimness, total disciplined effort, but when he spoke I saw him at midnight scratching on yellow paper in his dim library. And his voice touched on an odd pedal, some tatter of French about his Texas speech that propped him among our ancestors.

What do we make of him at the mike? It was getting warm in the auditorium, as the Boss asked all the black tenant farmers to recall the suicidal Second Peloponnesian War. The footlights glittered on his gold-rimmed glasses like a kept promise, a terribly large bargain, and we had

nothing to assent with but our sense of where we were, and
who. Now he moves to Thomas Carlyle and a gloss on the
Hero in History.

As he spoke, my stiff aunt was looking down at Ruthie
and me from the platform beside her husband. I nodded to
her. She had come back from the convocation of her sorors
in Austin. Archie brought her into our private dining car
in his complex and introduced us. Aunt Charlesetta was a
frightened, overweight woman. She sat there with that
smile painted on her face, and the four of us tried to ignore
the serving girl. The girl was wearing an extremely tight
red sweater above her white apron, those babies yanked
out like pistolas. She was flirting with the president, winking at him: "Won't you have *some*thin', Presydent?" She
giggled and rolled her eyes at him. He cautioned her quietly, and she pretended to be having a lover's quarrel with
him. Her eyes flamed at Mrs. W., as if to say, While you
were with your Sore-ors, we di'n't waste no time, the Boss
'n' me. The girl additionally flashed at Ruth, sex and race.
Again Archie told her to get on with her kitchen work, girl,
and don't be fresh now. And she came close, too close for
the comfort of any of us and blew at the back of his head,
blew toward his ear. *Pow!* Black Educator Ambushed by
Black Co-ed. But he took it with extraordinary patience,
his lips pursed together—the girl did *not* know where to
stop. Archie seemed as much hurt as angry; he kept his eyes
away from us, and again the lips pursed as he tried not to
hear with his hearing-aid. Finally Lady Washington said to
the girl, "Could you please get me another glass of tea?"
Just to make it clear, she held up her glass.

"And so here you stand, my seniors, ready to go out and
participate in the nation's life. To those of you who would
serve your race well, I say: a whole new world of promise is

auspiciously open before you, eager to receive the best you have to give. My delight is very great, to see you go through all those doors. Dream on it tonight, let your sleep be filled with images of opening doors. And once you go through them, do not do what so many in the talented tenth have done, do not forget to keep the pressure on, to keep those doors open for the generations to come. Be proud." And then there was a little click in his big throat, a genuine halting as he broke into a delicate premeditation that was everything. "Godspeed, my seniors. Carry the name Bundy in your hearts."

Dancing in the evening. The band struck up a fanfare and there strolled into the room, on Archie's arm, a gorgeous tall girl in a low-cut white gown. Her virginal satin and President's black dinner jacket, and their large white teeth—all of that touched us as it swept over us, as we brought ourselves up to meet them in music. Glory God, so that is it. We watched the thing go, all systems A-OK. And from the microphone behind the piano came a high, haunting counter-tenor, a silky falsetto: "There she is, Miss Bu-u-undy." I moved over to the piano. There in the shadows, frail with his eyes closed, stood Abner Washington. He was singing sweetly into the microphone.

For post-commencement we pulled out our plastic bag and I dug in the grass. In our little Honeymoon Haven, bent over the small metal machine I'd picked up from a Puerto Rican tobacco expert, I rolled us a couple of nice joints. In my shaving kit I found the little red bulb and plugged her into the lamp in our spare bedroom, now the Opium Den. We sat nude in music, passing it back and forth. She was still feeling upset from early in the day. George, the newspaper carrier, had been pointing out varieties of Texas trees to her, and she was nodding, taking it all in. Cottonwood, dogwood, soft pine. But his condition tortured her. George's about twenty-eight; so's his I.Q. He has blood bruises on his face because the guys kick the shit out of him for something to do.

I held all the smoke in, tight as a drum, and Thespian energy rapidly dissipates into quiet. I remember old poems, lyrics. In soft red light we smile and stroke. Somewhere out in the middle of the pasture a black graduate laughs, pissing on his diploma. Time passes.

I smiled to see my mind flum back onto her bare shoulder. This Little One of mine likes nice little serious bright boys, color immaterial, and you leave her alone for five minutes and she's got one. I left her one minute at a newsstand on Lenox and she got one: a five-year-old. They showed me his "caroon" hat. I didn't say "racoon" because it was a "caroon" hat. (Oh, when the Little One works in Harlem she does fine things. She asked her kindergarten class what was the sound of one hand clapping, and a Little Crusader shrieked, "Windy! Windy!" And she keeps up the good work down here.)

"What are you thinking?"

"That child."

She thought.

On the tennis courts a mother brought her four-year-old up to meet his Head Start teacher; the little guy came out of Mamma's skirts only long enough to kick Ruthie pretty hard in the shins. Ruthie waited a moment, then kicked him back. The boy's mother smiled.

My office was coming to a boil, and I sat waiting for anyone. Faculty men were supposed to wear ties whenever
they were on campus, but I thought I'd see if beads would
do. They're Pakistani beads, originally intended by him
for her, but I get them on alternate Tuesdays. So there I
sat in a black T-shirt with the blue and white brilliants on
my chest: Cochise Guru Garvey. Summer school was shap-
ing up as mainly a female affair; most of the boys had to
work or were getting taken to Vietnam to fight for freedom. I slept for five minutes after class there, with my forehead on the open textbook for Basic Communication, my
right ear absorbing a page of "Civil Disobedience." Then,
awakening, shading my eyes, turning, I appraised the landscape. In drama class we are going to RIOT. I played with
my brick prop.

A voice behind me said, "Mr. Green?"

I put down my brick and turned. Abner. On orders
from Mr. Big he was in my class; he sat in the back. I shuddered when I heard a girl call out to him after class,
"Toast, wait up." That was Abner's nickname on campus,
Toast. For the little flame-stripe on his face. He did not

seem to mind it. Now he stood in my doorway, wearing a
red sport shirt and blue jeans, and a gray cap on his head.
He came in and sat down on a straight chair beside my
desk. "Say, I took that Carlyle out of the library."

"Yes?"

"I liked what Poppa said Carlyle said. In his commencement speech. About heroes?"

"Ah."

"So I went to the library and I thought I'd read up on
him. The book I wanted was *Heroes and Hero-Worship*.
But it was out. So I got me *Sartor Resartus*." He carefully
mispronounced the Latin. "And what it means is 'The
Tailor Re-Tailored.'" He smiled at me and my beads.
"Man, everything is *clothes*."

I nodded.

He cleared his nose. "Well, all that talk about clothes
don't convince me. The way I figure, old Carlyle thought
so much about clothes he just couldn't put his pants on in
the morning."

Toast fought back in class; he didn't sit like the others
in silence with vague facial pain.

"Well," I said, "the less we say about Carlyle the better."

Toast shrugged. "Oh, he is trivial. Everyone is." He
looked into my eyes. "You name one person not trivial."

I played with my beads. "Take yourself. You, man,
you're not trivial, are you?"

"Well, no. I'm not trivial to *me*." Toast smiled. "But
put it on a percentage basis."

Each evening after dinner I'd slip over to the gym for
twenty minutes, where half a dozen boys would usually
have a basketball game going. They let me in for a nomi-
nal fee. Toast was always there; it was good to see his long
back, little layers of muscle working under the sleek layer

of sweat. He threw out wisecracks and shoveled in shots from thirty feet out. Usually he wore little leather straps, heavy leggings around his ankles. Playing him close I muttered, "Hey, man, why you wear them things on your ankles?" Driving round me for the bucket, Toast hurrahed. "It's the only way they know how to hold me down." Soul brother, ego brother.

Yet he was possessed of a peculiar gentleness. Walking home after lunch I'd stop and watch Ruthie gather the crowd of four- and five- and six-year-olds about her on the porch of the training school. In the afternoon heat she would tell the children a story, half Grimm, half Poe, no irony allowed. They seemed to trust her; that kid she'd traded kicks with, he held her hand. One day Toast came by and Ruthie had him tell them a story. I watched my wife and the young man and their children. Every once in a while Toast would spread out his arms and his voice would zip up into that counter-tenor and the kids would giggle and laugh, squeaking like hiccups. Look out, here comes Bo, and he wants to tell a story too. That crazy gal, if she had her way we'd spend the whole damn summer out on the lawn tellin' stories to each other.

He drew himself up on the chair. "I got to go, Mr. Green. Got to get the old man."

"The old man?"

"Henry."

I shrugged my shoulders. "Don't believe I've had the pleasure."

"You haven't heard about Henry?"

"Sorry."

"Henry—Henri Prudhomme." Toast stared at me. "You sure Poppa never told you about Henry?" Then he looked down and he mumbled to himself, "No, I suppose not."

"Where is Henry Prudhomme?"

"He's coming in today. On the plane from Atlanta. I'm goin' to pick him up."

I looked at my watch. "When you going?"

"Right now. I came over here to get the keys for the station wagon from Dr. Hamilton."

"Do you have any use for company?"

"Okay."

I put on my dark glasses and we walked together down the concrete steps. I would have to put off my lunch, but I wouldn't be missing much; all they served at the Student Union was bologna, unbuttered white bread with gummy salad on the side, and all the Kool Aid you could drink. I put a dime in the Coke machine. It kept returning the coin. Toast kicked it a couple of times and pounded on its face. Nothing doing. He unplugged it from the water fountain and gave it another kick for spite. "I know a place we can get some Cokes," he said.

We walked out into the sun. It was a furnace inside the car, the front seat blistering. Toast switched on the air-conditioner and gunned the engine. We pulled out and drove a mile over to the general store in Pastorius. The little building was swimming behind the heat waves. When we got out, the heat smeared up from the ground and out from the trees.

Three dogs lay grounded in gravel, asleep. Toast kicked a folded beer can off the step; in shade, the dogs did not move, though one snapped its tail slowly, a dead rope on the ground. Inside, through the fly-ridden screen door, one low light bulb was stranded in hot, damp air. The black boards of the floor gave slightly under us. Along the little counter flies were aimlessly weaving in and out of their minds; on a shelf stood three whisky bottles and a box of Kellogg's corn flakes. We pulled two Cokes out of the machine by the counter. When I walked with my bottle to a booth and sat down, Toast shook his head. He pointed to the back of the store, where a white waitress in a green uniform was sitting in a booth, talking with a man in a cowboy hat. Toast said to me, "We can buy it here, but we can't drink it here."

"Bull."

He shrugged and sat with me. But he only stared at the Coke. He was waiting.

The waitress said something to the man, stood up, and plodded to the front of the store. She was carrying a cigarette. Her blond hair was stuck to her forehead. She looked down at me in the booth. "Now, you boys know better than that."

I looked up at her. I made my face blank.

She tapped her cigarette, and the ash dropped off into the free-strike zone, on the table just beside my right wrist. I looked at the quarter-inch of gray ash.

She sighed. After a moment she said, "You boys can't drink in here."

I said, "Why do you suppose that is?"

Her face died.

I smiled.

She took another drag on her cigarette and looked at Toast. "You the kid with the nigger band that played at the Elks?"

Toast nodded at his Coke.

"We got facilities for you people over on Green Street."

Facilities. I said, "I'd be much obliged if you could refrain from calling me and my undergraduate 'you people.'"

The waitress stood there silent for another minute, and then looked back at the man in the booth and motioned for him to come forward. She stared down at me again. "We got facilities for coloreds over on Green Street."

Mr. Cowboy was tall and muscled and did not have teeth on the right side of his mouth. He came slowly out of Marlboro Country, forming his lips into a tight little line. At the table he stretched and said to me, without any speed, discharging air out of his nose, "Where you from, boy?"

He put his fingers under his huge belt. Then he stared me down: the green eyes did not move. He shrugged a shoulder at Toast, his eyes not leaving mine except for a flutter at Ruth's blue and white beads on my black T-shirt.

Toast touched me on the arm. "Come on, let's go."

"No." I turned to him, softly: "Wait a minute." I stood up, stepped out, and faced the cowboy. He had about twenty pounds on me, but he was an inch shorter and crowding forty. There was no one else but the waitress. I stared at Roughrider cleanly, and then very quietly I said, "We are going to stay here and drink our Coca-Colas." My first Adult Western. I laid it out with that soft clarity of utter confidence. "And you will let us do that." I was standing so as to make him existentially feel the sins of his utter imaginative paucity.

Mr. Cowboy blinked and stepped back. It took time to register in his brain. He said, *"What?"*

I kept my cool and my eyes narrowed; without malice, as a matter of simple, inescapable, natural fact, I repeat it. "You will let us do that."

So much for that shit, Beaunorus Green. Cowboy jerked forward and got me into some kind of East Texas karate wrist-lock, pulling my fingers, all of them, way over backward, and he rushed me straight forward, his knees in my butt, and the waitress opened the screen door—and we were all *amazed* that old Bo's fingers could bend that far backward—and I went sprawling onto the gravel. The dogs went on sleeping.

As I was standing up and brushing myself off, Toast came quickly out through the door and it banged behind him. We walked a couple of steps toward the car, and I was still brushing. Hate to get my beads dusty. My hand was on fire, hot water boiling.

Toast said, "I wish you wouldn't do that."

I held my wrist and stared at him. "I regret any inconvenience."

Toast blinked. He looked back once up at the general store and then took the gray cap off his head and whapped it on his leg.

Inside the store the woman was laughing, and we got into the car. For five minutes we didn't say anything; we took refuge in gazing out at the bleak landscape sweeping by. Toast slowed for a team of horses pulling a wagon on the right side of the road; he waved at the black man sitting in the front of the wagon as we gunned on by. Without looking at me he said, "How's your hand?"

"It's okay. I got another one."

Then he did look. "You want to stop and get some ice for it?"

I glanced at the scenery. "Next time, next time I'm goin' to lay that cracker out."

Toast's eyes brooded on me for a minute, and then he smiled.

We drove on in silence for a time. I said, "I mean, here we are again."

"Excuse me?"

"Oh, I was just thinkin'. In San Francisco, my freshman year in college, I left my date in an interracial multimedia discothèque, the Freaky Mother—"

"What?"

"That's what they called it, the Freaky Mother. And I went out to make a call, found the phone booth full of bodies, so I hummed on outside. It was midnight and suddenly there was all this shooting, somebody robbed somebody, bullets bouncing off buildings, and I couldn't run. I figured they'd think Black Me in my three-piece corduroy suit did it. So I walked slow and soft. A block away this gumball flasher roars up with cops all piling out, and they draw their guns and back all three pieces of corduroy suit, me included, to the wall. One of the cops stuck his old thirty-eight flush up on my sinus. They took me down to the station house and periodically they gave me slaps on the head. I kept screaming, 'You have no legal right.' And they'd slap me. I was a college boy with a black gal waiting in the Freaky Mother, and I'd say, 'You have no legal right.' And they'd slap me again."

We drove in silence. Finally he said, "I used to be nonviolent—even up to the time when I was out pluggin' my record."

"Your record?"

"Sure. I wrote 'Crazy Baby,' the flip side to 'Truly.' "

"I didn't know that."

"I was on a civil rights march. Old man Henry got me to go. And I was plugging my record, too." He nodded to himself. "You got to get something for yourself."

"Sure." The pain in my hand was easing now, and I kept doubling my fist, then stretching out my fingers.

"It was in Jackson, Mississippi. Station KASH." He grinned again. "The DJ, Bobby Ray Bright, he got me on. With 'Crazy Baby.' And we were talkin' and he said, 'so, how you makin' it here, Abner?' And I said, 'I am here to participate in—' And Bobby Ray Bright cut me off right there. He knew I was going to say I was in civil rights. We

went off the air for ten seconds"—Toast was widely smiling—"and he said to me, with us cut off the air, 'Baby,
what's a *mat*ter with you? Ross Barnett owns this station.'"
Toast laughed and patted his hands on the steering wheel.

I looked out the window at the parched Texas fields,
flat and yellow to the horizon. "So you marched."

"Oh, yes, but I didn't know any better."

"Didn't know any—"

"Well, you know, back when we thought civil rights was
one big peanut. Back in the times of the Farce on Washington."

"I see."

Toast slowed the station wagon. "But once, with old Dr.
King, in Montgomery. Once I didn't march. I just could
not."

"Why was that?"

"I don't get along with dogs so good." Toast whispered
the words in the air-conditioned front seat. We observed
a moment of silence and then he said, "A big dog scared
me when I was four years old. He bit my hand." He reached
his right arm across the seat and opened his hand; there
was a pair of tiny scars, jagged little spider tracks, on the
ball of his thumb. He pulled his hand back to the wheel.
"The cops in Montgomery had their dogs. I just could
not *do* her. I'm not afraid of anything in the world. Except dogs. It was a humiliatin' experience." He turned.
"But them police dogs are fierce."

I thought: That explains it. Our animal class. First day
in Dramatic Arts I had everybody do an animal (a hold-
over, I guess, from an old bad habit of mine: when conver-
sations get into an awkward little silence I've been known
to ask people what animal they'd most like to sleep with—
the Little One couldn't choose between a lion and a lamb—
and I really annoyed a lot of people with that question un-

til some crazy man in the East Village said to me quietly, "A spider"; somehow I never asked the question much after that). Anyhow, in class one guy did a bear and a real little guy did an eagle, and a lot of girls, too many, did cats. Toast's was hard for us to figure out; we thought it was wolf, finally got dog, and then the eagle got it. A police dog. And so that was it, the scar on his thumb.

I pulled off my dark glasses and rubbed with my index finger and thumb on my nose. I looked at Toast and he was smiling. I said, "What you smilin' about?"

"You."

"Me?"

He chuckled slightly and said, "Oh, the way you play with your shades in our dramatics class. You wave 'em around like you was a white producer or somethin'."

I put my glasses back on and decided we would *not* do imitations of people we know on Friday. Toast would have me to perfection. He might even take off on this little cracker escapade: Man, you shoulda seen that teacher of ours, the knee-grow thes-pian. He was just not Basically Communicatin' at all."

"I marched wearin' these shades," I said.

"Oh, I didn't mean nothin' uncomplimentary."

"Sure."

"No, I—"

"Some of us in the talented tenth your Poppa spoke about, oh, we spit at our image in the mirror but we hymn along on our way to sweet crabgrass in the suburbs."

"Well, I never said you belonged to the Urban League."

"No, I guess you didn't."

Finally I could see the buildings of the Dallas airport. Toast looked at his watch; we were, he said, just going to make it. We drove up close to the terminal entrance and parked the car.

Toast was eager to find his man. We moved over toward the big terminal windows, where we could see a prop-jet had just landed. Toast nudged me. "There he is."

Henri Prudhomme, out on the smoldering expanse of runway, was shuffling along toward the terminal, alert. He was a short old man, baked golden brown, the sun brightly bouncing off his bald head. He moved in a big floppy brown suit; somebody three sizes larger had given it to him. On his little feet were dark red corduroy slippers. As he came through the blades of glass into the terminal, Toast called out, "Henry!"

The old man saw him and lit up. Twenty years younger when called to, he came forward with his little valise in his left hand and his other hand wide, outstretched, firm. "Boy, I hoped you'd be here." They embraced. The old man's false upper teeth jostled around in his mouth as he laughed, hugging his boy.

Toast said, "This is Beaunorus Green, Henry. Down from New York, teachin' at school this summer."

"Hello, boy." He grabbed my hand and his owl eyes eat flesh.

Toast said, "You got your baggage checks?"

The old man raised the scrappy valise. "Boy, how many times I got to tell you? You get too much stuff, you can't *move*. I got my baggage"—he lowered the valise—"and let's get on with it." He shook his ancient head. "Oh, let's get the hell away from that *aer*-o-plane." To me he muttered, "Hate to fly—makes the angels jealous."

We started through the crowd, over toward the door. A little blond girl, white shirt and brown denim skirt, was standing by the glass doors. When she saw the three of us coming, she stared at Prudhomme for a moment and then erupted into a squeal, *"Henry!"* She came forward and flung her arms around the old man.

Prudhomme hugged the girl back and then they stepped apart and looked at each other and embraced again, and the girl kissed him and he responsively planted a big hard one on her cheek, and then they separated again. Prudhomme looked at her. "Now wait a minute, dear." He set his words out, clear things on a table. "I don't believe I know you."

The girl was crestfallen. She wailed, "Henry, don't you remember? We were in jail together."

Texans had stopped momentarily, faces slightly twisted at seeing the blond girl embracing the bald Negro. I glanced at Toast and he had an odd little pout on his face, his piece of distrust, looking at the girl the way he'd first looked at Ruthie in the White House living room.

Prudhomme was still quietly searching the girl's face.

"Albany," she said. "Don't you remember? Nineteen sixty-two? Albany, Georgia? My husband got your suit cleaned for you?"

Prudhomme's eyes focused, sharp, "Why, yes. Yes, of course." His little body became happy. "My dear, how are you?"

"Walt is coming in on the four-o'clock plane. We'll be at Jarvis this summer."

"Well, my dear, my dear. You must come out to the house. We live not far." He fished into his wallet and pulled out an old traffic ticket. He wrote a number on it. "Now you give us a call. On the telephone."

"Of course, Henry." She stood, her blue eyes shining. "Oh, it's so good to see you again. How are you feeling?"

"I think I got the old trouble licked."

"I'm so happy to hear that."

Toast and I were standing slightly away from them, watching; Toast seemed relieved when the little talk was over and the girl went to claim her bags.

We walked out into the afternoon sun and over to the car. Toast took the old man's bag and chucked it into the back of the station wagon; then we all climbed into the front seat, Prudhomme in the middle. His abdomen stuck out abruptly, an appliance on his tiny frame; that stomach was domed under his dark green shirt like an army helmet that had been strapped on his waist. He leaned forward and turned the air-conditioning vents away from his ankles, his little red corduroy slippers.

Toast said, "So how was the show?"

Prudhomme looked at me. "Been to Atlanta. Leadership conference, 'What Makes a Black Leader.' A preacher —looked a little like old Boss Bellinger—he opened her all up with a sermon. My, his voice was *melli*fluous. Could charm you right out of your skin. But, Lord, he gave a sermon on 'The Nothingness of Nothing.' What a hell of a thing to start off with. The Nothingness of Nothing. Lord, it *was* nothing."

Toast had his arms over the wheel. "You give it to 'em good, Henry?"

"You know I did." Prudhomme chuckled softly. "That little coed should have been there. They were all sitting around asking each other what it takes to make a good black leader. I said, 'He's got to be one thing. One thing, first of all.'"

I asked, "What's that?"

"Oh, my, they were all so quiet. Everybody wanted to know what old Prof was going to come up with." He shook his dark finger, a warning at the windshield. "I said he's got to be *one* thing."

"Yes," Toast said, "what was it?"

He growled. "A *jail*bird."

Toast nodded. "And what'd they say to that?"

"Not much." Prudhomme leaned back. "Ah, well, my people have their burdens."

At length he turned to me. "So, B. Green, you've come down to the Piney Belt for a little missionary work. Save some of the less fortunate members of your race from the pit of ignorance?"

I glanced at scenery. "I wanted a summer in the country."

The old buzzard studied me. He was quiet for a moment, his eyes walking around me, and then he said, "How many of you we got to put up with?"

"I'm your one and only. My wife's runnin' Head Start." I waited a moment. "She's white."

"Oh, *is* she?" He waited, sighed. "Well, I'm glad to hear you got a wife, whatever color she is." He pointed at my chest. "With those damn beads, I thought you might be a *ho*mo."

As we drove, Prudhomme fired local names at Toast, catching up on news. At one point he turned to me. "Why did you pick *our* little mental institution?"

"Washington's my uncle."

His eyes narrowed. "That I didn't know."

"Didn't you see the family resemblance?"

"I'll have to see you in action."

He made "action" sound like "combat." I pulled my eyes away from him again. "Besides, I wanted to see my uncle's school."

He laughed then. "Oh Lord, boy, your uncle's school. The white humanitarians saw they had to give us black folks a little vo-cational training." His giggle reeled around the front seat. "The Man says yes—come on, niggers, we're gonna set you up with some education. And what do

we get? Dozens of glorified high schools scattered all over
the South—colored agricultural universities, colored mechanical universities, colored normal universities—the
biggest mouthful of higher lowdown education in the
world. That's what happens when the Man says yes."
"It's funny," I said.
"It better be funny, Mr. Green."

When we finally pulled up to the Bundy neon sign,
Toast pointed the car down a little dirt side road, one that
I had noticed from our golfing afternoon; we went down
through dust and heavy trees. A hundred yards off the road
sat a cluster of old houses in general exhaustion. A separate community, beat, going back to Reconstruction. Prudhomme's place was the least ruined: a little frame structure
with a screened-in front porch and a gray garage out
back. Sticking out of the garage, an antique beat-up Hudson. A Hudson.
Toast pulled the school station wagon up to the
cement steps. I went around back and insisted on carrying in the old man's valise. As I walked behind them up to
the front steps, the bugs from the uncut dead grass
started buzzing around my head, and one crawled into my
ear to spawn. I had to stop for a second and coax it out.
When I finally got hold of it, Toast and Prudhomme had
already gone in, slamming the screen door behind them. I
went into the house alone. Set it down anywhere, boy. On
the porch, as I passed, was a little wooden swing, bright
red, hanging down on chains from the ceiling. I opened the
heavy door and pushed in. It was not the deep cold
of Washington's White House but a breathy cool gener-
ated by a tiny window air-conditioner and a pair of fans.
The front room was small; the old man seemed to like soft
chairs: there were three floppy pale green ones gathered in

conversation around a dilapidated brown couch on its last legs. I could hear mutterings, Prudhomme and an old woman's voice, back beyond the small dining room. I sat down and kept going deeper until I thought the chair had no bottom, but I finally came to rest a few inches above the floor, with my knees in front of my face. I peered through them, across the room: on the seven-inch TV sat a big gold-fish bowl with various fish aimlessly roving and blowing against the glass.

The screen door at the back squeaked and slammed; Toast came in. He smiled at me. I said that perhaps we ought to get going and he shook his head, no, and sat down on the far end of the couch beside a tall glass pink flamingo. The bird was a smart aleck around the mouth and eyes, a bird you didn't want to know. The old room was crowded: a pile of mail and *Jet* and *Liberator* and *Amsterdam News* stood on the coffee table and beside them another huge pile of *National Geographic*. Prudhomme came back in and picked up his valise and smiled at me, telling me to make myself at home, and then he went back into the bedroom. Shortly he called, "Green."

He was waiting for me in the little hallway. He pointed into a bedroom: the wallpaper was pink and black striped, a very tiny room, stuffy. On a single bed, just as I entered, was an old woman with very black skin and stark white hair; the hair was thinning on her scalp. "Mamma," said Prudhomme, "this is Beaunorus Green, down teaching at the university."

The woman opened her big eyes, eyes glazed and hurt. She moved her body slowly, something wounded under the sheets. She had barely heard.

The old man said to me, "Mamma's had a little operation. We're not letting her enter any dance contests."

Mrs. Prudhomme finally focused her painful eyes on me

and she smiled slightly. Prudhomme bent over and touched her on the shoulder.

She spoke up sharply, "Don't touch me so hard, Poppa."

"Now take it easy, darlin'." He patted the air above her shoulder, the damp nightgown. He looked at me, waved his hand quickly at his hip, and I went out of the room.

I repaired to the back porch and looked out at the foliage running green and yellow and wild beyond the clothesline and the big rusty trash can. Near the garage, cooped, pigeons were stepping in straw. Beneath the coop lay a venerable hound, asleep.

"Something to drink, Green?"

I turned and Prudhomme had started banging through his cupboards. He pulled down a new bottle of whisky and poured me a glass. Then he poured himself a Coca-Cola and scattered ice cubes into the two glasses and called in to Toast to fix himself something. He smiled at me and disappeared into the living room.

Toast and I stood by the sink, sipping; we could hear the old man on the phone, barking at somebody, pissed in a neighborly way. Again I muttered to Toast that we should go; he shook his head, his eyes brightening, and he took me through the bedroom opposite Mrs. Prudhomme's to a dark brown stairway leading down to the basement. There, two posts in the middle braced the floor of the house above us, the low-down ceiling. Beside a little screen door, escape hatch, squatted an enormous Voodoo god with an old cigarette in its mouth. In the low late afternoon light a midget fan droned on the floor like a small African animal. The walls were lined with big color photographs of Watusi dancers and a little orange and blue felt banner: FREEDOM NOW. A big watercolor portrait on the far wall looked like Ho Chi Minh. Toast and I sat in battered gar-

den chairs; we drank and he rambled on with Prudhomme
history, checking me here and there with quick glances.

When, at five o'clock, the old man came shuffling down
the stairs in his red corduroy slippers, he had the bourbon
bottle with him. He held it like a book. "So," he said,
"you've found the Zulu Club." He threw me the fifth.
Toast fluttered his hand negatively over his glass, but I
filled mine. Prudhomme was going half and half, Coke and
whisky. He sat down on the ruined couch at my right and
winced slightly, moving his hand gently over the great ugly
protrusion of his belly. He had a pain, and he dismissed it.
Toast put a scratchy Charlie Parker record on the ancient
phonograph in the corner; he wrapped himself around the
machine as if he could see the music.

Prudhomme said to me, "So tell me, boy, what do you
think of the great state of Texas?"

"Big."

He patted his domed stomach, gently. "Yes, we were
the *biggest*. Now that title's passed on up to the far north,
but we're still first in our cap-*ac*ity for illusion."

I nodded.

"Don't get me wrong. I love this state, boy. Texas and
Henry Prudhomme—both those wonders live on oil and
natural *gas*."

I couldn't keep up with him in the bourbon department. I was too hungry, not having eaten since breakfast,
quite unprepared. At seven o'clock I threw in the towel
and stood to excuse myself and go round up Ruth for a
cheeseburger at the Complex. But there was a rustling at
the back door and a large, throaty cry: "HENRY!"

In walked the Home Economics Department, Ophelia
Jones, on dress parade. Wrapped in a white summer dress,
she came forward, her enormous breasts preceding her like

escorts; she embraced the old man. He hugged her—
"Hello, colleague"—and then she saw me, over his shoulder, and she released the bald head from her bosom.

Prudhomme asked if we had met, and the woman
smiled for the first time at me, now that I was in the old
man's company. In a moment the little door out to the back
yard opened again and Homer Brown rolled in, nasal and
floppy. He shook hands with Prudhomme and then nodded
at me. Prudhomme told Toast to run upstairs to the main
floor and get another bottle and a bucket of ice. We sat
around, then, on the sagging lawn furniture, Homer and
Ophelia crowded together, four hundred and fifty pounds
on the couch, Prudhomme and I in chairs. Toast came
down and put the new bottle of bourbon on the table, the
ice-bucket on the floor. Then he asked Prudhomme if he
could borrow the record on the phonograph, and shortly
he went out. He did not seem to want to go, but he said he
had to take the school station wagon back to the garage. He
threw me a sporting smile.

For the first thirty minutes Ophelia Jones and I did not
know what to do with each other. When, in our conversation, I mentioned my uncle's name, Ophelia shivered as if
something reptilian had glided across one of her feet. She
made no secret of it. And at length she went up to see about
Mrs. Prudhomme. Homer asked me how I was enjoying my
classes. I glanced at Prudhomme and said I was concen-
trating on the one or two like Toast who were teachable.

"Teachable" stung the old man. He growled, "Now
what the hell you mean by *that?*"

Homer nervously crossed his legs and patted his top
knee, as if telling it not to worry.

Prudhomme straightened. "How do you know what's
in a man until it comes out? I was teaching here in nineteen hundred and forty-six. There was a student, a big big

boy. My, you never saw a man as big and black as him. Dumb Davis. That's what everybody called him, Dumb Davis." He poured himself a shot, handed me the bottle, and I passed it on to Homer, who wrapped his huge hand around it and set it ceremoniously at his feet.

"Dumb Davis. He got three F's in his freshman year. I gave him a B. Nobody could understand. In faculty meeting they said, 'Come on, Prof, this boy has got to *go*.' But I gave him a B—I thought there was somethin' there—and they let him stay on with a D average." He threw up his hands to the low ceiling in exasperation. "Teachable? You know what happened five years ago?"

"I don't believe I do."

"I was sitting upstairs on that front porch. A car drove up. That car"—he flung out his arms, spilling some of his drink—"that car was as lo-o-ong as this house. I *never* saw a car as long as that. You know who was in that car?"

I nodded. "Dumb Davis."

"He called out to me, 'Hello, Prof.' I didn't recognize him at first. I pulled my body up and peered out at him in the dust. He was dressed in a three-hundred-dollar suit, smoking a big long cigar. Then he came up the steps and I knew him. I knew Dumb Davis."

I toasted the man.

" 'Come on, Prof,' he said to me." Prudhomme was up now, acting it out. "Come on, Doc. You need a vacation. Let's go to California for five days. I got two thousand dollars to spend."

"And?" I said.

Prudhomme stared down at me, his face spread in a smile of conviction and memory. "We spent it *all*."

He backed away to the couch and sat down beside Homer Brown. "Dumb Davis is an oral surgeon in Kansas City."

Ophelia Jones came rolling down the steps into our Zulu Club and asked Homer for another drink. She nodded at Prudhomme, to indicate everything was all right with the woman upstairs. The old man went back into his drink. "Never underestimate your students, boy," he said. He kicked the midget fan, which was blowing too much air on his ankles. He scrabbled his hand around his mouth, like a man getting ready for the kissing booth at the county fair.

We refilled. The first bottle was done for. I am *terrifi-*cally hungry. Maybe I'll eat my beads. I put another record, Count Basie, on the phonograph and tried not to stumble as I lurched back to my chair. We sat silently, listening to the little fan and the music. Staring at the three of them, I felt uneasy, unplaced, generally out of it. A black dude in Texas. I looked up at the Ho watercolor on the wall, and then at the Voodoo god, and finally into my glass.

Ophelia Jones said, smiling at me, "You should have heard our beloved pres-y-dent, Henry. At Commencement he went into his old roo-teen."

"Old roo-teen?" I said.

"Now you see me, now you don't," she explained. She twirled her glass high, and her bosoms rebounded.

Turning to Prudhomme, I said, "You should have given the Commencement address."

"I should?"

"I mean, you'd talk on the platform the way you talk now."

"I would?"

B. Green groped. "What I mean is"—I turned a most pleasant smile over to Homer and Ophelia—"Prof has an integrated personality."

Prudhomme reached into his big shirt pocket and pulled out a pair of glasses. They were perfectly round lenses with solid black rims. He propped them on his nose and looked over them at me. "You're crazy, boy."

I shrugged my shoulders.

"An integrated personality, my, my," he muttered to himself. It seemed to exist for him like some new kind of diet cola.

"You mean, then, you would say what Archie said."

"Did I say that?"

"Sorry. Thought I saw you glidin' in that general direction."

Prudhomme scowled and shuffled in his red corduroy slippers up the stairs. "Green, you poor boy. You spent so much time around white folks you forgot how to think. I'll bet in the evenings, for relaxation, you read *Chaucer*."

I shall go after you and grab you and rap with my knuckles on your bald crown. Rap my knuckles hard, right on your bald head. Nailing down my verdict. Three raps. One, two, three. There, Prew-dum.

"Bo," Homer said, "he likes you."

I bowed my head.

Ophelia mellowed. "That's right, son. Prof don't hammer anybody down if he don't think you are salvageable."

"Me? Salvageable?" My beads are in my drink.

The woman's big face tightened. "But don't you get the wrong impression about Presydent. You don't know your uncle." Her eyes narrowed into a furious squint. Again, gleaming, she said, *"You don't know Archie Washington."*

Homer, beside her, stretched out his legs. "Now, Ophelia."

She was on to me. "First off, I thought maybe you were his spy."

"His *spy?*"

"How well you know that man, boy?"

"Well, I guess I've seen him about three times in my

life. The last time was my freshman year. He wanted me to go to where he was dean."

She nodded at Homer. "You see, I told you. He's just innocent."

"Now wait a minute, I wouldn't go so far as—"

She would not be stopped. "Oh, it's not just what he does here. Son, hasn't anybody told you about the Boston Tea Party?"

I said I'd heard of it. Wasn't that when them white folks—

"Archie," she said, "was scheduled to address the national convention of his fraternity. Oh, they have all the power."

"His wife," I said, "was at a big meeting, when I arrived. A convention of her *sorors*."

She nodded, pleased with my emphasis on "sorors." "Archie arrived in Boston at seven o'clock. By *eight* o'clock they had him fixed up with a date for the dance. By *nine* o'clock he and the date were drunk in his hotel room. By *ten* o'clock he had raped her. She was screaming and one of his 'brothers' came into the room and found Archie standin' there beatin' that woman like a rag doll. Blood was runnin' down her pink satin gown." Her big hands were trying to keep up with her story. "By ee*leven* o'clock his 'brothers' put him on a plane—packed him up and put him on a plane. They didn't know where it was going, Alaska or Bermuda. But they had to get Archie out of *Boston*."

"Where did it go?"

"Chicago." She nodded her head sharply. "Chicago. And his brothers called ahead to the fraternity chapter there, and two of them went down to take him off the plane, and you know what they found when they *got* there?"

I shook my head.

She sighed and a waxy, furious smile spread on her face. "He was just as conservative and dignified as you please. He had a little chat with those boys and then took the next Dallas plane." She pinched her body into a size smaller, prim with doom. "That Archie is a *devil*."

There was silence for a moment, and I mumbled, "Archie has to put in his penitential flying."

Ophelia studied me. "But it took him three thousand dollars to get clear of that one."

"Three thousand?"

"The *date*. The date wanted to press charges."

"So," I said, "the Boston Tea Party."

And just as I said it old Henry came back down the stairs into the room. He heard me—"the Boston Tea Party" —and then he looked from face to face. He did not like it at all. He glanced sharply at Ophelia but did not say anything.

It seemed we were going to let it drop, and then I got it. B. Green Sees Light. "The effigy," I said. "So that's what it was."

Ophelia rattled on. "Oh, yes, Presydent's been hanged in effigy in front of his own White House. And in front of his administration building. And once on his water tower. They put a sign on the last one—'Chippie Chaser.' "

I nodded. "I saw that little project." I looked at Henry. "There was a banana in his fly. A black effigy with a white banana."

Henry just muttered to himself, "Lord, if that's not the worst of both possible worlds."

With that, we sat in a moment of silence. Finally I said, "You'd think there'd be something more. You'd think the students would—"

"Oh, Gawd," howled Henry, "the Great *Up*rising. December seventeenth." He rocked up to playing the split end, waiting for signals. "The Great Uprising." He turned on his toes to me. "The boys posted their Theses on the door. 'This University Is Closed Until Further Notice.' " He giggled as he lobbed the words out and savored their trailing perfume.

I said, "How'd Presydent handle that?"

"Oh"—he rolled his eyes—"you don't have *too* much choice when the sign on your door says 'Join Us or Be Left Behind.' " Again the old man giggled, delighted with the memory. Then he growled low. "Ol' Archie Washington poured himself many a glass of whisky that day. Finally he showed up, dead drunk, and the cadre said to him, 'Go on home, Presydent, you're finished.' "

"And?"

"Oh, *hell*." He sighed. "Archie's sma-a-art. He slept it off and came back. He knew he had to be cool. So he neutra-lized us." The bald head nodded, acquainted, then shot up. "But that spark is sti-ill gonna catch fire." He turned on his heels. "They got rifles from the ROTC office. Not loaded, of course—those white regents don't give the black undergraduates any ammu-ni-tion. But my boys formed a rifle-ring around Freeman Hall." The old man shot into laughter, looking down at his divan. "Ask Homer. He was in there that day. He was a hostage for twenty hours."

The PR man needs air. Homer didn't dig it and got his big body up, reaching for Ophelia's hand. She stared around her in all directions with her hard eyes. As she allowed Homer to lead her to the screen door those eyes sliced me. "It's the truth, Bo. Oh, you don't *know* your uncle."

They went out into the darkness and the screen door banged loosely. I looked at my watch; it was coming along toward ten. Prudhomme stared into empty space and he was quiet now, lost in thought. An excluding silence sat there, all stopped up and gritty against his gums. B.G. looks down at the old man's red corduroy slippers. Now why you wear those things everywhere? I mutter, "Couldn't somethin' be done?"

He kept his silence a moment longer and then growled, half to himself, "Boy, that Ophelia talks too much." He turned, glanced at me, and then went back to staring at his far wall.

I said, "Shit, I'm not going to tell him."

But the old man only shrugged. We sat there, in an awkward situation. And beyond the screen door there were the voices of Homer and Ophelia. I put in a request for the bathroom and Henry said it was at the head of the stairs, boy, so I turned and made a genuine effort to walk straight. And while I was carefully watching the floor and thinking about my uncle—his checks over the years—I banged my head on a low beam at the foot of the stairs.

I fell into the bathroom and found the light switch in my hair and peed for several minutes into the white toilet. My brain wrestled with Achille T. Washington. I turned and smiled like a fool at myself in the mirror. The glass yields. Carefully I arranged the toilet seat and sat down for several minutes. I nodded off. Back there in my ninth year, after Mamma took me to a circus, I saved up and got the bicycle-shop man to make me a unicycle. I used to practice in the rain on the empty public tennis courts, weaving over my single whitewall like a small black drunk. And now I was riding the toilet the same way, keeping my balance in the rain. Wheet-ho-ho-wheep . . .

A rap at the door, Prudhomme's voice: "Beaunorus, you all right?"

I pulled myself up, shook my head, and opened the
door.

"Boy, you're unstable."

"It's the old trouble."

He glowered at me. "Well, zip up your pants."

I stared down at my gaping fly. No wonder he worries
if I'm a homo. I reached through my beads for the zipper,
got caught, tried to go the other way—

Prudhomme lost patience. He went into the kitchen
and pulled out of the small refrigerator a six-pack of king-
size Coca-Colas; with them in one hand and an ice tray in
the other he went into his bedroom. When he came out I
saw he had removed his false teeth, his upper plate, and
the top lip was collapsed, whump.

I stopped him at the head of the stairs. I had to get this
business straight. Archie Washington.

He looked at me, and the big upper lip was bouncing
slightly, like an awning. *"Well?"*

"Nothing."

And we went down.

I successfully navigated the stairs and remembered to
duck my head at the bottom. I congratulated myself;
Ophelia and Homer smiled at me.

Prudhomme came in on my heels, poured himself a
big Coke, and handed the others around. He turned to me
and said, "I see I got my work cut out. Where's your sense
of strategy, boy?"

"I left it in the back of the bus."

"Oh, Gawd," he said, "where would I be now without
strategy? Boy, I've faced mobs. Mobs." He stood up. "Men
coming after me with forty-fives. Back in the depression,
when I was trying to organize my black boys to face a posse
of Texas Rangers."

I wove over my piece of furniture. "All I got to say is"—
and I *knew* I should have shut up, I'm such a lousy drinker
—"all I got to say is this: It's taken my people a long time
to make their move."

He scowled. And exploded. "You're miseducated. You
been run through the whitewash."

"Now don't—"

"Boy, you're lookin' at a charter member of the Anti-
Tex-ass Legion. Many a time the vigilantes tried to feed
me to the Little Dixie alligators. Boy, go feast your eyes
on the slums of San Antone." He pointed out his screen
door. "Why, thirty years ago there was a sign down in
town. Do you know what it said? NIGGER, DON'T LET THE SUN
SET ON YOU IN PASTORIUS." He glared at me. "Boy, I been
through it all. I had my card in the UNIA. I booked my passage on the Black Star Line. What do *you* know? They
used to sell niggers in the Galveston market *by the
pound*. They burned niggers at the stake, and first they
chopped off their fingers and toes and sold 'em as *souvenirs*.
And you sit there all miseducated and Northern and tell
me it's taken 'your' people a long time to make their
move?"

I dropped my eyes, staring at my lap. Prudhomme was
still for a moment, and all we can hear is his breathing.

Then he said, "Now I knew I couldn't dance around
this Baptist empire quoting Marx." I looked up, and he
had put on a sweet smile; deeply he said, "Old Marx tells
us to have all our things in common and sell your posses-
sions and goods and part them to all men as every man has
need. Now that's Marx. Isn't that Marx, Mr. Phi Beta
Kappa?"

"In the flesh."

"The *hell* it is." He dropped his hands. "You illiterate

black college man, that's Saint Luke." He gulped his Coke
oratorically. "Oh, how I studied my Bible when I was
working for the NAACP. Forget the talented tenth; I
was out there with the sharecroppers. That's how you
don't get kicked out of town as a Bolshevisky. Say *Jee*sus
said it."

Throughout, Homer and Ophelia were smiling like
two abnormally well-fed black cats. Ophelia was wasting
the last of the bourbon in a glass half filled with Coke.

Prudhomme sat beside her and laid his hand on her
big puffy shoulder. "Boy," he said to me, "it's too bad you
couldn't have gone to college under me." He smiled. "First
day, I give all my classes a multiple-choice exam. And
you know the answers?"

"What are the questions?"

"Doesn't matter, boy. On that first-day exam the answers are all 'None of the above.'" The old man let out a
little laugh. "That's what you got to tell the Dumb Davises
I guess *you*'d call 'em the unteachables." He roared
up: "Black students, you get yourselves ready for a lifetime of multiple choices in the white world, and you learn
that answer—'None of the above.'" Henry chewed on his
slogan a moment and then turned back down to me. "I
told you about that sermon in Atlanta—the Nothingness
of Nothing. You know what nothingness is?"

"No," I said faintly and shook my head. "I guess
I don't."

"I DO." He reared up and held out his swollen abdomen at me. "I know what *Nothing* is. They all told me I
was going to *die*."

I stared at that stomach and then up into his man-
eater eyes.

"*Can-cer,* boy. They told me I had *can-cer.*" He

stared at that bowl, that army helmet, that appliance on his belly. "I was supposed to be cold and dead, *Stone* dead last January."

I opened my mouth, but the sound would not come out.

"*Dead,* boy. You know what it means to be in your house and feel your life drain out of your body? Your whole ad-ult life lyin' around on the furniture like the Sunday paper on Sunday night? And your sons and daughters come back and everybody looks at you with a sad, long face and you can't even hold down a bologna sandwich and they all just stand there—and they *look* at you and won't tell you what's the matter. All so sad and mournful." Suddenly he giggled.

"What?" I peered up at the giggling face.

"But I found me a doctor who told me he could re-arrange my intestines. Can't remember his name. Hell, I don't know. I remember his face."

"What did he do?"

"I can't tell you *that*. He reoriented my in-tes-tines, cut out all the rusty junk." The old man bowed with mock dignity, all bent over at a state function. "And here I *be*."

I reached down for a king-size bottle. I poured the Coca-Cola down my empty stomach; I could hear it splash into the lake of bourbon.

Prudhomme sat down. "Yes, the worst part of all was the way my sons and daughters stood there *lookin'* at me."

The conversation went on without me. *Him,* the old man, the death-defier, he was all over my brain. I was lost. And, on the second hand, that Coke—a quart of Coke on a gutful of bourbon.

Prudhomme shrugs, I think. He seemed to have taken a little chill. His eyes stared into empty space. Outside the door, the voices of Homer the Brown and Opheila the

Jones. If their voices are outside, maybe they are too. They've gone out again. They keep doing that. Why—boy —the party's over. She's scolding him about something.

"I just didn't know," I said, desperately trying to clear my head. "I don't know—"

The old man broke out of his meditation. He went to a little box on the edge of the table and pulled out a small cigar. It was a foul little thing. He lit it up and stood under a heavy cloud, regarding me, the wreck in his basement.

I muttered sadly, "Henry, I'm not as stupid as I look."

He came to me and patted me, his rough old man's skin grainy on my arm. "I don't mean to persecute you, Green." His hand on me: "We'd better get you to bed. That wife of yours will be out lookin' for you."

"No she won't. That's another thing." I started to say stuff, but it's way past closing time. I let him hoist me up, and I walked out to the yard, where Homer and Ophelia were standing with their voices. I looked down at the old man's red corduroy slippers.

But he was looking at stars and chomping on his Excremento Blunt. He chatted with Ophelia, and I went staggering by myself up toward the front of the house, where a big new Oldsmobile was parked. I stood away from the house and looked up at the screened-in front porch. A little red light was burning; it looked like the front porch was a mouth of a cave and there was a fire brewing somewhere back inside. Our red pot light: we'll sneak over here some night, Ruthie and me, sit under that weeping willow, and turn on. I staggered toward the red light, saying my beads. None of the Above.

Homer Brown touched my arm with considerable concern. "Give you a ride?"

"Fine." The quart of Coca-Cola and the bourbon were

going at it now, furiously laying alternate claims to my guts. I felt the brew rising and slammed it down; a terrific pain convulsed my chest.

Ophelia and Henry were walking slowly in the long, unkempt grass of his rural yard. They were talking about Mrs. Prudhomme. Homer got into the Oldsmobile and squeezed into the middle. I sat on his right, resting my chin on the cool glass of the window; then I rolled it down and rested my chin. I believe my eyes are crossing.

Ophelia came around and pushed in behind the steering wheel. Prudhomme walked slowly up to my side of the car, puffing on his cigar. He held it waist-high and the fumes started rising into my nose, a fuse, and just as the old man leaned forward to say good night I burst open the car door and crawled out and threw up. I held my head slightly up and the quart of Coca-Cola came spouting out. Man, I am a Texas gusher. Standard Oil.

The old man danced out of the way, a bullfighter, and I shot it all out and then stood shaking my head.

Prudhomme waited a moment. "Green, you feel better?"

I gasped and wiped my chin. "Hope I didn't hit your slippers." I sat back and, to my surprise, I did feel immensely better. I closed the Oldsmobile door all by myself.

Ophelia laughed. "Never try to drink Henry under the table."

I stared at the stream in the grass. "Say—awful sorry about disgracin' myself that way. On your property."

Prudhomme stood away and chuckled, puffing his rank weed. "Oh, a lot of black boys have puked on old Prof's yard."

Skittishly the Texas black gals came piddling by my office. They sat, smiling; when I would point to a particularly poor passage in their notebooks they would brighten and sigh loosely and bat their eyelashes at me. "Oh, did I write that? That don't sound like me at all."

Betty McKay, a girl who worked in the White House, was paying her way through college by doing the presidential cleaning and washing the presidential dishes. She sat in a yellow summer dress with tiny white straps up over her tiny tan shoulders. I leaned back in my chair and stared at the cottonwood tree outside the office window. From below came the sounds of half a dozen scratchy violins in the Music Department.

I said, "You can do better than Bundy."

She played with her white straps. "You really think so?"

"You should go to a school that will challenge you."

"My mamma doesn't want me to leave Texas."

"Okay, the University at Austin."

"No. No, I don't think so."

"Why not?"

She looked at me and said calmly, "Well, I hate white people."

I nodded.

"What I mean is we're going to have our revenge some day. And won't it be a terrible revenge?"

I looked at her Fundamentalist eyes flashing. She was scheduled, according to the *Bundy Gazette*, to go to the national Moral Re-Armament conclave in early September.

I stood up and shut the window on the violins. I went to the door and peeked out into the hall. No one was waiting. I shut the door, moved back to my desk, and fell into my chair. "You enjoy working at the Washington home?"

Her large eyes came up.

"Well," I said, "you *do* work there. How does Presydent treat you?"

"Oh," she muttered, "Mr. Green, you are Presydent's *nephew*."

"Everybody notices that. But I've heard a lot. He's wrong. Something's wrong with him."

She opened one of the books on her lap and batted the front cover back and forth between her long dark fingers. "Everybody around here knows."

"Knows?"

The book in her hands was very useful. "Couldn't we talk about the academic things?"

"I think we are. What does everybody know?"

She stopped with the book. "How he beats his wife. And all that."

"Yes, I've heard."

"My mamma is pretty upset. I think she's going to get Daddy to do something."

"I don't understand."

"Well, it's pretty dangerous working there."

I raised my brows.

"I used to go over at the lunch hour and answer his telephone. At his office, you know?"

"Yes."

"Well"—her eyes came up again, steady and quiet, looking straight at me—"President came over and so naturally I start to leave. But he tol' me to stay." Her voice went down. "President said, 'Girl, you appeal to me.' "

She was quiet, and I decided to share the silence with her. She wasn't sure she should go on. At length I said, "And?"

"He reach into his wallet and he hand me a ten-dollar bill. He tol' me to buy myself something pretty."

I sat forward and put my hands, palms down, on my desk top.

" 'President,' I said, 'my daddy buys my clothes.' " Betty McKay quickened herself. "But President just won't take no for an answer." She shifted around in her little chair, again playing with the book on her lap. "He kind of grabbed me, you know. So I ran out of the office and I ran so hard over to the dormitory. And when I got there I still was shaking—I was starting to cry a little—and I stood by the stairs, and I opened my hands and I had that ten-dollar bill all crushed up in there. Isn't that funny?"

I waited, watching her.

"I put it in a sealed envelope and I went back—he wasn't there—and I put it on his desk." She sighed. "It always makes me nervous now when Mrs. Washington says, 'You go help Daddy answer the telephone.' "

"And your own daddy?"

"What do you mean?"

"You said he was goin' to start something."

"Oh, that. Well, I tol' Mamma what happen. And now she and Daddy want to take legal action. Especially if he try me again." She reached up and pushed some hair back into place. "Mr. Green, what exactly is a affidavit?"

I told her, and then we went over her in-class theme on

A BAD HABIT OF MINE

I sing all the time and it irritate my friends. A number of them tell me I was not born to be a singer.

I know it's probably only a psychological effect on me. When I was a baby I was told if I sang when I was hungry then I wouldnt be so hungry.

I think I can break this bad habit of mine if I really think hard about it. And eat whenever I possibly can.

Ruthie and I were strolling out by the frogpond when a little caravan of cars came by. An old Ford pulled up at the stop sign, Toast in the front seat. I waved to him, and he leaned out. "We goin' to blow at the Paradise." He invited us to come along. I turned and looked up the road toward Freeman Hall: a stream of headlights, an undergraduate procession slowly building for a big time.

It was a little drive-in restaurant, greasiest cheeseburgers in Texas, the Paradise. The owner, Mrs. Stanley, presided at the griddle. All the Bundy girls had an eleven o'clock curfew, but a dozen of them jumped out of the dormitory windows—*whee!*—and were settled now, to stay. So here in the colored section of Pastorius, down in the depths of Mrs. Stanley's facilities, Toast and his band, the Soul Merchants, set up shop. Dozens of pint whisky bottles appeared out of nowhere, and the little back room was packed in the lightning of electric guitars. A pair of dull girls from my Basic Communications class were alive now, communicatin' like crazy with the studs hangin' around them and feelin' them up. By midnight those empty pint bottles were lying around on table tops and in corners, the darkened little barroom roaring with electricity and drums and brass.

I was standing away from the band and near the screen door that was mercifully letting in a little fresh air. But even there the room was so full of smoke and noise and boozy song that every sense was cramped. Useless to try to talk. I danced with one of my gals, but the floor was packed and we just struggled in place. Dancing with Ruth was one silly cat smoking an unlit pipe upside down; he was talking so fast the pipe rattled around in his mouth like a loose part.

At the mike, a smooth sadist in a billowy satin shirt. He called for silence with a certain rhetorical cruelty, nice. He told a joke, the point of which involved the white nympho's mistaking of a black male's head for his ass— the Little One ducks her head and the silly cat drops his pipe—and then our emcee says, "Okay, boys and girls, my good buddy Toast Washington is going to let you listen in on"—his voice smoothed out in a wave—'Crazy Baby.' "

The room was convulsed in a mating squeal. Loose and grinning, from the exit to the parking lot and dust trees, Cousin Toast stepped up to the bullet-microphone. He stood sideways, and he must have learned something in my class, for he was wearing shark-tooth blue beads on his white shirt. A capella, his beautiful voice took off like foreplay: one round syllable, crawling around the corners of the upper registers, feeling out major sevenths and popping, dodging, not letting itself get caught, running in and beating-ass out, throbbing like silver and finally ending up with yards of sweet breath down where nobody had ever been before, a little fast sigh below the belt, coming into "Crazy Baby."

He had to wait thirty seconds before he could go on. The barroom was too loud, too crazy, all of the gals yelling their heads off, crying. You could hear nipples hardening everywhere and all the gals' chairs getting a bit damp. Toast relentlessly pulled screams out of them, wringing them for ten minutes. He seemed to take it personally.

At twelve-thirty he squeezed through to me. His face was worried. "Man, you in a little trouble." He could hardly make himself heard over the electric guitars. He winced. "Mrs. Strout. You know Mrs. Strout?"

"Dean of Women."

"Yes." He eyed the Little One nervously. "She called down here. About her girls. Bein' out after curfew."

"Then it's the girls who are in trouble."

"Well, Old Lady Stanley got kind of mad on the phone. Mrs. Strout is always bothering her." Again he looked at Ruth, checking something out, and then he went on. "You see, there's rooms upstairs. With beds in them, y'know?"

We nodded.

"Course, people say that when Mrs. Strout was a undergraduate here at Bundy herself, well, she was no stranger down here at the Paradise. Anyway, she called about her girls bein' out after curfew. Mrs. Stanley—heard her on the phone when I was in gettin' a beer—Mrs. Stanley said" (here Toast did an imitation of the old griddle-keeper) 'Lucretia Strout, your new faculty member is down here with his white woman.' "

I dug in my shirt pocket for cigarettes. "Check."

"Mrs. Strout is goin' to complain to Poppa. That woman is somethin' meeean." He started to go, then said, "I wouldn't think nothin' about it, except he got a little static about that time up to the general store." He smiled. "When you laid that guy out."

I lit my cigarette. "Can that be our private little joke?"

"Well, he got this call from old man DeLucca sayin' to

keep that outside agitator outside of his store." Now he got up. "I just thought maybe you ought to know."

"Thanks, baby."

He crawled through bodies back toward the microphone and in a moment burst into new singing. He and his Soul Merchants joined together, chanting above the electric guitars. The roomful joined, all of us, in the song: "You gotta live. For yourself. For yourself and nobody else." Them's my sentiments, and I looked over at one of my little girls; in class she always kept her eyes down, her voice a whisper. Now she was wild, shouting, "You gotta live. For yourself. For yourself and nobody else."

I was so happy, seeing that girl. And I went out back for air and there were several cars parked, nosing at the rear of the Paradise, couples down inside them, unseen, giggling and moaning. I stared back in at Ruth. A giant, six three and two-fifty, was talking with her. He wants to audit her Operation Head Start classes.

We stayed for another half-hour and left only as the party was reaching its highest point. The smoke in the room was thick enough to be boxed and carted away. I pulled myself up and struggled with her through the sweaty crowd. Just at the door out into the front stood a skinny wreck of a cat, about thirty, tall and caved in with drunkenness; he looked like he hadn't had a good meal in some time. He was nodding and swaying and stroking a little patch of fuzzy lint under his chin. When he saw Ruthie and me coming his eyes reared up—liquid black at the center and liquid red around the black. I was trying to brush past him and then things came together and he lashed out to the rhythm and got Ruthie with sharp angry hands low in the belly, going for the box, and just as I turned back somebody much stronger and not drunk pulled him away but he got free a moment and slugged

me in the breadbox—that man, I can't breathe, that bas-
tard, what'd he do that for, I really wish these goddam
Texans would lay off my person—I heard yelling as I burst
doubled through the screen door and that air has got to
come back. . . .

"*Hey?*"

My fingers digging out my guts, I look up, and there
in the screen door of the Paradise is Toast, circled with
satin musical buddies in the electric lights.

"Hey, you gonna be all right?"

I waved my hand, leaned on the Little One, and we
tottered off through the passionate cars.

But back at quarters she was the one in pain. Sometime during a break in the dancing she'd gone for the ladies' room. In her stall she heard a couple of black gals
breeze in the door and they were deploring white meat.
At the mirror: Oh, goddam white women, stay away from
our men. Who's that bitch think she is? . . .

It was rough. With me on the couch, the Little One
sat alone, couldn't be touched, staring into close space, just
staring and all cold, the voices of black women in her ears.

After the John Wayne war movie in the Bundy Summer
Film Series, a wet, hot wind was blowing around the campus, shaking the trees. Every minute or two, heavy clouds
in heaven would light up all over, a great sheet of white
behind the gray wool bags. I threw myself briskly down
the road and stopped only for a minute to watch the wet
wind sweeping across the black surface of the frogpond
and laying the long water-grass low. Miles away a bolt of
lightning shot down, a ragged power line scratching to the
distant horizon; it was followed several seconds later by a
blistering clap of thunder, two mile-wide white hands
smashing together. I scuffled through the gravelly driveway, went into the apartment, and there under my door
was a white square envelope with my name on it. The message read:

> FROM *the Desk of Achille T. Washington*
> Beaunorus,
>   See me please, today.
>
>   A.T.W.

I clomped on into the bedroom with the message in

my hand. Storms always scare her; she thinks they're out
to get her. When she was a little girl she thought Hitler-
thunder was going to get her, and she wrapped herself up
at the bottom of the bed.

"Hey," I said.

She murmured, "Who's there?"

"Who else?"

"Oh, it's you." She kissed me and then saw the message.
"Oh," she said, "that came while you were at your war
movie."

I had her read it. "I better go," I said, "it does request
my presence *today*." I stared at the Little One a moment.
She was not pleased, but I went out.

A new bolt of lightning shot down, closer now, a half-
mile away, and the thunder rolled just a few seconds after
it. It was going to be a real East Texas thunderstorm, catching the tail of a tornado up from the Gulf. The big outside
lamp on a post over our driveway flickered for a second,
dimmed way down, almost off, and then came back up.
When I crossed the road and got to the frogpond, it was
very, very dark. The pond water was oil. By the time I
got to the White House big drops of rain were starting to
fall, black separate circles on the white cement walk. All
but one of the windows were dark. Then I saw a shadow
move across the lighted window, and I decided to ignore
that presidential doorbell, the NBC chimes. I knocked.
At length the door opened. Betty McKay.

"Mr. Green." Her eyes widened. She was wearing an
apron and held a dishtowel in her hands.

"Evenin', Betty. Got a note the Bossman wanted to see
me."

She stepped back, one step. "He want to see you *now?*"

"I got a note." Waiting, standing. "May I come in out
of the rain?"

She was whispering. "Oh—oh, yes."

I stepped into the darkened front room. Oh, those long drapes hanging in scooping folds all along the far wall. I focused down at the glass ornaments on the coffee table; the tiny glass rocking chair, my mother's sign, was picking up a spear of light from the lamp in the dining room. I whispered, "Is President in bed?"

"No. No, he's not in bed. He's back down there." She turned and pointed with the dishtowel hand. "Down in his study."

What say—let's the two of us stop this whispering. "Well, perhaps I ought to go down."

She started to reach out, to touch me. Then she stepped back and smiled. "He's there waitin' for you."

"Is he working on something?"

"Oh, you know he's *always* working on something."

I waited and checked around the emptiness of the room. "Is Toast here?"

She shook her head. "No." Then she brightened. "He's pickin' me up later."

I nodded. "And Mrs. Washington? She—"

Betty seemed a little irritated with me. "No, she's not here, Mr. Green." She seemed to be saying, Want me to draw you a picture?

So I turned and at the head of the stairs leading down into the study I could hear dance music floating up from a radio. There was little light on the stairs, only a vague warm flicker as if from a candle. I went down softly, reaching out for wood paneling.

I turned at the stair base and stared ahead into the back-cellar study of the White House. He was sitting with his back to me, at a card table. On the tabletop was a heavy brown candle, half down, flame flickering. He had not heard me: his hearing-aid wires were sticking out

from his head. Someone had unplugged him. Across the
room I could make out an old, huge radio, massive Philco,
like a chest of drawers, crouching, twenty years old. In the
middle, above the masked speaker, a little rose light was
shining. Beneath, something moved: Dixie, Aunt Charlesetta's cat, a hill of gray fur under the Philco. Bossman himself had not yet turned around. He was swaying slightly in
his chair. Drawing close, I could see that he had a deck of
cards. He was slowly dealing them out, one by one, onto
the tabletop under the candle. Along the wall to the outside the windows were open; through the screens and the
open back door, mingling with the music, came the sound
of rain. I made a wide safe circle around him and ended
up standing back, just out of the candlelight, in front of
him. He did not seem to see me, did not hear me. He
looked relatively young—the deafness is due, after all,
not to age but to a defect. Finally he became slowly aware
that there was someone else in the room and he looked
down at the cards and reached his hand in slow motion toward the candle; stretched over his table, he looked up
through his gold-rimmed glasses.

I had expected him to jump out of his skin, seeing me
loom up in the semidarkness. But he merely took five
seconds to focus on me and then he said, "Good evening,
son."

So goddam drunk he was sober. It was drawn up from
decades; he stared, totally conscious and dead drunk, eyes
boring into my face like a white man's instruments. He
was immaculately dressed in his black suit and white shirt;
his black tie was pulled down from his neck two inches.
Slowly his right hand moved, as if someone beside him
were gradually bending his arm, up to his hearing-aid.
"I did not hear you come in."

"I got your note," I said.

"My note?"

"You said you wanted to see me."

He smiled "That I did, son."

Long silence. During it, he motioned to the chair opposite him at the table. I sat. Then, again taking great time, he reached down to his right and pulled up a tall drinking glass and without a sound, gently, laid it on the table. Like a piece of machinery, he reached down once more and pulled up a half-empty fifth of Jack Daniels. "Over there"—he stuck out his fingers, stiffly relaxed together, his hand like a paw—"you may find yourself a glass."

I pushed back my chair and went over by the open screen door, where the rain was pattering outside, heavily in the leaves of the trees. By the radio I found a tray and some glasses on it; I picked up one and I came back and sat down. He pulled up the bottle and poured a triple into the glass. No ice existed.

"Yes, Beaunorus Green," he said, "Lucretia Strout tells me you were down at the Paradise the other night. With your Ruth." He sighed and pulled on his liquor. "The Paradise is off limits."

I looked at him.

"You may find it odd," he said, "that I should be so strict. Last fall I had to cut down a hundred yards of hedge by the water tower. That is where the boys were taking the girls. They were out there at night just like animals." He snapped that word "animals," a nasty little ferocity, and I blinked. But then he drank, and I drank, and he went on. "Most of our students do not come from a desirable family background."

Shit, why was he talking like that to me?

"In high school you could find them walking the streets or in the fields at three in the morning. They have never known discipline." He slowly repeated the word "discipline." "The American university is usually a place of liberation. A place where young men and women can experiment with new freedom, new ideas. But"—his voice dropped—"we cannot afford the luxury of freedom here." The last word, "here," was heavier than the rest, and he pointed with one steady index finger down on a seven of diamonds in front of him, bull's-eye on the center diamond. He was absolutely in control of himself. "Do you see that, Beaunorus Green?"

"I see," I said. Then, quietly: "And you want me to steer clear of that general store."

"Oh"—he sighed—"that old man DeLucca is a damn fool. I don't know how many times I've had to—"

"Yes," I said, "you must catch a lotta shit down here."

He let the sentence sit for a moment, and then he said, "No, no"—a funny little low, swaying sound—"I've told many a white man where to—" He turned, caught himself, and said, "It might be better, yes, if you took your Coca-Colas on campus."

"Sorry to be causing you trouble."

He waited and then slightly smiled. "Beaunorus, you keep my switchboard buzzing."

I lifted my glass and the bourbon was beautiful, soft and thick, carpeting my throat on its way down. I listened to the music on the radio and stared at my uncle looming in candlelight opposite me, his eyes fixed on my face. He was looking for something in my face. He slowly did something to his hearing-aid. He saw me staring at the appliance and he said, "When I was a young fellow, like you, at my first teaching job, I spent a weekend in Nashville. I rode in with my good friend, Richard Osgood. We were standing outside a movie theater in Nashville, looking at the posters. A white man and his girl came down the street.

I did not hear her speak to me. Later Osgood told me she had spoken. She said, 'Let me pass.' I did not hear. The white man pounded me in the kidneys. He threw me down and ground his heel in my groin. When the man had left I pulled myself up to go. I asked Richard why he had not helped me. He was too scared to move."

It had taken him some time to tell the incident, and now he bent down and picked up the bottle and poured more into his glass. (On Monday afternoon as I swung round the steps, Himself was hearty with the Little One at his office door; to her he was saying, "Well, how's my favorite teacher?" I flittered into the shadow and listened to him jive.)

He stared into the candle. I joined him. Then I got uneasy and checked out his face. He opened his mouth, yawning, and a lumpy gray shape, a mouse, his tongue was moving around in his mouth. He finished yawning and said to me abruptly, "How old were you, boy, when your father died?"

"Four."

He shook his head. "Our father—your grandpappy—you know the last time my brother Bill and I saw our old man?"

"No."

He sat back in his chair and his head fell forward on his chest. He looked like he was dead. "The last time we saw our daddy he was hanging from a pine tree. With blood on his pants."

I froze up and waited.

His head came up and his eyes opened wide; the light of the candle was dancing on his gold rims. "He was a fighter, your grandpappy." He seemed to be reaching, reaching across a terrible expanse of space.

We observed a silence for a full minute, pondering. Here we are, my paternal grandpappy, the fighter, caught that night in the torchlight, white women singing and watching. Hang ever' nigger t' a sour-apple tree. More awful shit-silence.

His whole body seemed to come together, to shift, to pick itself up, atoms suddenly realizing what they are here for and darting to the center. "Excuse me one moment, son."

He pulled himself up out of his chair; he was walking slowly, steadily. In a minute, with right words, I would be on my way home in the rain, going home to red lights and soft red thoughts. But he was climbing his stairs.

I was alone with Dixie. I went to the radio and listened to the dance music, soft and easy. I reached down to touch the cat. It moved, slightly, and I could feel its heart bumping against its gray side like a slow rock. The cat droned darkly, considerable horsepower in neutral. Up there, the front door opens and closes. There goes my Betty, sweet little gal. Toast has picked her up. Girl, you appeal to me. I went to the window and watched it rain, the trees metallic and green out there, reflecting the one electric streetlight.

The Little One said that he said I was wrestling with a good-sized ego. I would have liked to hear him say that. She reported his opinion: "Ruthie, you're more mature than Bo is. Now don't you go running yourself down on account of him. You deserve some of the spotlight." Oh, I would have loved to be in on that conversation. What'd you say, baby? "I let him know I knew what he was doing." Still, I'd like to have been there. . . .

But he is coming down the stairs. Briskly. He sat at our table and a ring was in his voice; he waved a pack of Kents at me. We lighted up together from the candle. Helpfully, he looked down at the cards, picked them up, and shuffled them. "Are you a poker-player, boy?"

"I have played some."

He was very good at the cards; drunk, he was able to make them jump. "How about a hand?" He was just plain folks, and I kept my eyes on his eyes, two to two.

"Well, there are only the two of us." I turned and pointed under the radio to the cat. "Unless, of course, we deal Dixie in."

Archie regarded cards. "Oh, Bo, you're not serious." He reached for the Jack Daniels. "How about Showdown?"

"Fine."

"Dollar a bet?"

"Suits me."

"You don't mind if I deal?"

"Uncle, I trust you completely."

He banged the deck on the tabletop, and the candle wavered. I cut the cards. He picked up the deck, played with it, and threw out a card to me, and then his hand circled back for his bourbon. "Six." Then the hand was careful, teasing over his own card, and the hearts slipped up—the card seemed to pause, softening itself into the air, and it slid red on the table.

"Ten, my bet." He stopped and dumped out the Kents on the tabletop and handed five to me and kept five for himself and brushed the rest of the cigarettes off onto the floor. He put his long chip into the center. "On the line. One dollar."

I put my cigarette out to greet the poker pot.

Archie said, "This afternoon I talked to one of my old fraternity brothers. Were you in a fraternity in your white college, Bo?"

"No. But the Alpha Delts went through agony—soul-searchin'— before they handed me my little black ball."

"Old Jackson"—his eyes went hazy behind the glasses —"we were in the same class. I will never forget our initiation. They didn't let us pledges sleep for sixty hours." Then his mind switched back from the siding and he said, "Showdown," and the card came across to me, falling first drunkenly on its face. I reached for it, flipped it. "Jack." I looked at the one eye.

"I declare," he said, "I don't think any fraternity in this country, black or white, ever had an initiation ceremony like old Beta Beta Tau." He dealt himself a card. "Nine here. Possible straight." He looked down to his hands. "Up it a dollar."

I put another cigarette into the pot, four of them now, two from him and two from me, white tubes lying together.

He held the deck of cards against his white shirt. "They took all our clothes except for our shorts. They painted us white. Oh, Bo, you should have seen us. We had to carry eggs between our legs in our shorts. We played *Rug*by"—he laughed—"and every time you crawled under the rug you'd break an egg. I had seven in my trousers."

I stared at my two cards, just checking.

He smiled. His smile was very deep and familiar. "Old Thurmond had to put his nose up against mine"—he leaned forward—"and say, 'I love you, I love you, I love you.' " Deliciously he fingered the cards. "And I had to put my nose tight on his and say, 'I may be deaf, but you're a homo, I may be deaf but you're a homo, I may be deaf but you're a homo.' " Laughing with extraordinary middle-aged pleasure, he briskly put his young body over the table and dealt. "There's your six on my side. Too bad for you. Still a possible straight over here." He meticulously picked up another cigarette and laid it down in the center. "One more dollar."

He had dealt out of order, hitting himself first, but I let it go when he lifted the deck and laid a jack of hearts on me. "Well," I said, "it appears I have a pair."

He seemed momentarily confused then; he smiled. "I guess we'll go on. You came out of that one smellin' like a rose."

I put my cigarette in the middle, six dollars in our pot. The basement room lighted up when a flash of lightning came down nearby. We are in a black recreation room in Texas; it's all right. Presydent, let's just say I can't stand it no more. My paternal grandpappy hanging from a pine tree and then the whole family blow up, my dead daddy—all the fight gone out of him—taken in to the Green household, formally adopted. But I should not be a Green. I am Beaunorus Washington. Why didn't my daddy keep his *real* name?"

"Bo?"

I stared at him. "Sorry."

"What were you thinkin' about, boy?"

"About bein' a Green when I'm supposed to be a Washington."

He slumped slightly toward me.

"I mean, my daddy's name *was* Washington. Before —before it happened to Grandfather."

"That's right, son."

Again, a silence. I coughed into it and tried to find myself again. Come on, go on with your fraternity initiation when you was painted white and the banana is white too hanging down and play strip-poker with your Distinguished Colleague nephew. And then let's the two of us go on out and stand in the rain.

"Your fraternity?" I said. I really don't want to play cards.

He tilted back in his chair, onto it again. "We had to eat grasshoppers and smoke big ceegars in a telephone booth. We'd blow air into each other's faces to keep alive."

"Sounds like fun."

He stared at me. "It was. Isn't that odd, Bo? It was. Dressed up in shaving cream and eggs and fish guts smeared on our heads. We had to crawl up into the chimney and scrub her down." He guffawed. "The only way they'd allow us to clean our heads was stick 'em in the toilet and flush."

I waited, watching his head, and then he was with me. My eyes watched the seven coming across. "That's your seven."

"Well, now." He sighed and regarded the cards. "Bet them up, Bo."

"You can't play to an inside straight. My jays have got it."

"Would you like to double the pot?"

"One can hardly refuse."

"Then double it we do."

He slowly pulled himself up and went over by the radio, reached down into a liquor cabinet, and brought out another fifth of Jack Daniels. He came back and propped the bottle on the table.

I said, "Black Label. Afro-American stuff."

He smiled. "I try to keep abreast of the times." When he opened it he passed the bottle back and forth under his nose. "My, *isn't* that a lovely aroma?" He poured into his glass, but I held my hand over mine. I'm not going to repeat my famous Texas oil gusher, not with it raining so hard. I thought of Henry, the old man; he was propped up in bed scrutinizing the *Liberator,* eating cheese. His teeth are on the dresser.

"I am much impressed with your taste in women, Bo."

I glonked my eyes up at him. He was straight to me. I flumped around in my chair. "She's got a lot of crazy ideas."

"Does she?"

"Her idea of family. She wants to pick up children all over the world. All colors. She can't see what the problem is—my children, other men's children. I think she read some book somewhere about society doesn't have to be based on the family unit."

He kept quiet, our eyes on wires, and then he sighed, sat back, and dealt himself an eight.

He couldn't beat me: he could not fill that straight, and even if he paired up I would still be jacks high.

He laid the deck on the table beside him. The radio was playing the last dance: "*Dream,* when you're feelin' blue; *Dream,* it's the thing to do." I had been lost in the music; then I pulled myself together, for he was looking at me again, all on top of me with his eyes.

He was on another tack. "Do you want children?"

"Sooner or later." I thought for a moment. "I want— I want a son."

He smiled. It was like music.

And only an inch of the candle left. I said, "A woman is a strange creature."

He yawned once again, and his mouth was huge. His eyes were idly on his cards. He dropped his head forward, and I stared at the top of it. His hair was beginning to thin there. "I remember," he said, "when I was in high school and old Mrs. Johnson made us read *The Scarlet Letter.* Did you ever read that book, son?"

"Yes."

His head was still down, the top of it pointed at me. He

muttered to his lap, "That poor woman. Lord, that poor woman."

I will get up and walk round the table and pick him up and carry him up to bed. Uncle—oh, Lord, that poor woman—let me tuck you in. I don't much care whether you are a conscious villain or an unconscious victim; what say, shall we tango on upstairs? I wish my girl was here.

Still with his head down, he said, "That woman is worth a hundred of me. I adore her."

Then he caught himself again; he had been walking around on top of a skyscraper, reeling, one foot off the edge, and then coming back on, reeling, one foot again over, there he goes, look out below, and coming back onto the ledge. "That woman is worth a hundred of me."

"I know how highly you think of your First Lady."

He looked back up and smiled at me, a sharp little smile, made out of compressed air.

Muzak, electro bleeps from the USAF. Steel birds at this moment are circling the world. Knock-knock. Who's there? Presydent. PRESYDENT *WHO?* And it occurs to me that before that rain stops one of us is going to kill the other. I tried to knock it out of my mind, but our just being there in the candlelight—it walked over me, and I was ready for physical damage. I could smell it.

He held his hand over the low candle, so close that the nervous flame must be starting to dig up and blister the palm. With his flesh being roasted, he stared into me. Now —put out the light, and then . . . he is looking for himself in the pupils of my eyes. His hand is cruelly hurting itself. And one does not blink. If I quench thee, thou flaming minister . . . both of us, we are being looked at.

He took his hand away from the candle. He put his scorched palm on top of his other hand. Softly, finally, he whispered, "Son, it's a bitch."

There was a considerable silence. And then he let out an unmusical little whistle and stared into his bourbon. Under his breath he said, "When you come right down to it, there is one thing that you can count on in this world."

"Yes."

"When you come right down to it, in the final analysis, a white man will always turn white."

I waited and then said, "And a white woman?"

He just sat quietly.

I got up. Outside, it was still really coming down. I stood watching the rain on the lawn. And as I was trying to think, slowly, from behind me, the low voice said, "Beaunorus, you *have* been hearing bad stories about me."

Here it comes. Six guns, the Texas stand-off. I gave thought to my face, its reconstruction. "What do you mean, Uncle?"

"Beaunorus Green, you know what I mean. In a Negro university rumor is a powerful weapon. Our people are very gullible."

"You've noticed that too?" I turned and went back to the table and sat staring at the wildly burning butt of the candle.

His eyes are round. "You never questioned them, did you?"

"Uncle, I don't quite follow you."

"You assumed." He sighed and waited. "You brought your white girl down and you were afraid the coloreds would behave poorly in her eyes."

"I don't think you can say that to me."

He grinned. "Boy, there are so many things I could tell you. Your poor old father."

"What?"

"You know about your father. He was a little crazy."

"Do you think everybody in Texas is crazy?"

He waited a minute. "I believe so. We're all just playin' out our diseases. That's all man ever does—all playin' out our diseases."

"So much for history." I looked at him across the table. "Ruthie's parents, you know, they had to clear out of Germany in 'thirty-six. She's got a friend with blue serial numbers tattooed on her arm."

He nodded.

"You think Americans could do that to us? Exterminate us?"

He waited. "Boy, you mean you thought they couldn't?"

My eyes stammered at him and then I said, "Archie, I—I don't think we've finished our game of cards."

He glanced down at the cards and then back at me, his eyes glowing like fine bourbon held up, straight, to the light. "Why look here, son, you're absolutely right. You're sitting there with a pair of jacks and me with just a possible inside straight that I've got to fill. You have me, boy."

I put in the last cigarette.

"Would you like to bump it?"

"No."

"You don't want to take my money. Is that it, boy?" And when I shook my head he said, "Well, then, what say we just play for a straight hundred dollars, the whole hand?"

Oh, come on, man. Screw the white man's greenbacks. None-of-the-Above shit. Uncle, let's play for the thing that means the most to us. You put in your school. I'll put in the Little One. Fair? Bundy versus Ruthie. Winner take all. Oh, I can see me now—my inaugural address: "Distinguished colleagues . . ."

"Well, boy?"

I was about to suggest my idea, but I simply nodded.

"Son, I've misjudged you. You *are* a poker player. One hundred dollars. I declare." He studied the hands spread out and then said, "Bo, I'm a gambling man." He delicately put in his last cigarette and then dealt me the card, a seven of spades: two pair, and there it was—more than two pair, the seven he needs. "Well, now," he said.

I looked at the board. I should have advanced the big bet.

I have won.

It didn't mean much, I fell into it, but put down this one little fact: I *did take* him. Galoop, galoop—so happy, let's go to the Boston Tea Party.

Before I could speak he flipped over his card, the seven of clubs, and his straight was filled, impossibly, neat as a pin. He waited for a moment, letting it all sink into my eyes—say good-by to five twenties—and then he exploded in laughter, a huge burst. "Oh, *boy*," he shouted, "don't you *ever* let a man deal his own cards." He laughed until it looked as if his hearing-aid would burst, a plug, straight out of his head. "Boy, you got no nigger sense at *all*."

We sat in cascades of his laugh. Like fabric, wadding, filmy thick all over the room in folds and drapes.

I stood up, went for the stairs. "I gotta use your john." It took Distinguished Colleague a minute to find the bathroom. I emptied the world's best bourbon out of my bladder and bathed my face. In the mirror my eyes were steady. I snapped off a few sections of rose-print toilet paper, blew my nose, and sent the tissue down into the plumbing. Then I went back to the stairs and as I started down I heard the screaming of the cat above the radio blaring and my uncle's laughter. I could see little darting lights flickering on the walls. I stumbled down the stairs; the candle was on

its side and he was roaring; Dixie's tail was high and wav-
ing and exploding, a yellow fire whip that ran behind her,
popping off the fur, crackling like burning human hair.
Archie was slumped over the radio with his big bourbon
glass, quite empty, hanging in his hand. He laughed and
shouted, "*Cat.*"

I ran for Dixie, reached to the pawing legs, awkward,
and I cradled the big flaming tail starting to spread. I
patted with my hands, stumping to the open back door,
and went out into the night, throwing the cat to the rain.
I ran forward, over the little roofed patio and out into the
storm, the grass at the side of the house, and I fell on Dixie,
fell to smother brightness of the firelight with my chest.
Put your arms around me, Dixie. I lay rolling against her
until the fur sent smoke to my face, making me cough.
There was a bad smell in my nose as I lay with my arms
around Dixie, covering her in the rain.

I lay on my back, blinking up at the sky. The rain
whipped down, catching in my eyes. From the house there
came out, now, no sound. He had turned off the radio. He's
gone to bed. Don't forget to put out the cat, Beau-nor-ees
Green. I'd like us all to do everything possible to make our
distinguished colleague comfortable. I rolled over and
looked at Dixie: she was pulling herself together, whining
to herself. She padded, with all the dignity her burnt fur
allowed, back under the roof of the patio. She sat, softly
crying, and stared at me. What's the matter, black boy,
don't you have enough sense to come in out of the rain?

How very, very soft it is, when you run to the bottom and hang on. We do not shut the door. The body, brazen from fire, melts its blood and bones. And we are at peace in rain. A peace too warm for crouches or for warnings, more like saying to the warm personage under you, "How you tonight?" It would be good. Come now, let us wrestle in a red light of candles. All of us. Something downright comical about it. All of us in bed. Henry, no. Snoring on a throne, after declaimin' a bedtime story. Honk honk hee hee. Toast is just smiling in sleep. Archie and I, we have a hand apiece on her breasts. Toast keeps smiling and Henry flutters his lips, wheew-ooo. The voice is sweet from the ground.

I sat up shaking, brushing the wet grass from my clothes. I pulled myself in under the roof of the patio. Dixie was looking very uncomfortable, but the damage was slight, just burned fur; she would pull through. The blood of all men and animals is the blood of one body. I threw myself down on a damp green chaise longue. I stared across the campus and at the trees swinging in the rain, the land stretched out, crumpled with underbrush;

it was heaped up and rolling, an old blanket on an old bed. That blanket of Texas land seemed to be moving, as if there were some giant under its bedclothes, and I could hear, through the rain, crying; the giant was having terrible dreams, and his green sleep was severely troubled. He groaned. The blanket of the land moved and shifted in my eyes and I could hear low crying and indistinct words. Poor giant, that it should rain in your bedroom.

I sit here in hard helium and on our right you see trees with doodles of spider legs among the branches—peer— thousands of Texas leaves outside the White House window and the light, the rain below them, splinters them into huddled flat machines and shadows. I hit the dirt.

Try not to watch the leaves, sweeping and kissing. Ashes blow. Hear the thunder a hundred miles away, soft and deep: buffalo sweeping up a plain. I scratch my head. Poor Texas giant is trying to sleep, and Archie and I know all that is real in this world is the open center of an open eye.

BEAUNORUS GREEN?

HERE!

You are Archie's boy.

Pokerwise? Sexwise? Racewise?

NAME YOUR OWN DEAL.

And look at this White House. Here at the back she's the Black House. Charred boards, signs of a fire. Uncle likes a fire.

A small piece of the ground over there is moving. A small domed piece of ground, a muddy paperweight, decided to move. All physical laws suspended. In the darkness and the rain I stood up. I walked toward the little piece of land. It's a turckle. A real live turckle. The turtle could not, surely, have come all the way up from the frog-pond, but there on the dark sloping lawn of the White

House the Vietnamese orphan turtle came, an inch at a time, slowly forward, its clawy flipper stuck in the green grass. I started out for it and bent for it—we was going to play the Dozens—and a blast of lightning from straight over my head came crackling down, with all the power of the sky, blasting a tree across the yard. My brain rang. I couldn't see, and electric cotton—the remains of a hearing-aid—loose wires were sticking out all down my ear canals. I faded back to the porch and You gotta live for yourself For yourself and nobody else and *all you turckles will have to make it without B.G. from now on.*

I was not going to try to go home with all that sky doing all that Lone Star damage. I curled up in my wet clothes on his green chaise longue. A Green nigger in a green chair. I was dreaming that I was back over at the apartment and it was A-OK, Zip Luper sitting in his chair asking me if I was going to cop a few zees and I said surely I was. I am giving my Oscar speech in Santa Monica and suddenly I stop, rear back, and heave the statuette like a brick—sailin' out into the audience like into a store win-dow. T-Birds and Oldsmobiles a few years old are lined together under fluorescent blue-green lights. The lawn, beyond the gravel driveway, is defoliated radium green and there are spiders of rag-blister grass on the red dirt. A cricket wanders on Dixie's back. And I give up the stream of my blood, the fierce pressure of accumulation, the waste of days. I began to be needled by Toast, his image, floating, darting into familiar scenes of my boy-hood in Modesto . . . cowboys and Indians . . . Tarzan on a vine . . . landing soft in dusty jungle grass over your head . . . somebody's coughing . . .

I woke up in the patio and it was hot at dawn. My head was fuzz throbbing. The rain hadn't helped a bit. The sun was up somewhere, though I couldn't see it from the patio, and the sky was bright blue. I got up and started through the drying grass for the apartment.

I was staring up at the sky, rounding the corner of the White House, when I stopped and sank back under a dripping tree. There up on the flat roof, straight as a store-window dummy, sat my uncle, the President. He was sitting in the porch swing high on the flat front roof of the White House. He was in his white short-sleeved shirt, and his arms were fixed like poles beside him. He was looking at the sky, trying to stare through it, trying to stare through the blue and come out on the other side. He did not move.

The leaves sprinkled a little chill water down onto my neck as I stood moving under them, watching the man on the roof. I couldn't walk out in front of him, for he would see me and call me. God knows what he would have to say about last night. Dixie? She had not been on the patio when I had awakened. That cat is a truck. Am I going to stand here in my shoes all morning? I don't want to look at the man in his porch swing any longer. I'll make a break out back for it and circle around by the auditorium. That's it; if he should hear me, turn, and call, I shall ignore him. But no, that man will not do any hearing this morning. Archie did not move, did not even breathe. He was just staring, solid up there on the roof, eyes riveted on something unnamed in the brilliant blue sky. He looked as if he had been painted there.

"This morning we're celebrating the Viet Cong's latest assault on Danang." (In the back, absently listening, Toast was doodling, drawing something in his notebook.) "Once again, millions of Uncle Sam's electronic eyes could not halt ten skinny little Asians—colored men—from destroying millions of dollars of star-spangled white men's equipment."

Toast kept on doodling; with his eyes on his paper he said slow to himself, "Hoo-ray for colored men crawling in the bushes all over the world."

After class we walked over to my office together, talking about the war and the black man. Suddenly I laughed.

He looked at me, questioning.

"Oh," I explained, "late one night last spring I was ridin' a big green-topped New York City bus on Broadway in the high seventies. Needle Park we call it, where the junkies hang out. I was comin' home all alone from a movie and I was sittin' in the middle of the bus and at one stop all the old white ladies around me stiffened up. I

looked up at the front door. We had ourselves a new pas-
senger, and he was one big noise."

Toast and I went into my office and sat. I held forth as
we lighted our cigarettes. "You see, it was a black boy on
the bus steps, somewhere down in his early teens, out of
his mind. He was rubbin' his head with an empty Coke
bottle. He reeled back into the open doors, callin',
"Later, baby," to a dark empty place of street. Then the
bus moved back on out into the piddle traffic and the kid
addresses his attention span to the fare box. A long, long
time chappie stood there, and I watched him, everybody
did. He rocked away, breaking his moorings, tennis shoes.
Oh, man, he rubbed that Coke bottle on his head like it
was hair-straightener. At the next stop somethin' Jewish
went on out the back, and our boy was still bent over
starin' into the coins. What seemed to have happened was
that he had got to like the pattern and to watch it move
round."

Toast grinned. "I thought this had somethin' to do
with the war in Vi-etnam."

"It does." I leaned way back in my chair, remembering.
"Now the driver, a curly Italian fellow over the big wheel
—guy about my age—he snaps a lever and sends some
small change down into the guts of the coin-eater. Several
seconds later the boy looks up. And the coin-eater goes
on digestin' with a regular grind. It goes on like that
and then we hit a stoplight and driver squashes the
doors whimpf open again and says, 'Pay up or get off.' But
our boy just waits. He fasten his rovin' eye on a chunk of
flat space between him and the driver, more toward the
latter. Continuin' to conk himself with that Coke bottle,
he says, 'Look, how far uptown you go?' And the driver
says, 'Hundred twenty-ninth and Amsterdam.' And as the

light changes the boy says, 'Glad this bus goes up there. My brother's waitin' for me, to pay.' "

I slammed forward in my chair and put my hands on the desk. "Right? You got it, Toast? The bus with the green top and the silvery sides, that's mine, baby, you wait for it."

Toast nodded, and in the middle of a conspiratorial smile he ejected a smoke ring that flattened out like a halo over the desk.

"Well, the driver indicates he has no choice—and I guess he doesn't. He says, 'Pay or get off.' Boy-o'-my-heart expels low words. The driver twice says, 'What?'—first because he can't hear it and second because he can't believe it. So then, for the third and last time, the boy draws. himself up and says, 'Vet'ran. Vet'ran.' And driver's toothpick recrosses to left field, whink. Driver is in a locomotive cab, looking down at a boozy yardbird way down there alone in the morning ice. And above the endless giggle 'n' grind of the coinbox our boy wonder speaks the piece that says everything about the black man and the war."

Toast said, "What was that?" He was looking at me oddly.

"He says, 'I fought in Vietnam so that you could drive this bus.' "

"The *kid* said that?"

I nodded. "And then the driver's right bicep twitched, a flied horse flank, and he said, 'Yeah, that's all I needed.' "
I leaned over the desk. "Now, see it, Toast: the boy's only about fourteen at the outside and he says with utter self-confidence, 'I fought in Vietnam so that you could drive this bus.' And then he bides his time. Nothing much happens, so he puts on a little pressure—'I'm not alone, my boys is here with me, the cats I run with'—and he motions behind him with his bottle to those doors still wide,

and we're blocks from where he got on solitaire. And the streetlight changes again, like an idiot. And it just looks like we're goin' to have to call it a draw, this driver and the kid. Neither one can move until the other does, and all the passengers are sittin' there like baggage, waiting."

Toast said, "So did they kick him off the bus?"

"Hell, no. I was watchin' it all and I called up from the fifty-yard line, 'Hey, let's go.' And then, poppin' my voice up an octave: 'Hey, baby, what's matta wi' you?' Well, our black veteran catches my double-barreled cry, and he *re*sponds, '*Yo!*' And Lord, Lord, he was lookin' all over that bus, up to the roof and on his shoulder and in his Coke bottle—baby, here I am, come get me.

"Well, at last he turns and sees me. 'Say, Jack, gimme dime?' 'Ho-kay,' I said. And that kid walks back and sways over a seat where those white bus ladies go to rubber together. The bus doors slam shut and away we go. As the blocks roll by no fare is forthcoming from our team, none at all, and the two of us brothers just sit sweet whilst everything stays fine. Real fine, stopping to take in and discharge, rolling up that Great White Way."

We sat in silence in my office for some time. I laughed, remembering the incident, reliving it, and Toast was smiling easy, eventually leaning forward to put out his cigarette. We were stuck, though, a bit lost as to how to talk.

Finally I said, "Well, you goin' to work after school's out this summer?"

"Guess so."

My eyes went from his face to the closed office door. "What you plan to do?"

"Oh, Henry's trying to talk me into going back on down to Bogalusa."

"And?"

Toast began to move around in the chair. He grinned.

"Once I was in the tiniest jail cell you ever see. No bigger'n a pay toilet." His eyes closed, he said, "Man, I had the funniest dream." His lips smiling: "There I was all cramped up, and I dreamed I was dancin'." There was just a hint of the counter-tenor, "Crazy Baby," in his voice; he repeated the word: "Dancin' and dancin'."

Slowly, in the silence, I said, "What do you do when those crackers get you down and start workin' you over?"

"Well, now, first of all, to prevent disfigurement of the face—"

"Disfigurement of the face?"

"Well, you put your back to a wall. If you can get near one." He was looking at the wall behind my head.

"Near a wall? Your back?"

"For your kidneys." He stood up. "But hell, we're through with all that."

I stood with him and we went to the door. It was time for lunch.

"That marching and praying, we just had to quit that. Especially the praying—it *did* get on one's nerves."

We went down the stairs of Freeman Hall and out onto the campus.

"Hell, I don't know about you, with your white wife and all, but I never wanted to be integrated."

"Come on, Toast, she's sort of white, but she's not White Womanhood. I couldn't have married U.S. white meat."

He was looking at me.

"Man, she is *la petite*, the Little One. And we've worked out a beautiful thing."

He looked away, embarrassed and good, nodding. "I see the way you are."

"Okay."

"I meant those old integration marches always going

into the worst neighborhoods. All they got is wall-to-wall
honkies. Now why would I want to live there?"

"Beats me."

"I mean some of those people can't even speak the
English language. It's ridiculous."

Going across the lawns toward the administration
building, I stared back at the trio of white brothers. They
were bunched in gray business suits under the trees. We
were having a Career Day; those white brothers in Madison Avenue Stetsons over there, from Dallas, employers
("Three niggers into the front office"—A.T.W.) had
agreed to participate in a panel on Opportunities in Industry.

Toast and I were crossing the parched lawn with the
crowd of kids coming from class when a window behind us
flew up; a voice came spitting gravel out of the presidential
office. "You look me in the eye, Archie, tell me you're trying to send me out to *pasture?*"

We turned. Henry Prudhomme—his sharp little
figure was standing right inside the open window. He was
shouting out his words, half to the man inside and half to
all of us on the lawn. "After thirty years of my life to this
college—the only *professor* it had when you were here—"

Archie's body intervened. We could see him pushing
Henry away from the window, but the old man began to
yell, laying it on, and he could barely catch his breath.
"Keep your hands *off* me, Archie T. You try your rough
stuff on Henry Prudhomme, and it's going out about those
contracts for your *Com*plex. You black Billie Sol, I'll kick
up so much dust—"

The office window came crashing down. On the front
lawn Toast and I looked at each other, and both our faces
were working; a dozen students turned and ran together,
charging back into the building. Toast and I followed

them; I was shaking, muttering to myself, "Get him, Henry, get him now."

Crowded and jammed in the hallway I stayed back against the wall, behind stacked-up students; Toast had moved up into the front lines, staring about him, and his face was frantic for action. The door to the presidential office was thrown open. There he stood: Henry, in an old gray suit and red slippers, on the thick gold carpet. He was slamming his hands up and down in the air, furious. "Look at those students out there. You try to re-tire old Prof, and this whole school goes on the picket line."

Henry looked out, his jaw loose, shaking, and then Archie himself stepped again between Henry and the outside world. The door to the office slammed shut, a hollow sharp blast. Behind it, muffled, the old man's voice heaved up, blind.

I declare, those two old people are on their honeymoon. Ruthie and I came hand in hand up to the porch, and Mrs. Prudhomme was dressed in a blue housecoat with little pink roses on it; Henry was dolled up in style, a three-piece black suit, a funeral suit, ancient and shiny, and a spanking white shirt and white socks and black shoes. The line of white hair down on the side of his head, the fringe below the bald crown part of the outfit. Running across the dome of his stomach, a silver chain with a glittering silver medal hanging down from ribbons at the center of the black vest. Henry called out to us, motioning us in; I opened the screen door, and we sat in metal chairs opposite them. It's the young folks, the children, payin' respects. And the old folks sit on their little swing like it's a loveseat hanging from the low porch ceiling on two heavy chains. They had hung it too high; no one shoe of those four shoes can touch the floor. They rocked back and forth, two old little children.

"Rather warm to be out on the porch," I said.

Mrs. Prudhomme was feeling much better. "Oh," she said, shaking her head, "I don't like these air-conditioners.

So Poppa brings me out here for an hour in the evenings."

I looked out across the twilight to the other old houses. On the porch across the street half a dozen home folks were sitting and talking, their voices low and lazy in the air. Then I stared back at Henry in his black suit.

The Little One said to him, "That's quite a medal you got there." She gazed upon it.

Henry was pleased. I never introduced them; when I found them one day surrounded by dogs they were already on to each other, completely, and now the old man bent his bald head down to look at his medal. "Oh, I got a drawer full of them. My public-speaking prizes. But this one is the glitteriest of them all." He perked up to say it, and some of the old fire began to kindle in his eyes. "It's the one I like to wear."

I said, "So you were in public-speaking contests?"

"*Was* I?" He stopped the motion of the swing and peered across the twilight at Ruthie and me. "Why, when I was in college I went all over this land on those forensic tour-na-ments."

Mrs. Prudhomme nodded. "That's how Poppa won me. I saw him up on the platform and I said, 'I'm going to get me that man.' " She giggled, a schoolgirl.

"All over this land. Up to Lincoln and down to Tuske-gee and New Yawk. That's where I won this little treas-ure." He played with the medal in his tiny fingers. "It was an o-ratory contest. I had to win first prize. Twenty dollars. So I could buy a wedding ring." He turned and frowned at her. "I had to win first prize."

"You did, Poppa." She held her old wrinkled hand out at us. Ruthie rose, half standing at her metal chair, and scrutinized the thin gold band on the old lady's finger.

Henry said, "I never memorized my speeches. Always figured something brilliant would come to me once I got up on that platform. But this speech, it was the only one I ever memorized. I had to get Mamma her wedding ring. So I worked and I worked on that speech. The only one I ever memorized. And I forgot it."

"That's the way it works," I said.

He smiled, and someone was pouring energy, life, into that old body. "My Lord, that was back in nineteen-nineteen. Was it that long ago? Up in New Yawk. That oratory contest in a Jewish synagogue."

"A synagogue?" Ruth said.

"Oh, Lord, yes. And I forgot my *speech*." He threw back his head and let the words bounce up to the porch roof. "It was down to just two of us. Rudolph Martin—oh, he became quite a *surg*eon, they tell me. And couldn't he speak? Oh, Lord, he was as smooth as silk. The chairman of the occasion was the Honorable Roberts. He was a big Harlem lawyer. That synagogue was packed. And they announced my name and I got up and I started to speak. I got halfway through, and—oh, Lord, isn't it funny how the human mind works?—it went right out of my head. I looked up, and there on the balcony was a clock. It said, Henry, you got fifteen more minutes to go, and *noth*ing to say." He popped down off the swing. "My old speech coach —my, Miss Beecham, what a wonderful lady she was—she always said to me, 'Henry, if you ever forget or get mixed up, pause, don't hesitate.'" He was convulsed with a little giggle, standing in the middle of the porch. "That was all that was in my mind." He lobbed the words out, slow and vast: "*Pause,* don't hes-i-tate." He giggled again. "But my speech wouldn't come to me. It *would* not come. I swear, my mind was never a bigger *blank* than it was in that New Yawk synagogue."

"So, what'd you do?"

"You never saw a man p-au-au-se longer than young

Prudhomme. I hooked my thumbs in my pants pockets"—
he did it now, on the porch—"that was one of my tricks.
I walked along the platform and bent over just a little, like
I was lost in thought." He scowled. "Lord, I wasn't lost in
thought; I was just plain *lost*."

Ruthie sat back in her chair, brushing her hair away
from her face, all caught up in the man and laughing.

"Pause, don't hesitate. Pause, don't hesitate. That was
all I could think of. I walked and I walked"—Henry
walked and he walked, in front of us, to the end of the
porch—"and I got clear to the end of the patform, I
couldn't walk any farther, and it *still* wouldn't come to
me." He stood there at the end of the porch, and behind
us on the swing the lady in the blue housecoat giggled.

"That's when I got my idea," he said. "It's an old trick
I learned from Booker T.'s nephew. Oh, he was a great *de-*
bater. And he had this *de*vice—he'd stop in the middle and
then he'd look up and shout, '*Think.*' So there at the end
of the platform I suddenly whirled around"—Henry spun
around on the porch—"and I looked back at old Honorable Roberts, sitting in the chairman's chair, big and fat
and sassy. I pointed my arm at him and stuck out my finger and I shouted, '*Think, Honorable Roberts! Think!*'"
Henry popped up and down, breathless with laughter.
"That's when the rest of my speech came to me." Muttering to himself as he sat down beside his wife, he said, "and
I won first prize of course."

The Little One especially liked that, the muttered
addendum, first prize.

"After Honorable Roberts had announced me as the
winner and gave me my check he shook my hand and said,
'Mr. Prudhomme, when you turned and said, *"Think,*
Honorable Roberts, think!" I must say I was so *moved*.'"

Henry cackled. "Oh, he wasn't moved half so much as *me*."

We sat then in the deepening hot twilight for another ten minutes. I looked at Ruth for some time. She was utterly happy in her eyes. She reached out, with a little grin, and clasped my hand fast. Finally Mrs. Prudhomme said she figured she had had enough fresh air for now, such as it was, and so Henry and I helped her back into the house and on into her little bedroom. She said she wanted to sit up and so we hauled a couple of pillows in from Henry's bed and put them behind her.

Henry and Ruth and I walked back into the front room. A few nights before, the Zip Lupers had had a little party. An old friend of theirs, a short chemist, a graduate of Bundy, was there, surrounded by his endlessly repeating family. While Zip tried to explain football to the Little One, I got the chemist in a corner with scotch, and his button eyes sparkled while we chatted. He was a real professional. As he left me to dance with one of his daughters he had tossed over his shoulder, "Oh, don't you worry. When I was here, a crook was the president. Now they just got a bigger crook." So now, in the Prudhomme living room, I said, "That Uncle Archie sure gets a man down."

Henry growled to himself. "A traitor to his own name."

"Washington? What—"

"No, no. The middle initial. T. Toussaint. That's Archie's middle name."

"Isn't there a way for him to go out quietly? He could get a job somewhere else, maybe not a presidency—"

"Where could he *go*? Every president in the South *knows* this man. Who would hire him? The faculty that has left here has spread his story all over this land."

"The faculty that has left?"

"Why, surely. In the five years he's been here, Archie

has fired sixty per*cent* of the old order." Henry let out a hollow little laugh. "And when Archie *fires* you, you know what getting fired *me-e-eans*."

I waited. Then: "Would you say the faculty is better or worse now—better or worse than when he arrived?"

"Hell, it's better," Henry said.

"Well, then?"

The old man was staring at the little goldfish bowl on top of the scrawny TV. The bowl was lighted, and the fish were absently, gently gliding. Suddenly Henry started up, staring at Ruth. "How do you stand it, married to this B. Green?"

She smiled from him to me.

He rared back. "Boy, you don't follow my *ar*gument. I never said your uncle was *stu*pid. He's cra-a-azy."

"Oh."

"He could be a *fine* president. He's one of my *boys.* I taught him every *good* thing he knows. Right over there in Freeman Hall. But he just didn't listen to me lo-o-ong enough. No, Beaunorus, don't you make a mistake. Never underestimate the enemy. Your uncle is a most intelligent man."

I said, "One wonders why Mrs. Washington stays with him."

Henry sank back into his chair. "Well, now, I think maybe Charlesetta's a little sick in the head too."

Ruthie was sitting there, very still. Into the silence she said, "Why do you say he's crazy?"

Henry turned on her. "Young lady, do you know, once a white man—old Cletis Anderson, Archie's friend—he called down and said a delegation from a colored college in Oklahoma was coming over for a little *con*fab. He wanted Archie to see them for the evening. Have a little re-ception. Now you know what Archie said?"

Ruthie shook her head.

"He said—I got it on authority—Archie said, 'Andy, you don't expect me to spend my whole evenin' with a crowd of *niggers?*' "

I smiled. I heard Presydent saying it. I didn't feel about it like Henry did.

"Well," the old man said, "now we're getting our support. We have a saying in Africa: you can't kill a louse with one finger." He shook his head and under his breath he said, "I'm going to preach on that little text."

"Preach?" I said.

He stared around him. "Now look here, you two have made me late." He shuffled into the back bedroom and we could hear him talking low with his wife, and then he returned to the front room. "You want to go?"

"What is it?" Ruthie asked.

"The Reverend Prudhomme's church. A mile down the road."

"The Reverend?" I said.

"Oh, my daddy's been dead for twenty years, but his poor church is hangin' on." He went past us to the front door and snapped on the little red porch light. "Didn't you know, I'm the son of a preacher who was a son of a preacher who was a son of a preacher?"

"It doesn't get any better than that."

"Boy, I am the grandson of a slave. My granddaddy was a slave and then a preacher and then his son a preacher. That old *church*"—he giggled—"Lord, Lord, I use it for my sub-versive purposes." Then he pulled himself together. "I waltz down there on Sunday evenings and spread the *new* doctrine. They save me a spot. That's why I got my *med*al on."

We followed him out under the red porch light. He was moving briskly, his little body in its black funeral suit blending into the humid darkness. The Little One had to trot to keep up with us. "Henry, I never suspected you of being a preacher."

He didn't look at me, just said, "Lots of things you never suspected." He waved to the porch on the other side of the road and shouted out a name; his own name came back, floating on a woman's voice. The fireflies were out in full force, darting and winking. "I go there," he said. "It's my filling station."

Ruthie said, "Aren't you taking your car?"

"Hell, that auto-mobile hasn't run in five years." He was breathing hard, and he touched the big disease, the rotten thing growing out on his stomach.

"You okay, Henry?"

"Oh, I just can't get myself accustomed to this can-cer. Now they tell me the old devil has popped up again, raised his head in my bile duct. I didn't even know I *had* a bile duct. So they'll cut that one out of me too, I guess."

Perched on top of one tree was an ornament: the moon. I looked down at Henry's bald crown shining in the moonlight; little beads of sweat gleamed across it. He was looking straight ahead.

"Yes, yes," he muttered, "the worst thing is that Archie T. could do a perfect job down here at this old service. After his ee-naug-ural, after he'd been so sweet and holy, I was invited to the res-i-dence with all the rest. A swell affair. And our local old black preacher"—here he giggled —"I remember, he was with Archie by the big color TV. And we were all balancing our cookies and lemonade. Poor old Preacher, he said, 'Well, Dr. Washington, you've done right well.' And Archie looked the Reverend straight in the eye, he didn't flinch, and he said, 'Brother, it all comes from servin' Jesus.'" Henry turned as we walked. "I saw that man. That *man*."

"Henry," I said, pullin' the Little One along beside me, "My uncle kills me. I mean it, that man just kills me."

"Oh, he'll never kill you, boy." Henry's laugh oozed out and fell into a soft place. He looked at Ruth and then at me. "No, he'll never kill *you*."

Sound pitching into the darkness, erupting from the lung.
And a little electric organ, rolling jazz bass, rocking on the
Texas night air.

We went through dusty trees. The church looked like
a general store: a small board building with no steeple. A
bright square of white light came out of one window. We
walked in under the small wooden cross. Hot sweat
crowded in the air, buffeted by the singing. When we first
tramped in, I wanted to turn around and touch the Little
One. The drenching sound, bursting the ear, like the night
we had gone to Paradise with Toast and his Soul Merchants. Two dozen men and women, half that many children. No Bundy faces.

We sashayed along behind Henry, down front to an
empty pew. Some of the old people looked up with curious
eyes—the eyes of the parents at Bundy's commencement,
watching the Little One and me. Up on the stand at front,
by the huge preacher, stood a young cat with a little beard.
Now what in hell is he doin' here? He should be sittin' on
the steps of the Paradise. The last week in spring, when I
was in Manhattan, I was walking along 125th and a glossy,
friendly voice from a dark doorway said softly, "Hey,

motha fuck." I turned and saw a young brother, a cigarette propped in his big lips; he smiled. "Hey, motha fuck,"
I said, "your motha's got no drawers." And this young cat
here, in his green suit, he looks like that boy in Harlem
and he has no business to transact here, holding that white
towel. Maybe the preacher is his father.

The hymn was blasting out; all joined. The Morning
Star Baptist Church. Three times the congregation
marched around the little wooden sanctuary, and Henry
and Ruthie and I marched with them: a ba-ba-boom rolling bass on the electric organ. After we had finished and sat
down I put my hand down to my leg to stop the thigh muscles. Nobody seems to know enough to sit down. All flesh
moving: a big frantic family and old pa preacher cleans his
ear with a match. A fat old lady got the Spirit. She clapped
her hands thirty times in ten seconds and fell full length on
the bench. The other brothers and sisters fanned her with
their hands. An old shriveled lady, Withered Sister, stood
up and gave a speech.

As the service rocked higher and more old women
fell along the benches I turned and stared at Henry. He
don't seem to have his quota of natural rhythm; he sat
there, frail, breathing in little earnest efforts. Ruthie bent
over in the pew and began to shake. A woman in a yellow
dress came to her and smiled at me and did not fan my
girl. The woman said, "Easy, honey. I can see you is in
the Spirit."

The enormous, baggy chocolate preacher arose from
his chair and towered at his pulpit. He played jazz on
Holy Word. Sometimes the voice sounded as if it came up
from wet soil; then, up from fissures in black rocks. He
planted his big sparklin' 11-E black shoes and rolled back
and forth. Singin' Scripture. When we looked away, his
speech-song, the timbre, pulled our heads back, his voice

like a rope. After five minutes he moved. Slowly he descended from his pulpit, down one step, then the second,
to the church floor. When the Spirit hit another woman,
Preach pulled himself to her and stood roaring, his hand
on her head. He raised his eyes up and the water ran down
his neck. All that bulk in one human form. "Lead us not
into temptation. Deliver from evil. Thine the Kingdom.
Power and glory. Ever and ever." He began to sing. "Going to Heaven," he sang, "going to Heaven to meet my
bossman." And, at that, Henry rustled slightly at my side.
"Going to Heaven to meet my bossman." Preach went heavily back to his pulpit, where all the words now ran together
and there was only, in The Morning Star Baptist Church,
a stuffing of dull, vast sound. And the Little One clasping
my hand, squeezing, labor pains.

The young man in the green suit wrapped a white
towel around the preacher's neck. The young man was a
handler in the ring. Then Preacher walked down from
his high place and came to the front pew. He looked at
Henry and leaned over to me, while the hymn went on.
Word gets around; in his big, soft voice he said, "We are
glad to welcome our visitors from the North."

I didn't say anything.

He looked from Ruthie to me. "Would you like to
give us a word?"

Henry's wide eyes were unblinking. And Ruthie
slightly shook her head, a little twitch. "No, thank you,"
I said. "We'll just worship with you." That young man in
the green suit, he was glancing at me and the Little One.
He did not want her here.

The preacher turned his vast damp form from me to
Henry. "You ready, Professor?"

The old man nodded, and the preacher rocked his bulk
back to the pulpit. "You all know Dr. Prudhomme." He

held his palm down to Henry and sat in his throne behind the pulpit.

Henry stood up, immaculate in his black funeral suit. He mounted the stage. For one moment, flanked now by the big pa preacher and an enormous deacon and the boy in the green suit, Henry was very small, delicate, so delicate and belonging to no worlds, we coughed here and there in our pews. That little round head, I can hold it in the palm of my hand, that high little bald crown, sitting there alive—now isn't it funny the way the human mind works?

Henry stood and looked at us, and the church fell silent. Perhaps he's forgotten what he was going to say. Pause, don't hesitate. Then he held his little old hand high up over his head, and we're still waiting, hushed, and in the light the little hand becomes a little fist and Henry barks: "I-mman-uel Kant."

Hang on to your pew, baby.

Henry throws out each syllable of the name. "I-mann-uel Kant asks you, Do you exist?"

Across from me people looked at each other, and I saw a woman, an old flat Haiti face, nod up at him, smiling, as if she had just been reading Kant that very afternoon.

"DO YOU EXIST?"

Think, Honorable Roberts.

"How do you *know* you exist?" Henry descended a step and put his hand on his stomach. "This one black body. How do I know it *exists?*" His hands cupped and rolled on his guts. "How do I make ONE man out of the TWO men I am? Do I bleach my chaste African SOUL?" A large vein bulged, knotting, on that bald tiny crown, and the medal on ribbons dancing. "Do I bapt-i-i-ize myself in the whitewash? Do I speak a twice-told ta-a-ale?" He stepped back up onto the platform, and all of us, seated here, move one step up with him as the words come rolling out from inside him, spreading and burning in the room. "The flames of history are lickin' up into our sky. From the time Sherman himself sliced into Georgia, rolling toward Savannah"—oh, how he loved that word "Sa*van*nah," wielding it—"flames, O my people, licking up through history to Watts and *De*troit and all our cities. We look up through history, we look up through the flames and we hear the words, 'I come to bring the swo-o-ord,' and then we see—we see it red, orange, burning as deep and true as the flames, and then, scarlet—WE SEE—Christ's blood streaming in the firm-a-ment."

I reeled back, the blood streaming in my eyes, and Henry went on with his work: he forged the blood of suffering into the sword of justice, power. That vein on his little forehead extended, knotting itself even larger, and then when he finished he leaned forward with a great shout: "Our black MANHOOD."

He sat among kings.

The boy in the green suit descended, almost running, to the organ, and he plunged, plugging himself in; with his left hand banging, stabbing on the bass, his feet smashing deeply on the pedals, he had no mercy: the sound ripped inside the head, blistering through our eyes, and all lines are overloaded, ear canals buzzing and whistling and shorting out as the boy's whole body tormented and loved the organ. A great iron door a hundred yards high slammed shut in the jungle; tall pink birds rose shrieking to flood the sky above the steaming trees, staining the sun, blood streaming in the firmament, and at last their clotted power held up heaven.

We did not retire to the Opium Den. In the white light of the little living room we sat, quite dressed, with two

small glasses of straight bourbon. She tried to talk about
the service, and I said I'd rather not. Really, I would rather
not. That hurt her—several things came up in quiet—and
I would not talk about it. Bad silences, that was what we
were having. In clear light.

    She stood up and walked outside. After a few minutes
I went to the window and stared out through the venetian
blinds. The Little One was standing there, fifty yards out,
looking up at the sky. I kept watching, and her little body
sat down, her complete form on the alien grass.

The night air was absolutely still in my office, all clogged up. Toast and I sat frying beneath the naked bulb. We were having a three-day weekend, the campus almost deserted. I stared out into the emptiness; one light was burning over in the laboratory, where the sixty-two-year-old dean of men was still trying to get that experiment right. For his Doctor's. And somewhere out there, solitary, a man was walking, whistling "Do You Know What It Means to Miss New Orleans?" I listened to it and his slow clicking footsteps beneath it, going away.

I pulled out my cigarettes and offered the pack to Toast; he took one, broke off the filter, and we lighted up. Puffing, I returned to the window. The smoke sprayed on outside and died in the heat. The lonely whistle was almost gone now, down by the frogpond. The music seemed to come out of a movie somewhere in my childhood—a faint tenderness.

I sat myself once more on the sill. "So, you enjoying the course?"

He took a long drag, opened his mouth, and then there popped out one of his perfect thick smoke rings. I watched the white doughnut walk forward in the air. Toast said, "I like the improvisations and that stuff. But the literature part"—he shook his head—"you teach us Molière and Shakespeare and all that, man. What we got to do with that junk?"

I played with the cigarette, delicately on the sill, trimming the ash. "We read *Othello*. Didn't that have anything to do with—"

His head went on shaking. "Man, I'm a pretty bad-educated East Texas Negro, but I'm not as stupid as he was."

"Stupid?"

"Of course he was. I mean, if he had just sat down for *five* minutes with that goddam Desdemona they could've cleared the whole mess up."

"I see."

"Boy, that is a long way from reality. I don't have time for readin' that kind of stuff."

I put down the cigarette and watched it burn its way into its own filter. It was hot, and the whole vacant building smelled empty around us, dull echoes of nothing. "You should have time for it. Your life, you know, is full of choices, and the more you got in the bag, the more—"

"Oh sure." He finished his cigarette and put it out in his fingers, shredding it. "I'm swimmin' in possibilities." He grinned at me watching him. "I can become a schoolteacher at a place like this. Maybe work myself all the way up top, just like Poppa. I could go in a big-time way for religious work, I'd be a great Gospeleer. Or I could keep up my pro-fane music and work clubs and get real big and play at the winter carnivals at white universities on the basketball court. At intermission me and the boys would stand around out back in the snow narcotizin' ourselves. Or I could strike myself out into industry, and some concern somewhere could prop me up as their knee grow." His eyes, through the whole steady speech, had been on the mutilated remains of the cigarette. Now he affronted me. "Yes, indeed, I am up to my eyeballs in vocational objectives."

I looked at him. "What does your poppa want you to do?"

His eyes blanked.

"Don't get me wrong, Toast. I appreciate my Uncle Archie."

"Appreciate?"

"Of course. He is an extreme human being." I laid the Dr. Pepper bottles on their sides and rolled them with my feet across the dusty floor, one after the other, and then I went back to gazing out my window. The light in the chem lab was out; old Dean Crocker had gone home, another inch closer to that Doctor's, that degree floating in his dreams over the decades. I stared down at the bare grass and brown hide of the Texas earth. Come on back with me to my good old days, Cousin, and we will set ourselves on star-spangled unicycles, hooting like owls and riding all night over scrubland, you and me. We must keep the possible world from dying. I spoke. "America is a very destructive place."

"You're right there." He stood. "Well, I guess I'll be gettin' on back."

He was on his way to the door, and I caught him. "I wonder what you'd say about something your daddy told me one night when I played poker with him."

He turned. "Poker?"

"Yeah, I know my Uncle Kingfish pretty well."

"You do?"

"He stacks all my decks." I really could not let Toast go. I had to have this boy. "Oh, yes, between burning up cats and terrorizing Charlesetta, he has himself a little free time to stack a deck or two."

His eyes, first time, gathered something he had not known. His mouth hung slightly open, waiting.

But I didn't go into it, decided to let him cope with what I might be aware of. "He said to me that there's one thing a black man can count on in this world, one thing, in the final analysis—a white man will always turn white."

Toast scratched his right arm. "Maybe one out of a hundred, maybe one would stick with me when the real trouble hits." He smiled. "But it's one hell of a lot easier on the nerves to figure the percentages and let it go." He moved in his chair. "Hell, for ten years I was a we-shall-overcome nigger."

"Oh, come on, *ten years*—"

"That's right. I went on my first march when I was nine."

I paced and then stopped. "Toast, I told you, Ruthie's no white woman. She's my woman. But her skin *is* white."

He waited, then smiled. "Well, I guess you're just going to have to live with it."

I took the mandatory eight-count.

We rapped around, trying to get back on the track, and finally I just said, "It's all wrong."

Toast glanced up. "Pardon me?"

"This damn school. They're never going to improve Bundy. It was never any good, and it's never going to be any good." I paused. "You can tell that to the Bossman."

He turned away. "Oh, he knows that. I guess we all do."

"Well, then, come on. You have talent. You could make it. I never heard a voice like yours. You're one big cat."

"Thank you."

"*Thank* you?" I leaned forward. "Why don't you haul ass out of this place?"

He stood, silent, and his eyes seemed to have locked on the darkest corner of the office. "Poppa loves this school. Do you know that? He knows it won't ever be no Harvard of the West, but—oh, man—it's every*thing* to him. It's his life."

"I don't think anybody questioned that."

"You haven't seen him work and work, every night. Writing and telephoning and going to meetings and having those receptions and worrying. This school is his life, and he worries all the time."

"I'm sure he does."

"Hell, most of the teachers aren't much. You know that—always balling things up. If he wasn't strong, they'd *never* get anything done."

"Toast, man, I'm not plugging for a sweet little black gentleman. But it's not a choice any more between a doormat and a lunatic."

He waited. "My father is not a lunatic."

There was a silence. I said, "He's going to kill somebody."

Toast looked at the floor, fussed it with his shoe. "I know all that stuff Henry says is true—about Daddy being a product of the system."

"Henry's been in that system too, you know."

He looked at me. "You think Henry'd be a good presydent? I mean, I love that old man, but—"

"Look, Toast, in a week, a month, a year, your pappy is gonna kill him some people."

"Oh, I don't know—"

"His wife or some fancy little co-ed or Homer Brown or Henry—or you. He is going to take lives. We stand here in this goddam office and it's as simple and factual as us standing here. The lives are already gone."

Toast waited, and he was thinking hard. "I live in his house."

I watched him.

"He works his heart out for that school. It's in his blood. He's no Tom. He wants a *good school.*"

"Of course he does. But he's so far out of control he can't—"

"Oh, shit. If he was to resign you know what they'd do?"

"No."

"They'd kill this school. They'd close her up."

I looked at him. "And we are to think of that as a step backward?"

"They had a plan last year, those white bastards, they wanted to make Bundy a home for the aged and *in*firm."

I said, "Bundy Colored Agricultural and Normal Home for the Aged and Infirm." But then I wished I had not said that, for he was trying to get his point across, and he had been thinking about it for a long time.

"Poppa said, in his *ad*dress when he was made the presydent, he said, 'I did not take this presidency to preside over the liquidation of this institution.'"

I nodded.

"You *don't* understand. If those bastards close the old place up, that would put a hundred and seventy black people out of work. Now, where all of them going to *go?*"

"A problem."

"And the kids, a thousand of us black kids. You really think *half* of us could get into somewhere else? I mean, you got to see things the way they is. Maybe twenty or fifty or a hundred years us black people'll stagger on into the Great Society. But that time's long away. And Bundy is one hell of a lot better than zero." He quieted down. I thought he was through, with his saying of that, but he suddenly turned and looked at me. "I mean, it's *so* good just to be with your own people. I mean, I went to Whitey's school for a time, and even with the people who were trying to be nice, god*dam* I got tired of having to explain everything all the time. There was this white chick, one of your big ac-ti-vists, and she was all right, but she used to come up to me in the hall and, damn, damn, she was all the time touching my *hair*."

I smiled at him.

"You got to see where I'm coming from. I'm black and I just want to be with black people. We got to be with our own. Here at Bundy, we can be. We can be black as hell."

I sat.

"Black schools are a good idea," he said. "You just got to get good people. Black schools are a *good* idea."

His face was a little out-of-phase hysterical; he thought he wasn't getting through to me.

The previous evening, just at twilight, I had seen him with Henry down by the frogpond. They were crouched down, sitting in high grass. I stood up by the Training School and watched them talk, bent close together on the bank of the pond. Some janitors and construction workers came rattling down Opportunity Drive in a pickup, singing, men harmonizin' on the flatbed, goin' home. The men waved their arms in the air, and Toast and Henry waved back. In twilight, up above, the stripped-for-action birds swooped and shot around, dropping like rocks, then soaring again. And Toast and Henry were crouched there in the high grass, lobbing pebbles in the water, conversing. It was private. Henry was bending forward, serious. I had never thought that old man could whisper, but he seemed to be doing it, imparting the secrets of the tribe.

I looked at Toast, upset and guarding himself in my office. "Does Henry really start off his course with a multiple-choice exam?"

Toast smiled to himself, remembering. "None of the Above."

"Right."

"Yeah." He shrugged. "I dug that." His eyes came up to me. "The old man, he did a fine thing with his life. He's touched a hell of a lot of people. If he could do it, I can. In my thing, in my time." Toast kept his eyes on mine. "That's what I am trying to tell you, about black schools. We are at the bottom"—he bent and tapped the base of the chair leg—"really the goddam bottom. And Henry's right—None of the Above. We got to come *up* from the bottom with all you learn *down* at the bottom." He sighed. "If that's not it, then we better forget it, and just settle for a parody."

"But, man, that's pretty much what it is. Bundy is a parody."

"Oh, I know. Mostly. But there's something else. And there's the future." A little silence again, and I thought we were going to go easy on things now. But he suddenly caught it all up again, turning on me. "Why did you come down here?"

"Archie asked me."

"No, I mean, why did you *come?*"

"To monitor the lunchroom."

He reached over sharply and took another cigarette. I did too. He pulled out a matchbook, scratched, and lighted us both up. As I mouthed the cigarette end into the small flame, I said, "There was something I didn't know that I wanted to know."

"About your Southern soul brothers, you mean?" He shook out the match.

"Oh, come on now." I looked at him, then looked away. There was a silence, and I said, "Lobster soup."

"What?"

"That's what I was eating last summer about this time. In the South of France. With Ruthie. Goddam lobster soup."

He blew another smoke ring, a beauty. It refused to dissolve. It blammed into the wall and stood there, circularly attached. The silence lengthened nowhere. I regarded his shredded knee-high Levi's. "You just can't go to France." I was talking to myself. "You can't do that."

He looked at the cigarette he was smoking. "I never really thought too much about it."

And now he's on his way. I joined him at the door and cut the lights. We walked on down the steps together, and it was peaceful, not so sticky hot, in the starlight. I said, "You know something?"

"What?"

"Here I am *teaching*. But sometimes I think I'm stupid."

"Naw, hell, you're not stupid. You just talk stupid."

I stared at him. I started to laugh, to laugh loud and long, and then I stopped and only said, "You know, I think you're on to something there."

"I find it's true of a lotta black people."

At that I did laugh. I threw back my head and I felt very good. Jesus, this Toast is my A-number-one boy. Dear teacher . . . I banged him on the shoulder. "It's you and me, we gotta live for ourselves and nobody else. Come on.

Come on over to the apartment and let's smoke a little pot."

He held back. "You got some?"

"Like you say, I only talk stupid."

He looked at me. "I *would* like some smoke. It makes me feel real quiet, like a big body of water."

"Absolutely."

And so he fell into step.

"Ruthie and I, when we get real stoned, we paint up."

"Hunh?"

"We get nude and paint each other."

He looked at me. He wasn't too sure that was a good idea. Especially tonight. If we're all going to have a little arts-and-crafts contact comfort this evening . . .

I was very happy. Toast and I and the Little One are heading for a major breakthrough. And then as we went up the driveway to the quarters, Toast stopped. "Maybe I'll wait out here."

I looked. There, nosing into the apartment by the Luper T-Bird, the presidential Cadillac. "Maybe he's just trying to persuade Zip to stay on next year."

"Well," Toast said, "if it's all the same to you, I'll wait here."

I shrugged, suits me, and I went on ahead. At the apartment door I stopped, and Toast was right: he was in there, in with the Little One. I wondered if he'd brought his cards along. I knocked.

There was a silence inside, and then more silence. I stepped back from the door, and at last Ruthie was there. She was wearing a stupid little cotton blouse that she'd worn to camp ten years ago, I can't get her to throw that thing away, and black short-shorts. She grinned, a little flustered.

I stepped in, peered around, and there he is, the

Boss, nursing a drink on the coffee table. He was wearing a goddam hula-hula sports shirt, and in my opinion he looked ridiculous. I said, "I hope I'm not intruding."

The man looked up, with his bare arms crossed. "Evenin', son. Ruth and I were havin' a real high-powered discussion."

I'll bet you were. Girl, you appeal to me. I glanced from face to face, and I said, "I don't want to interrupt your discussion."

"Oh," he said, reaching for his drink, "no interruption."

"I want to get some stuff. Got a dramatics boy out there, and we're goin' over lines."

Ruth said, "At this hour?"

"It's okay."

"We're surely lookin' forward," Himself said, "to this evening of skits you're cookin' up for us."

"Well"—I crossed upstage right—"I hope you will look back on it with a similar pleasure." I went into the Opium Den, turned on the red light, and closed the door. I stood for a moment over the grass-bag. Easy, Bo. Just take her the easy way, Beaunorus Green. She can handle herself. That's what we have counted on for some time.

I was rolling the third joint in my Puerto Rican machine when the door opened. I covered myself: we haven't had a position paper from Pres on pot yet.

But it was the Little One. "Hi."

"Hi." I went ahead with my work. "It's Toast—I kind of thought it would be nice to turn on, the three of us. But something tells me Pres wouldn't work." I heard the toilet flush down in the bathroom.

"It might be fun to try."

"Well, thanks anyway." I licked the paper and then

put the triple threat in my shirt pocket. I looked at her. "Is it going all right?"

She nodded. Oh, that goddam nod. I have seen it before. It was half a blush, half a conviction, and she put her hand on my arm. She was saying it was all right. She was relying on something I had only glimpsed so far. "Well," I said again. And then I told her what Toast said, my not being stupid but only talking stupid.

She laughed and came forward, one fluid motion, and she kissed me on the neck. "Bo, I love you."

I turned, embarrassed, and the bed in the Opium Den was littered with Head Start art work. I was uneasy, and the toilet flushed again—I saw him standing over the bowl, contemplating bubbles. We're all playin' out our own mental diseases. The bulk of him. Yes, it's his *bulk* that is the problem. Absently I leafed through the crayon masterpieces. One was incredible; it was a little black kid with the most enormous black dong. Just a little guy on a red piece of land, and the black penis was so huge that it was hard to imagine his imagination. I held up the paper. "What was the assignment?"

She looked at it and nodded, smiling. "I told them, 'Draw a picture of yourself.' "

"And this is what he did?"

"Uhuh."

"Certainly does reinforce a lot of stereotypes." I shook my head.

She said, "Do you suppose his mother ever said to him, 'Don't play with *yourself*'?"

I laughed. "Oh, Ruthie." I pulled her in to my chest and hugged her tight. "You *are* a goddam miracle." And then I heard my uncle's steps on the bare linoleum. Whispering, I said, "It's okay? You're sure?"

She nodded, the top of her head against my chest.

"You know what he did to me that night."

Into my chest, her muffled words: "He's not like that."

I waited some time. "I see." I broke away. "Well, Toast and I, *we* are going to turn on."

"You're sure you don't want to come in? The four of us?"

Still whispering: "Ruthie, a guy can't turn on with his father."

"Why?"

I shrugged. "You aren't stupid, you just talk stupid."

We went out together. "Well, I'm going to go over this stuff with him."

Archie was looking at me, letting the silence speak for him. He slowly reached down for his drink. I took one look at her and went on out. Oh, my Lord.

It took me a minute to find him. He had repaired to the frogpond and was sitting in moonlight, watching the water. I came up slowly. "Hey, baby."

He turned. "Was he in there?"

"Yeah."

Toast turned back to the water.

For the next twenty minutes we were both wrapped up in that scene, the apartment, and I turned once to survey the Caddy parked in the driveway and the dim light against the venetian blinds. Toast was very quiet. But with the first joint we loosened a good deal and it was lovely. Passing back and forth, in the moonlight, we listened to the bloop and splash of life around the water. I thought again of him and Henry in this place, the two of them. At one point Toast said, "How come you never got drafted?"

I was holding in smoke at that juncture and had to wait a moment. Then I said, "I'm allergic to eggs."

Toast thought it was the funniest thing he ever heard of. Nigger allergic to eggs. He lay back in the grass and he laughed: HA . . . HA . . . HA . . . HA. It was a long time between each laugh, and I knew he was very susceptible. By-by, time. High in the grass—his sense of humor went way out, as he said, just like a big old body of water, and in the moonlight he was thinking. Egg, no, I won't go. We kept the joint alive down to the last millimeter.

On the second he said, "You know, I said I had a lot of vocational plans. What's yours?"

"I'm going to be a actor."

He took the joint and before he pulled in on it he said, "On Broadway?"

I watched him. "Sure. For a few months I worked in the CENP. That's the Committee for the Employment of Negro Performers." He was really gone, my boy, high as the sky. "We spent some time picketin' in Shubert Alley."

Time passes. "What'd you get?"

I took the joint. "Sore feet."

He had a little run of slow giggling, very slow, a 45 played at 33. "It ain't much of a career."

"Well, in New York a actor who works in a play—*one* play a year—he's in pretty sweet. And if that play runs three months it's a miracle." I tugged in my stuff, watched a giant bullfrog, wondered if it was a prince, and then said, losing some of my smoke, "If you're black, you get half that much exposure and a third of the pay. So you end up recitin' great lines to yourself over racks of dishes in Chock Full o' Nuts."

My homeboy is blipped. "They good?"

"Whoot?"

"Colored actors?"

I shook my head; the joint returned. "Sure, some are beautiful. Beautiful. And lots of new things opening up."

He thought a long time. We weren't sure just what about. He was humming to himself. "Sometimes I really think I should go into show business."

"I think you should."

He sat forward. "You do?"

"I do."

He sighed; his arms embraced his knees.

"What does Archie think of it?"

He took the reefer, tapped it like a cigarette. "I guess he just wants me to have a good life."

"And your mamma?"

"Oh, last time I saw her—" And then he stopped. He looked at me with a quick little agony, his first sharp motion in an hour. Maybe it was the pot, maybe just being there on the bank of the frogpond. "Charlesetta's not my mamma."

I fell back, with all the stuff in my head. "I hadn't known about that."

He sighed in the night air. "No, she's not nobody's mamma. She's barren."

The word "barren" was a little too much for me, and I looked back at the quarters. The Caddy was still shining in the streetlamp clear and strong, and the dim rich light was there in our apartment window. A shadow moved across it.

"No," he said, "she's barren. That's why I didn't live with them for a long time. I was not formally adopted until I was fourteen."

I kept quiet.

"My mamma is real pretty. She *was* real pretty. Would you like to see her picture?"

"I would."

He sat forward and reached behind him, into his hip pocket, for his wallet. He pulled it out and elaborately opened it up. He was fumbling for the picture in the plastic flaps when a little piece of paper came out, fluttered, and fell slowly over and over onto the grass.

"You're losin' something." I picked it up. It was very small, and there was printing on it. "May I?"

He leaned toward me, his shoulder brushing mine. "What is it?"

I held the paper up. I couldn't quite read it in the moonlight. So I struck a match. Holding the flame close to the paper, I read, "The danger, if any, I expounded, was from our proximity to a great human passion let loose. Even extreme grief may ultimately vent itself in violence—but more generally takes the form of apathy. . . ."

After I had read it, with the match flame licking at my fingers, I stared at him. "What is that?"

He was picking self-consciously in his wallet. "Oh, that's nothin'. I just read it somewhere."

I shook out the match, flicked it toward the pond. "No, what is it?"

He took it back from me and slipped it in with bills. The wallet with his mother's picture—whatever it might have been—went back into his hip pocket. "That's by a English sailor named Joseph Conrad. He wrote a story called *Heart of Darkness.*"

"What's it doin' in your wallet?"

"Oh, we read her in English class. And I just thought that passage was sig-ni-fi-cant." He lay back in the grass. "I guess you could say it made quite a impression on me." He then spoke the lines on the paper aloud, pausing for some time on words like "expounded," "proximity," and then, concluding, just sitting there listening to the sentiment.

I never did see his mother. The third joint of ours was probably smoked, but we lost track of just what was where —not like being drunk, it was just that there was so much *time* between everything. I got onto his rhythm, and every few minutes I would have to remind myself that it was time to breathe.

Just before we fell asleep he took one long drag and looked at the moonlit water for all the clues in the world, and then he smiled. He smiled the greatest smile.

"What is it?"

He blinked his eyes fairly rapidly and said, "Old George."

"The paper-carrier?"

"Yeah."

"I've been meanin' to talk to you about that. Can't you stop those guys from beatin' the shit out of him all the time?"

"Oh," Toast said, "it don't matter." He kept on blinking his eyes. "I was just thinking of something poor old George said to me once last year."

I expected him to go on, to *say* it, but in the silence he seemed to think that I knew. I didn't. So after a respectful pause I said, "What did George say?"

His pause was equally respectful, though less focused. At last he said, "I met him one morning at about five-thirty o'clock, and he was carryin' the Sunday paper. I said, 'Hey, George, how you this Lord's mornin'?' " Toast turned to me, "That's how you talk to old George Mo-ron."

I nodded.

"He said to me, 'I came into this world with nothin', and I figure I'm just about holdin' my own.' "

I was lost in the point. I treasured it. Smoke. And then my cousin loomed up in my mind, singing to young blood in the Paradise. I heard the feeling and repeated his words, a reminder to the night: "You gotta live for yourself. For yourself and nobody else."

"Oh no," he said. And you wouldn't have thought he was party to his own song. Dreaming, he said, "No, man. I got to live for me and mine." His voice was the soft flutter of wings, sleeping wings. He drifted, stationary, decisively gentle and at home, almost an echo: "Me and mine."

Losing ourselves in it, we slept.

When I awoke, the moon was down and a big car had just whummed by on Opportunity Drive. I sat up, sober as a judge, and looked around me. The taillights of the car were up there now, moving on.

Down in the grass, he slept. Hallucinating. I whispered "Hey—hey, man." He rolled softly in the grass. There's no point to waking him. It's summer, and there is little better to do than sleep here. I looked at him, as he dreamed in peaceful times, and Beaunorus Green is not going to pull him out of that. So I struggled up and went back across the road, back home to the bed waiting for me.

I was at my door. I shuffled a moment on the cricket-covered mat, the night is on its way to being over, and I went in. I stared at the full ashtray on the coffee table and the two empty glasses. Stale cigarette smoke was in the air, and the lights were on. Quarters, hollow. I listened to the silence and then went into the kitchenette and stared at the brown fridge before threading my way back through emptiness to the living room. Still stale. I went into the john, peed in the bathtub with a certain rhetorical flourish—never able to spell "Beaunorus Green" clear to the last n—then turned on the shower for a minute to Keep Clean. Bedroom seems to be empty. Well, it won't be the first time. I shed clothes. Naked, I tap-danced aimlessly back out to the living room, turned off the lights, and then I saw what the thing was. A sliver of red light from under the door of the Opium Den. Cautiously I proceeded. I gently opened the door, and she was there, all there.

Ruth was sitting nude on the bed, there in the spare room, never as nude as that.

I came in.

She did not speak.

Naked I padded, and there seems to be a layer of sand on our floor, a wisp of topsoil. Archie T. It has occurred as it had to occur. I am in the red light of his tent, his crusading Roman tent. UNCHAIN THE JEWESS. SHE HAS FOUND FAVOR IN THE EYES OF ACHILLES AUGUSTUS. His tent, his Caesar tent. And what was it like? Oh, come on, what was it like? On his halfback's chest, iron filings. That man is never nude; he is stripped. Barefoot, on his linoleum, the contracts, a new "unit." I seem to be looking in the dust for a footprint. Crusoe on the beach. Only I am black and so would the footprint be, if I could find it. My eyes rattle up sharply onto her fine quick body, nude as complete feeling.

"Bo?" She looked at me.

I stood there in the doorway, naked to her nudity.

She sighed, sitting there on the side of the bed, and her arm moved to her face. Her hand was lost, touching her cheek. The oddest little smile, and then: "Nothing happened that you didn't want to happen."

"Hey," I whispered, "don't, baby." I was waiting for some gentle words, but she only nodded. A motion of the head.

BOOK TWO

We got into the habit, evenings, of strolling the campus. With her beside me, looking at it all, my eyes kept fixing on a dogwood tree, a moldering bench, a stray bald tennis ball, an empty pack of Winstons. My eyes were all caught up in negligible objects. Midsummer, when the Texas heat was unbearable, even after dinner, we saved our prowl for late at night. Zip's daughter had a corroded bicycle; we took turns on it, and when I'd scoot out my knees would pump up to my chest. Little Sadie had fixed a queen of hearts with a safety pin on the front spokes and an eight of clubs on the rear; as I rode I went rat-a-tat-tat, a motorgun. I'd coast, hold my arms out in the moonlight, and the humid breeze curled in through my open shirt. Often, turned on, I'd pause and sit and chew the fat with a star. I'd talk to the star about that night, with Ruthie and the Pres. There were so many things I could ask the star that I couldn't ask her.

And I always had to take five minutes at the White House. Parking the little bike, I sat and stared; as the night thickened, the house itself would focus, sharpen, and begin to glow with the heat saved up from the day. If I went early, sometimes there would be a parade: summer-school business, long-range financial problems, little parties; trucks or Caddies, depending, they coasted up and the people went in to see him. But usually it would be quiet, prairie quiet, and the vastness of Texas would begin to stretch out and insinuate itself there, and I'd sit back against a tree, staring, hypnotized, chanting. Then home to the Little One, not to talk about it. I was very sad; the Little One was very sad. Always, before, we had talked. Our Great Gift, said a Good Guy once, was that we did not repress things. It all came out, for better or worse. I remember his saying that. But now we were—for all our talk—not quite on speaking terms.

I was out at my White House observation post one mid-July night around eleven, munching on an apple, when a female voice cried out, wounded, in the residence. I sat forward. Uncle's voice, too, bellowed out from down by the garage. Shadows flitting, bulging across the windows; and again she shrieked. There was a slamming of several doors—bang, bang, bang—he was chasing her through the train. I looked around me, and Opportunity Drive was empty.

There was an abrupt, full silence from the White House, the swollen quiet that comes after something irrevocable.

I waited, watching, and for half a minute nothing happened. Then the front door opened and she was there, my Aunt Charlesetta, in her nightgown on the porch. She was being very quiet about it, closing the door, and then she turned—and here the good lady comes, racing, almost falling, down the walk. When she got to the street she stopped and held her hands up beside her face; she was looking to her right and left, trapped by all the empty moonlight. She touched her hand up to her scalp and moaned, a hollow little complete hurt.

I moved out. I threw down my apple on the way and came, half running, to her.

She stepped back. "Oh," she cried out silently, "*oh*."

I loomed up as bad as the man she was fleeing from, one of his boys. We were surrounding her. Texas is a mighty big place. Her nose was bleeding, a dark profusion over her lips and down in dribbly spots on her nightie.

"Let me help you," I said.

She fumbled off, lame and horrified, in another direction.

I trotted beside her for twenty yards, asking, imploring, all caught up, and she was my own blood, my kin in terrible distress on the pavement. Her big breasts flopped full and low against the sheer nightie, the stains of blood. Breathlessly she whispered, "Go—go away, boy."

I slowed, stopped. I stood watching her full ghost figure melt jerkily into the darkness, down toward the string of faculty cottages. I didn't know who to go for. I ran back to the trees for my little girl's-bike, and was wheeling out when I saw him. Archie, in black pants and an undershirt, thick like a weightlifter, on the porch. He was there. He was sniffing the damp night air, a bull, and I sank down against the bicycle frame—if you get down and just stay still, they'll go right over you—but then the King roared savagely round and tore back into his White House.

"Last night he almost killed her."

She was sitting on the tweedy couch, stripped to the waist, and the air in our quarters was stifling. She was wearing the black short-shorts, the same pair she had worn that night.

"He what?"

"He inflicted considerable damage. And the First Lady ran bleeding into the night."

"How do you know?"

"I saw it."

There was a silence. "Why didn't you tell me last night?"

I waited. Well, here goes nothing. "I gather—stop me if I'm out of order—I gather you and he are not going to have a summer affair?"

She winced and seemed to want to cover her upper nakedness.

I picked up my lighter and threw it up and down, a cat on the corner with his fifty-cent piece. "It's funny," I said, "I look at him in the hall, we pass and exchange pleasantries. No different. It wasn't different after that night I

played poker with him. And it wasn't different after—
after you and him."

"Same here."

The two words caught me quickly, below the belt.
Same here. I held on to the lighter, snapped it open, and
struck fire.

She was biting her lower lip again. She does that when
she thinks. And I stared on down at the nipples.

She seemed almost to speak. She was speaking without words. And she was holding on to herself.

It was the first I'd demanded. Okay, man, blow it to
hell. "How was he in bed?"

Listening to the fabric tear, she started to answer. "It
wasn't—I didn't want to—" but then she cut off. She in-
habited the whole lighted room.

I knelt down over the table. "Don't you see, baby?
We really had it made. Against all the odds. We were in
the sunlight, walking on soft, long grass. And now it's
pitch dark and we're walking on a cold floor and the word
is out that there's a lot of broken glass."

Holding herself: "Bo?"

For some obscure reason I went into the bathroom and
got down on my hands and knees and—oh, get hold of
yourself, Beaunorus Green—I began to scrub the bathroom
floor.

It was almost morning when I shot up in the empty bed
and felt around me. No Little One. I put on my robe and
weaved out into the dark living room. She wasn't there.
I felt a spasm, she's making the scene in the White House
basement, and then at the front window I caught sight of
a tiny red light, a cigarette end, moving far out in the
darkness. I watched it for a moment before going into the
kitchen for a glass of chocolate milk. I poured it and sat

at the table. Sipping, I watched her outside, walking slowly back and forth.

I went to the front door and said, "Ruthie, you shouldn't be out there in the cold like that."

She came toward me, stopped to stamp out her cigarette. "It's not cold."

I followed her back into the apartment and shut the door. "Hell, I know it's not cold."

She went to the kitchen table and lit up another cigarette. "You're afraid someone might see me. God forbid anybody should think that we aren't just Happy Bo and his Little One."

"Cut it out."

"I really want to get away from you sometimes. I get tired of being your 'Little One.' "

"Do us both a favor—"

"You tell me that you need me to make you feel real. Who do I have to make me feel real?"

"Archie, it seems."

She looked away.

"You and Archie." I laughed, hollow. *"Damn."*

She took another drag of her cigarette. "That night, here, he told me about when he was a little boy. He wanted an ice cream and went into a white store, and he had a nickel. The man at the counter said, 'Ice cream for black boys costs six cents.' And he didn't have the penny, and the storekeeper wouldn't sell him the ice cream." Ruthie looked at me. "Archie wasn't telling me that to say something about 'race prejudice.' And he didn't say he felt rage or anger or—I don't know, I just felt his hurt. I felt it that night, the way sometimes he just knows things. It's almost the way an animal senses you, knowing whether you're going to pet it or throw rocks at it."

"Oh now, come on, baby. Ice cream? That's why you slept with him. Pity. Poor Archie. He didn't get the ice cream but now you give it to him. Ruthie Vanilla."

"It's not that at all. I guess it was something of a—well—a contest."

"Oh, I can just see you arm-wrestling in there."

She put out her cigarette. "He has power. And—I had it too." She was flushed, staring at me, and abruptly she looked down at her lap. "And then, after, it just snapped. Snapped. He said, 'I better be gettin' on before your hubby comes back.' And—I hated him. He just couldn't resist that."

"Ruth, goddam. How can you tell me that?" I pulled her up and started to shake her. "He *used* you, baby."

She pulled away from me. "I didn't know what I was feeling. It was good before, when we were talking. I was so much *with* him. And then, after . . ." She looked up. "And you could have stopped it. You saw what was going on when you came in."

Nothing Happened That I Didn't Want to Happen. Face that, Beaunorus Green. I grabbed her and shook her again. "You don't know what the fuck you're doing. You wanted to come down here for the darktown strutters' ball." I was hurting her now, and I wanted to hurt more. "My mamma told me never to marry a white woman. Because one day, she said, that white woman's going to look at you, Beaunorus Green, and you'll just be a nigger."

"Bo, stop that. Don't you see? I was attracted to him for something you *lack*."

"Oh no, oh no." I was all out of control now, pulling her with me into the spare bedroom. "I got what he's got. It's the same color. And you're gonna feel it now."

"Don't, Bo." She was trying to get away.

"I got the same thing, and"—I pushed her down on the bed and lay over her squirming body—"I know what you want, baby."

She stopped struggling and went dead. "Prove it if you have to, but don't expect me to help." Her eyes, a blank stare.

"Damn it, Homer, why did you do that to me?"

His voice came out through his presidential door, out
into the deserted Sunday-afternoon hallway. I had prom-
ised the kids that I would have their midterms back on
Monday, and now I found I was missing one; on my way
back up to the classroom into the administration building,
I stopped, hearing the weight of the men.

"But, Presydent," Homer's voice pleaded with agoniz-
ing slowness, halts, "I had to . . . I mean you was in no
shape . . . and she was most frighten to *death*—"

The King's voice broke back over him. "I pay you to
handle my public relations. And you *crossed* me, boy."

A fist went down on a desk. Then the sound of getting
up, striding around the desk, a chair going over, Uncle's
voice exploding, "*Damn* you, boy." And as I fell against
the wall, outside, I heard it in there: Presydent closing in
fast on that fat black electric bunny-rabbit, trapped.

At ten o'clock it began to look like a success. The Marshalls and the Lupers were dividing our floor between them, dancing to old music on Horatio's phonograph. Ophelia and Homer and Ruth and I stood in a kitchen circle around Henry; the old man leaned back against my brown fridge. Over the music he was saying, "Oh, now, don't you tell me about registering voters. First time I ever went to register, they asked me to recite the Constitution. Lord, I'll never forget that day." He giggled. "It was the Reverend Prudhomme's work. My daddy knew that's what they always asked. For three solid months before my twenty-first birthday he took me into the parlor, and every night we worked her over. Memorizing, memorizing. That was prohibition, you know, and I memorized her right down to the last amendment." Henry raised his huge eyes to the ceiling and stood, then, rolling the ice in his drink, lost in the sweet memory. " 'After one year from the ratification of this article the manufacture, sale, or transportation of intoxicating liquors within, the importation thereof *into*, or the exportation thereof *from* the United States and all territory subject to the juris-dic-tion thereof for bever-

age purposes is hereby pro*hib*ited." He got to laughing as
he recited, and ended up crouched, almost doubled, catching his breath. He laughed himself out and then straightened back up, saying, "Took me almost two hours. The
registrar stopped me when I was five minutes into it, and
then he gathered his clerks around him, three of those
crackers, and they opened their books and they read along
with me. I didn't look up. Oooooh." He rocked on his red
carpet slippers. "I was twenty-one years old and all dressed
up in my Sunday suit, scared to death, and my daddy was
waiting outside, and he would have *killed* me if I forgot,
and so I stared and stared at my shi-i-iny shoes."

I said, "Did they register you?"

"I was the third Negro ever registered in this county.
My daddy was the first. Then there was Warren Dawson,
but they killed him before I came up."

There was a silence, and we sipped our drinks. Henry
went on then, periodically casting his wide owl-eyes down
into his bourbon. At one point in his history I lobbed a
safe second serve: "Yes, as you look back, you must feel
real satisfied."

He put one hand up onto my shoulder and patted me
in a paternal way. "Before I came waltzin' over here," he
said, turning his eyes on me, "I took out the supper gar-
bage, and I saw my two old hounds had turned over the
trash pail. Behind the Zulu Club, you know. Lord, they
were having a feast. Lickin' their chops and talkin' to each
other. I listened—and you know what those two old dogs
were saying to the evenin' air?"

"No."

His hand went away from my shoulder and down onto
his big abdomen; he rubbed his belly and rolled the word
out of his mouth: "Sat-is-fied." He put back his head, staring at me, and continued in deliciousness: "Sat-is-fied."

I smiled.

"That's the difference," he growled, "between man and dog. Man is *never* sati-is-fied."

I glanced at delighted Ruth. She was wearing the party dress I'd bought her for her birthday, purple and red, *so* short. I glanced back at him. "But tell me, Henry, if you're never satisfied, how—how can a man live?"

"Carefully, boy, carefully."

Ruthie smiled. "Then an old Marxist believes in freedom of the will?"

He studied her a moment, then his drink, and he shortly popped up. "Well, I'll say this—I like to see it." He touched his lips delicately, smiling at her. He certainly did like Ruth. They had an understanding. Why did she have to foul it up with Archie?

Henry said, "Oh, yes, yes, Lord, if I only can keep my *health*. Then I'll have some freedom of my *will*. When I finally re-tire, I'm going to write me a book."

Ophelia was conspiratorially smiling and nodding at us. "Yes, Prof's been working on his book for some time." She giggled, and the bosom goes bazoom. "You ought to hear the title."

I looked at his shirt, the great bowl attached to his tiny frame. "The title?"

Henry smiled at Ophelia and then said to Ruth, "You've heard that beautiful voice of Billie Holiday?"

Ruth nodded.

"Oh, that poor woman. There at the end—she had a hard life, you know—there in jail, narcotics, smoking a *car*-ton of cigarettes a day. Lord, how could a songbird ruin her lungs like that? Well, old President Roosevelt, FDR, he had Billie Holiday up to the White House to sing for him. And she sang for old Franklin Delano Roosevelt, and oh, she sang like an angel, you know, and after the com-mand performance old FDR came up to her and he said, 'Miss Holiday, you sing so be-you-tifully, but tell me, why are your songs so *sad?*'" Henry regarded my girl. "And you know what that lady of color said to FDR?"

Ruthie shook her head, don't know.

"Well, she was quiet for a moment. And then she dropped her eyes and said, soft and pretty—she sighed— 'Oh, shit, Mr. President.'" Henry threw back his head and filled up the kitchen with laughter. On the way down: "That," he said, "is what I'm callin' my book."

Gladys came in, swinging her little body. She was all a-laughing; above those high Oriental cheekbones her eyes danced out through Batlady glasses. After a few records we decided to let loose. The driving moan of Ray Charles, singing responsively with his audience, filled up the room. Gladys bolted what was left of her drink and threw herself into the dance. She began to twist and pull her skirt up on her thighs, toe-heel, toe-heel, ducking her head at me, her short hair bouncing all together with her steps. I looked at Ruthie. The Little One can't dance, can't completely dance. Once she said to me, begging an hour of instruction on our floor, "Couldn't you teach me, up to my limits?" And that is the question. Teach *her* up to her limits? B. Green passes.

Toe-heel, toe-heel, skirt up and arms out, Gladys moved. Girl, you appeal to me. I hitched up my pants and swarmed out to the floor. Her eyes lighted when she saw me; she stopped for a moment, took off her glasses, and kicked off her shoes. She kicked the shoes over behind the television set; then her mouth went wide, laughing, and she started again toward me. Don't just stand there with your teeth in your mouth, man—*do* something. I looked back at her, that taut shape in motion, spinning, her bare feet slapping the floor, and I picked up the blind moan of

Ray Charles. Cock-rocking, I turned to jelly around the shoulders, a mechanical man from the waist down.

She was busy with her own body.

Eyes down, I danced very, very close to her, come close, black woman; we are touching, and her Passionella eyes shoot into mine—see, little missy, it's a mile deep in there, no? She was beginning to shimmy; her tight little breasts were burning, and she pulled her teeth down, biting on her bottom lip. Perhaps one of us should sit down. Ma-*ma*. Chung-katcha, chung-katcha—I may blow my cool.

I laughed.

Gladys slowed herself. I stared at her little bare feet, not slapping the floor now—not a Grinding Queen; she is a Servant Girl at a party of the Jungle Lord. I have my fun with her (what else can I do?). I am a poor old black man with a mahogany body. I shuffled. Then I threw my legs up and out—up and out—and gnashed my teeth, bellowing like a coal-black bull, turning from Gladys, me a dazed bull with bright swords in his back—in an act of nature everybody wins!—my cheeks filled, and I am one nigger in heat and I begin to ravish consciousness ironically in the air.

She stopped completely. "Don't." She said it with a stinging little pout, spitting it out like a slap. She stood, idly dancing in place; she smartly tapped her thighs, her hot embarrassed eyes darting up at me.

I broke through the crowd to the open front door. As I went out, panting, I heard Buddy Marshall in the stairwell. His folks had brought him over to spend the night with the Luper kids; Buddy had gathered them in their pajamas around him for a bedtime story. As I headed for the gravel driveway I heard him say, "And then the Indians shot Jesus dead."

I stood in the driveway for a few minutes, mopping my forehead and face and neck with a handkerchief.

Ten past eleven, as I was making my way out of the kitchen with a fresh drink, I stopped. Archie. He was in his black suit, standing just inside the door; his eyes were squinting behind the hard gold-rimmed glasses. I hadn't invited him. *No, Beau had not invited him. We noticed that.* And now there he stood in the doorway, his mouth an intensely drawn line.

I greet him quietly.

He seems to have misplaced his public self. He was frowning as if something was hurting him inside; his brow was wrinkled, tense. He managed half a smile. "Good evening, Beaunorus. I hope I'm not interrupting your festivities."

"Uncle, you could never interrupt the festivities of the Little One and me." Well, pretty lame, unworthy, and I was standing there with egg on my face. *And I am allergic to egg.* "Have a drink?"

"Thank you, no." He was looking toward Henry's circle in the kitchen. "I'd just like to borrow two of your guests. For a moment."

"Surely."

He nodded toward the Opium Den. "As I remember, we had the phone installed in there."

Well, as *I* remember . . .

I cleared a path for him to it. One of the secretaries was in the bedroom with Homer Brown; when they saw us come in, they looked up, and Homer's eyes caught Archie's. Homer hustled the female and himself past us to the door, like a huge kid caught by the cops necking with his gal in the graveyard.

Just as they had almost escaped, the president said softly, squeezing fire and grease out of a tube, "Homer?"

Homer turned around, large and frightened in the door. "Yes, Presydent?"

The voice was deeply patient. He sat on the bed at a Sunday-school picnic; he sat straight, with both his feet planted on the linoleum floor. He knew, exactly, all his distributions. "Homer, I wonder if you could bring Jim in here. I'd like to talk to you boys."

"Presydent, that's what I'll do."

I stared down at my uncle there, and his eyes were on the phone on the bedside table. This room is too clogged up. And now the room begins to fan with electric sound.

In the middle of it, he suddenly looks up and says under his breath, "Shit, boy."

I think maybe I'll get the hell out of here. I met Homer and Jim coming in. I turned for a moment; Homer was looking at the floor, and Jim shut the bedroom door with his foot. He's gettin' good at that.

I nodded and looked beyond, into the kitchen, where Henry was standing with the Lupers; Henry shouted out a punch line of a joke and it was followed by a whoop and a burst of laughter. All clear, all clear.

I went out to the front. Standing in her pink party dress on the gravel driveway, Ophelia Jones. The dress flowed around her, blooming; it made her seem even vaster than she was.

"A nice party you givin' us this evening, Beaunorus."

"Well, don't stay out here by yourself."

She turned, staring back at the apartment. "I thought I'd get me some air. I wasn't expectin' your latest guest."

I was not looking at her. "I didn't myself expect to be visited by royalty."

"You don't mean Archie is *crashin'* your party?"

"Not exactly. He had to see Homer and Jim about something."

"Yes, I suppose he did. If you know what I mean."

"Don't believe I do."

She lowered her voice. "You heard about Archie's little escapade? Our President's latest adventure?"

"No." Ah, but I have. I have heard. And seen and tasted.

"Your Aunt Charlesetta is in the hospital."

So, that. I said innocently, "Hospital?"

"Bo, you know what Presydent did? That man got after her. He fixed Charlesetta. He pulled her hair out by the root." She clenched her fist, grabbing an imaginary bunch of black hair in the darkness; she pronounced the word "root" as if it were "rut," in the singular, "by the *rut*." Her face was working. "He made her nose bleed and pulled out her hair. She ran out of the house. In her *night*gown. Can you imagine that?"

I looked back across at the faculty apartments; Zip Luper had stepped out onto my front porch. I thought it best to keep quiet about that night, when I had seen it. To Ophelia I said, "How did she get to the hospital?"

"Homer."

"Homer?"

"Oh," she said, "our stock in Homer went way up that night. *Way* up. Didn't think he had it in him. But just like Henry say, you never know what's in a man until it comes out."

Ophelia looked at the porch, where Zip was standing. We are out of earshot. Ophelia turned and motioned up beyond the frogpond to the string of faculty cottages and the darkened White House. "Charlesetta went out, running across the lawn in her negligee. Right up there. Oh, that poor woman, not knowing where to go. Now, Homer, he lives in that cottage there, the one next to Presydent, you know."

I nodded. So the lady went to Homer.

Ophelia was completely *in* her story, replaying it. "Well, Charlesetta saw his light. She went up to his porch and rang his bell. Homer told me. He said, 'I did what any Christian gentleman would have done in the same situation.' "

"A Christian gentleman," I said.

Ophelia leaned closer toward me, and the pink party dress fell down away from her enormous front. My jaw fell accordingly. "Homer took her in," she said. "Oh, he was just *fine,* saying, 'I shall stand here in the door. And he will have to get past *me.*' "

Ophelia spoke her set-piece rather well, and it was obvious that she had spoken it before. I saw Homer in his little straw hat and Madras sport jacket—he also seemed to be wearing white boxer shorts—standing in the doorway with his face all bloated up for the harvest: Presydent, thou shalt not pass. *Homer is smarter than I am.*

And—and so. That is where my poor bleeding aunt went, where she went on to, after she left me swamped in empty moonlight.

"Homer drove her to the hospital. In her nightgown. But Presydent found out where she was. He got in that big Cadillac and he went storming over there. He beat up a *in*tern trying to get in to see her. Charlesetta said, 'Don't you let him in here, or he's going to kill me.' She said, 'I won't see Archie unless he's accompanied by two po-lice officers.' " Ophelia was completely lost in her story; she was not looking at me, she was recreating Charlesetta Washington in her nightgown, in her hospital bed. Ophelia's whole life was there, in the consciousness of that hospital bed. Her big mouth wagged, open. Then: "They called the

police. And the po-lice escorted him in." Exhausted, after
a major effort, she sagged. "My, I gather it was quite a
scene."

She took a step back toward the driveway, but suddenly
her eyes were wild, and she turned, as if frightened to be
seen talking with me. Her voice went low. "Of course his
cruelty to women is well known."

"Yes."

"Like that Marshall party."

"The Marshalls?"

"You remember when I came in? Late in the evening?
You noticed I didn't sit down?" That seemed very important to Ophelia, for she repeated it. "I didn't sit down."

"Yes."

"Well, you left before the *fun* started. Did you know
Presydent attacked little Gladys Furman?"

"Gladys?" I looked back toward the apartment.

"Presydent attacked her, oh *yes* he did, in Buddy's bedroom. You noticed we didn't see much of *her* for a week.
She stayed indoors, her face was beat so bad. Presydent
even had his *clothes* off."

My Lord, it gets worser and worser. I was only half
hearing her then, thinking about the Little One, who came
out of it with never a mark on her.

"Oh yes, Jim had to dress him again and drag him
home." Ophelia was silent for a moment, and then she drew
herself up. "And the *tra*gedy is, everybody *knows*."

No, that is not the tragedy.

She peered at me. "This is no state secret. But Archie's
in cahoots with Anderson on the board of regents. Anderson wants Archie in there."

I said that perhaps we ought to get back to the party.
Either that, or sleep with her. Beau and Ophelia, yards
on sheets. You know, it's not a bad idea. It would certainly

be a change from the Little One. I looked at Ophelia and smiled slightly. Ma'am, you is the Big One. I'll have to get Toast to write a song about it. "The Big Un 'n' the Liddle Un."

Before we reached the driveway Ophelia whispered, "He's got a *gun*, you know." She stopped on the grass. "Charlesetta came over to my Home Economics practice cottage one night. She said, 'Archie's going to kill me with that gun of his.' It's a pistol. I told her to take the bullets out of it. And she said to me, Charlesetta said to me, 'Ophelia Jones, if I take the bullets out of that gun, Archie's going to kill me with his bare hands.'" She stood looking at her hands. "It's a *crime*. Can you believe it? Some nights he holds her up there, a hour at a time, and they just sit, and he holds that gun at her head and he says, 'If you make one move, I'm going to kill you.'"

"He told me that he thinks 'that woman is worth a hundred of me.'"

Ophelia laughed. "Oh, that's another story. I wouldn't say Charlesetta's worth more than *five* of Archie. *Six* at the outside." Then she whispered, "He's after *us*, you know."

"Us?"

"Henry and me. He denied my annual budget request for Home Economics. He's cut off my stipend."

I saw Archie hacking away at Ophelia's stipend.

"For my professional meetings and all." She sighed. "And he's gone after Henry, you know. And Henry was teaching college before Archie was *born*."

We started back in. Zip Luper, on the porch, was carrying on with his daughter; just outside my party, he was kissing her good night, holding her up high and snuggling his face into her shoulder and neck, smooching with her. "My big blonde, my bi-i-ig blonde." And the black child squealed with helpless laughing.

Ophelia went on back in and took refuge with Henry holding forth in the kitchen. I stood in the outer hallway for a moment, watching Zip with his little girl, and then I glanced out the front door. A white shirt, far in the darkness, across the frogpond. Someone coming in the darkness. Now he crosses the highway and is heading for my place. All alone, in a hurry, coming out of the night.

When he got to the gravel driveway, I recognized him. Toast. I stepped out to the porch, "How you makin' it tonight, scholar?"

He stopped. His eyes were anxious. "He in there?"

"I reckon he is."

"I got some news for him," Toast said. "Can I see him?"

I led him in. He nodded at Barbara Marshall on the couch. I rapped on the door of the Opium Den. After a moment Jim opened it; he looked at me, not knowing what to do. "Abner," I explained. "He'd like to see his father."

Inside, I could see Homer on the bed holding the phone to his chest and Archie beside the window, looking out at the darkness, lost in the darkness like a sheet of metal. Toast brushed past me; then Jim muttered something to me, nothing understandable, and closed the door.

Apparently Toast's arrival settled something. I had just gone out into the kitchen, trying to get near Henry again, when the bedroom door opened and they re-entered the room: Uncle Washington, Homer, Jim, and Toast. The big boys, fraternity men; they had just extended the hand of brotherhood to the rushee. Back in the smoke-filled room. But Toast did not look like a pledge. He stopped, his head bent down, looking at the floor, nodding, and his father was intently talking to the top of that head; Archie held one arm out, being firm, making his point clearly, and again Toast's head nodded, yes. He turned and waited another moment, listening, and they were frozen there in their sharp shared sense of the thing.

I caught my boy on the porch. "Sure you won't stay?"
"No. Thanks. I'm kind of busy tonight."
I looked back at the apartment and then at him. "I suppose they keep your hands full at the White House."
Toast stared at me, blank. "Night."
I followed him a bit, watching him go up the road again, disappearing into the night. I almost called. But he was going about his father's business.

What say, Bo, shall we call this party to a close? I strolled up to the frogpond and stared at the black water. We usually have a good supply of smart little birds; they play all day above the pond and zip across the sky and drop like stones, straight down, and then dart up again—so where are they now? Come to our party? Perch on guests, carry messages from one to another. I sure got one to send to Ruthie. It goes: "Come home. All is forgiven." Before you deliver it, bird, let me cross out the last word. There, that's the truth. I stared at a large bullfrog breathing like a round machine on a round rock. Night, he said. So where are you, birds? Asleep in trees. That's what we'll do in Dramatics, we'll fly. The whole goddam class is going to fly out the window and we'll soar and dance on air over this pond. Man, that's acting. And at the dark hour before dawn the birds fly down, real birds, down, close to the water, brushing it with their wings, dipping their wingtips in the water, like a painter dips his brush in the paint, and the birds fly to where Toast Homeboy is standing, and with their wet wings they paint his face. They touch up that little place on the right side, to make him complete. They restore him. He's a lovely piece of Florentine art, and then the flood hit him. But now's

okay, now's the time, and your eyes open to the flutter of
wet wings. In the morning they will find footprints on the
yellow grass, footprints on the dawning silence. This boy
—the land parts, opens, gives him up—and here he comes
to me and we join hands, running, chased through moonlight by the angel. In the following century the team finds
on the dirt our footprints: here is where a pair of black
boys prowled, up to no good—and suddenly the footprints stop. Where the angel caught us, lifted us like real
brothers.

I crouched down. Here we got on to it. And I
am allergic to eggs. The music from the party rocked
across the night. There was no music that night. Just the
Little One, mystical, waiting for me sleeplessly. I squatted
there beside the frogpond, and I looked through my fingers at the moon in the water. The moon was quite lovely
in the water. I yawned and shivered.

When I went back in, Uncle Archie was sitting with a drink in his hand, sitting straight on the couch beside Jim. So, he's going to stay. They looked uncomfortable, the two men there, unspeaking; they were watching Gladys having her way with Zip on the dance floor. I moved to the couch, nodded to Jim on President's right, and then— what have I got to lose?—I sat down on the left.

Presydent turned to me, slowly. "Well, son."

The rock record had been turned up, and I pulled my head back, shapes swimming in front of my eyes, a roomful of party. Ruth, in that fine party dress I got for her, she was excited and eyes-dancing, not body-dancing, against the wall. Beyond, in the kitchen, Henry was still holding forth. I said, "Professor Prudhomme is a great man."

"Henry?" the smile reappeared. "Yes, old Henry is a great teller of Texas tall tales. He's a real character."

"Not quite what I meant."

"Beg pardon?" The hearing-aid moved toward me.

"Well, he's more than a character."

"Oh, I see what you mean." His head nodded. "Yes, Henry's had quite a life." The President turned and faced me; his smile endured. "I'm sure he told you?"

Ruthie makes her way around Gladys in perpetual motion; the Little One turned our way, and Uncle put up an arm and asked her to sit down. Stately bed-knowledge. She looked at him and at me, and for a moment I thought my lady was going to panic. But, no, walking, she came over, and Jim stood up on the right, I on the left. Archie moved in my direction—yes, indeed—and Ruth came down, a little faster than she intended.

"Evenin', child."

It lay in my ears, lay in my brain. As he softly let it out he was fulfilled upon her. That's what he had said at the moment, that moment, as he slightly raised himself: "Evenin', child."

I think I'm goin' to turn in this brain on a new one. I've had this one for some time, but now it just keeps dyin' on me. I think I'll get me one without a automatic shift.

I left them there together, and while Jim passed on to Barbara I went out to the front porch. Uncle's big black Cadillac—it was parked in front of the next apartment unit. Not here in this driveway. Hidden over there in the trees. Now why the hell did he do that? When I came on back in, everyone was gathered at the kitchen. Except for Ruth and President. They sat, a couple on the couch. He was speaking slowly, in low tones, to her. The Little One held a drink in her hand, her knees close to President's knees and her body leaning away from him; with her free hand she was fidgeting with a cigarette. She smokes so damn poorly. In the kitchen Henry was carrying on about something; Carolstyne Luper and Barbara Marshall were with Homer and Ophelia, spectators at the table.

Yes, there he is, good old Henry, always talkin' in the kitchen. He was leaning his perfect little brown head back against my brown refrigerator. He was telling a story about the time he had a ticket on a train in Tennessee and when he got on they wouldn't let a nigger sit with the white folks, but he *had* his ticket, they had to admit that, and so "to *pre*serve the great system of segregation" they made him ride all the way in a private *com*partment, fit for a king, with a private lavatory. He told the story with his usual unstoppable flair, but the hour was late and fifteen minutes later Henry had lost track of himself—he seemed tired, hoisting himself up for punch lines, then dropping low—and he started to tell the same story again. I stopped him.

I held my glass in one hand and with the other I reopened the spare bedroom door, peering back out at Ruth and President on the couch together. If they try to come on in here again, they'll have to get past *me*. And beyond, the old man, tripping over his punch lines. I love the old buzzard. I closed the door. So you love the old buzzard? I'm sure you do. Henry's an old gentleman. But let's not tell ourselves he's God's gift to America. I sipped my drink. Now Uncle, he's a different story. Out there with our wife.

Presydent is the man we put our money on.

But we got big things in mind for you, Bo-nor-eees. Green Power. You're Archie's boy because you know the name of the game. I began a little soft-shoe shuffle on the linoleum. "Me and My Sha-ah-ah-dough." I turned and put down my drink and flopped at full length on the bed. Humpidy-humpidy.

Henry looks in. Hey, boy, what you doin'?

MASTER BAITIN'.

Cut that out, boy, you'll drive yourself feeble-minded.

WELL, I AIN'T GOT FAR TO GO.

Outside, a slow blues was deepening on the phonograph.

Somebody gimme a hand up.

I stopped at the front door and leaned back slightly,
toward the couch where they were sitting. He was very
close to her, and he still had both his feet planted hard on
the floor. She was talking to him earnestly. The bourbon
in his glass looked like it was solid. It was not liquid; it
was carved and set roundly in his glass. Presydent smiled.
He was in the middle of showing his even teeth. He looked
extremely strong, packed.

I am now one-quarter of an inch high and I am going
exploring in my rival's face: I kick up my highly visible
heels in your cordovan lips in the shadows and now I flow
down your blood and give the word in your heart, and
end up—through your ballistic thighs, the scenic route—
in your feet. I checked to see if I could see myself surface
on his ankle, crawl out through his nylon sock.

Henry Prudhomme, Ophelia, and Homer came out
into the living room. Henry said it was time to go, and he
glanced at the pair on the couch, my Ruth and my uncle,
a world unto themselves. I staggered, rubber legs, on
outside. Homer had brought his own car; he thanked me
for "a most enjoyable evenin' " and then drove away. I
walked with Henry and Ophelia over to her car. Ophelia
was eying me oddly and Henry was eying me not at all.
Slowly I said, "Look, I know all about his most recent
outrage." The one we can talk about. "Is there anything
I can do?"

The old man glanced at Ophelia, then back at me. In
the darkness his skin was falling, tired on his face. He
stared down at his red carpet slippers for a moment, and
he kicked absently in the gravel. "Lord, you'd think that

after all that man has done, somewhere along the line he would have got it." He sighed. "Sometimes it's hard to get a man." He shook his head. The fire had gone out of him, the wind out of his old patched sails. He stood there, party over, repeating that Archie Washington had just gone too far this time.

"Agreed," I said.

He waited a moment and then said that now, maybe, they had a chance to get him.

I looked at my hands and brushed them together. "What're the odds?"

He turned his eyes back to the apartment. "Who can tell? We hope he's gone a step too far. Anderson is going to have to talk fast to keep Archie in after this." He sighed and shook his head. Henry is old now, old and tired. He pulled his ancient lips back away from his false teeth and rocked on his red carpet slippers. "All these years Archie Washington has been sitting on a powder keg with his pants on fire. Now it's going to blow up. That's what I thi-i-ink." He snorted. "I been out knockin' his hustle. Now we will *see*."

Ophelia asked Henry if she could drive him, but he preferred to walk the hundred yards. The lady got in behind the wheel, and I stood for a moment beside her window. She patted my hand. "Good night, Beaunorus."

I watched Ophelia's purple taillights go on out to the highway. Henry stood with me and muttered something about her to the night air. I wasn't sure what it was, but I didn't ask because it wasn't said to me. I sighed. "That man in the White House." I looked at ancient Henry. "Isn't there something I can do?"

He contemplated his slippers. "We got a chance, I

think. Now he's done this thing to his wife. I got an investigator coming down." He nodded firmly. "A *criminal* investigator."

"You hired him?"

He turned back toward the frogpond, facing away from the apartment. "Oh, no, I got the faculty a better deal than that. This man is comin' on be-half of the state. He'll be coming to us Sunday, tomorrow. He's going to spend *four days* rounding up evidence." He turned on me. "I've been getting the letters out, you know."

"Letters?" (He does *not* just flap his lip in his own breeze?)

"Oh, anonymous. Mostly anonymous. But I got some people to write on their own and sign their *names*. Alumni." He nodded, his eyes back to his slippers. "Those letters have been rollin' in to the board and we've got some results at last—a real investigation."

"Does he know?"

He started down the road toward home. "Oh, boy, what do you expect? Of course he *knows*. Archie's got some people around here in his *pocket*." Without turning around, staring ahead into the darkness he said, walking away, "See you, boy."

I contemplated his back. That old man has escaped, whole, with his heart.

I followed him. "Look, Henry, I want to help you. I'll testify."

The old eyes narrowed. "Boy, you be careful."

I sighed. "Send the state man around. I'll tell him."

Henry slopped forward on his slippers, old on the dirt. "Boy, you sure you want to get in this mess?"

"I *am* in it."

"Now, we don't have no need for repetitions of old

rumors. Ophelia, my *Gawd*, she'll take care of that. No need for you to testify unless you got some eyewitness testimony."

"You better believe it."

He looked at me for some time. Then he shrugged. "Well, we'd both better sleep on this." On his way home he looked back a moment, wide-eyed, considering, and then he was gone into the prairie night.

On the way back to the apartment I quickened my steps, and my heart began bangin' around in there—yes, oh, yes, hang on, Little One. I am possessed of an idea: Presydent, I don't think I ever thanked you for making us feel at home here with the Bundy family. Man, do we feel at home. I walked in and passed quickly to the master bedroom. The paper, yes, it was there on Ruthie's bedside stand with her watch, and my fingers snapped the paper up. I went back out into the living room.

Here I stand—myself of Thespic proportions—and this is our school newspaper, the *Bundy Bee*. I had been looking through it, hot off the press, and now I stand thumbing through it, facing Ruth and the Red-Hot Violator on the couch. I called his full name, Achille Toussaint Washington, and requested his careful attention. Behind, against the walls and peering out from the kitchen—Jim and Barbara and the Lupers.

I glanced down at Uncle: he looked like he was facing a hard sun; his face was tortured by something jabbing out from behind the eyes. I had seen that expression once before, when I had taken over one of the practice pianos below my office. I filled up the room, accompanied myself: *"La Donna è mobile."* That was part of my old act, and I had won two tickets to Hawaii—for Mamma and me—when I was fourteen, singing that on the Stockton TV channel, *Stairway to Stardom.* Mamma was home rootin' for me, lookin' forward to hula-hula lessons—and I *got* 'em for her, just like Henry got his gal the weddin' ring—and I was sittin' on my unicycle, rockin' back and forth, lustily singin' Verdi. I had quite put my heart into it, and was surprised, a few years later in Introduction to Music, to discover it was not a military song. Sure sounded to me like a military song. Damn you all, I still sing it like a military song. At Bundy I was sitting there at the piano, my vibrato wandering all over left field, when Archie walked into the room. The piano was turned around and pushed back toward the wall opposite the door; the minute he stepped in, I saw him. He stepped suddenly outside himself. His face was a split second behind his eyes; he saw me and another face appeared, but just a tenth of a moment too late. When he came in he was angry at all that noise, that uncontrolled Italian bombardment that one of his students was making. His face was burning, eyes angry behind the gold-rimmed glasses. But when he saw that it was I, Presydent brought out the other face and smiled, and I shut off my voice, sudden silence, and he was still angry at the noise, but he only said, "Son, what big lungs you have." He stood laughing, kidding me. But for that tenth of a moment there had been three of us in the room, and I had seen that menacing face, that face burning against its will—the face Presydent turned up, now, to me in the center of the room.

"Where is it?" I said and I licked a finger, turning the pages. "Ah, here she is." I folded the paper. "The story goes: 'The students in Agriculture tried their hands at butchering in June.' " I stopped. "Check." Then I went on with my reading. " 'They experimented, also, with all processes involved in slaughtering.' "

I made a slaughtering-process gesture—can that really redeem us all? and I leaned forward a step. B. Green

caught himself, unicycled. "Now, there's the part I want
to know about, Mr. President. Point of information. It
says here in your *Bee*: 'Close supervision was given
by the head of the Agricultural Department, Mr. Horatio
Sanders. Also, President Washington played a vital role.' "
A sour giggle worked its way out of my mouth, but, grabbing it in midair, we looked up. "Now *there*'s the part I
don't understand. What is this vital role you play—in the
slaughtering process?"

The room was hushed—Bo standing there with the
paper in his hands and Achille Toussaint on the
couch with her. Nobody moved to break the silence; it
deepened into electricity, buzzing with lack of sound.

President shifted his weight. He looked at Ruth. "I
will say good night."

I walked over to the couch and helped the Little One
up, pulled her up; she winced, unsteady beside me. I
turned—I'm not going to let go now—and I said crisply to
President, who was moving away, "Sorry to hear your First
Lady was indisposed."

⎯⎯⎯⎯⎯⎯⎯⎯⎯⎯⎯⎯⎯⎯

I sit black and lean and expensive-looking in my kitchen window. Nobody in here but us dead pigeons. Sent my old lady to bed with a bitter pill. "Didn't even have the courtesy to say good night to your guests," I said to her. "Old Henry just had to wander off."

She reared up. "Why didn't he come say good night to me?"

"Because," I said, "you were *occupied*."

She stood for a moment, attacked with her eyes, then roared off to bed without a word.

The Little One banked her whole life on an idea: if you don't understand something, sleep with it.

Next weekend my Thespians are gonna strut their stuff for the assemblage. After, we'll have some punch and cookies in the Complex. If he comes up, claps me on the back, and says, "Good show," I'll kick his butt.

I wish my leading lady weren't a teen-age drunkard— "Hee-hee-hee, sandwiches?" Toast wrote a skit called "Love in These U.S." and he's such a sentimental chappie. All that happens is in two playing areas: a black guy and a black gal necking on the left like the Total Groove, all tangled up in each other; and then on the right a white-face boy and a whiteface girl saying "Why?" "I don't know why." "But *why?*" "I don't *know.*"

We will see how it goes. And fifteen minutes of darkness with music by the Soul Merchants. In the last half-hour we do what comes to mind.

From the bedroom, her voice: "Bo? *Bo?*"

My own voice, stage whisper: "It's all right, baby."

And back to sleep. Not knowing quite where she is.

Pause, don't hesitate. A Christian conscience should sear you. Soul Brother Speaks. Like Watts, a Motown tune, Pause Don't Hesitate. Shootin' 'n' Lootin', Settin' Fires 'n' Slashin' Tires. The way it was, you see, is that back there they used to come from miles and miles around. When the posters went up, Bo Holdin' Forth, why hell, them black folks would pack themselves into their wagons and bring the kids and dogs and cats and possums and beavers, and they'd all pile over to the Lyceum to see the soul freak-out on the electric unicycle.

> All you bastards out there in TV land,
> This here is the voice of God,
> The voice of Bo God comin' at you,
> Comin' at all you black *sinners.*

Go, brother. Christ's blood.

> The voice of God comin' to all you black niggers
> And comin' to all you car-a-mel black boo-jaw-zee
> Guzzlin' your Dewar's White Label,
> Suckin' your Menthol Trues,
> God's goin' to kick you in your black gizzard.

I threw an arm out to the window.

> I come to bring the sword, bros. The *sword.*
> Glory Jesus, you're saved.

You're saved, black soldier, with the box of chocolates in
one hand and that disvirginized child in the other.
You're saved—that colored woman in the balcony who is
bein' taken in adultery.
You're saved, Toast, and Henry, and Ruthie, and Homer.
And yes Ophelia's saved and yes Barren Charlesetta,
Hell, save her too, and yes save Buddy and
You're saved, Presydent. No, not you. You are definitely
not saved.

Pound the pulpit. Go, baby. Go, baby, *go.* For yourself.
For yourself and nobody else.

I pulled out a cigarette. I don't know what in hell I'll
do. Turn state's evidence on my own blood? My uncle?
How can I do that?

Watch me.

Tonight, this little party, it was just a preview. I
sighed. They'll all remember you, Bo, especially Presydent. Party sure did break up fast after my bit with the
newspaper. He couldn't exactly turn around and kill me.
As Henry has said.

Archie Washington flunks his all-time multiple-choice
exam. Pres says, "*All* of the Above."

I sat in silence—it was hot in the apartment, even now
—and I just sat there, sleepy-like. I finished my cigarette,
then leaned back and stared for a time at my lap; I started
zipping down my fly and then I zipped it back up and then
I zipped it down again. Someday I may play an elevator.
Absently zipping, I realized how quiet it was in my
kitchen, how utterly still, and I shot my eyes up at the
brown Texas fridge and it was smiling at what I was doing. Bo quickly jerked away from his zipper and put his
hands up on the table. Which, after a moment, made me
laugh in my nose. The brown fridge buzzed.

Over here you see Gladys's glasses. That's just not like Gladys, to leave a party before somebody beats her up. I played with them, finding them on the couch table and recognizing the Batlady rims. I put them on. Christ, what a weird left eye on that girl. Perhaps Presydent put it out of commission, and this is her post-Marshall prescription.

I stood up and turned off the light. I sat back again in the little fuzz of leftover light from around the corner in the bathroom. I took off my shoes and socks, then my shirt. The stale smoke of the party lingered like used conversation. I put on and take off the glasses belonging to Gladys. I never got through to my students about Dostoevski. Toast was right. I had read to them a passage from Father Zossima (and then I was going to have them embody it on the stage for some time): "Love a man even in his sin, for that is the highest love on earth. Love all God's creation, the whole and every grain of sand in it. Love the animals, love the plants, love everything." One stringy coal-black girl about six-two with no breasts, she sat there putting her long head up, smelling the air, Bambi with Man in the forest. "If you love everything, you will perceive the divine mystery in things. Once you perceive it, you will begin to comprehend it better every day. And you will come at last to love the whole world with an all-embracing love." I turned to Toast. "What do you make of this?" He blinked his eyes, drew on his cigarette, and muttered, "It's harder than it looks."

I smiled in the kitchen. Kinfolks.

Oh, shit, Mr. President. B. Green in Newark feel considerably better. Driving the tank with a load of guerrillas to the front, he sees it in the rear-view mirror: he is being followed, followed all day. Green laughs. He laughs easily not frightened. They stop followin' him. So do his own people. Let's face it: I am driving an empty tank.

Well, Mr. Green, I guess you'll just have to live with
it.

I muttered in despair and took off my jockey shorts. I
sat back down in the post-party kitchen. Looking around
my loins—is my Ruthie lonely down here this summer?
I hung my head and said, "It's all in the laps of the Voodoo
gods." Or maybe Henry is right; he said it's all a mystery,
what makes a man love a woman, a woman love a man. He
said it's all according to the secret, mysterious demands
of the "feetish." It was a word. A word managing to mean
foot-fetish and various lulus not in the index. Or, he said,
maybe it's that Ruth rhymes with truth.

That is pretty.

Now BEAUNORUS GREEN reappears in his Marat/
Sade spec. Marat Me, rising from the bath: you'd really
hear the click of binoculars against bifocals when Bo comes
up out of the bath, black old bare-ass Bo on his unicycle. Jeesus, what a gorgeous creature. I moved down onto
the floor and tried not to think. Naked black buttocks bite
the dust. A posterior for posterity. I guess I'll just sit here
until I'm a old man. I made it into a little blues tune, and
it wasn't half bad. I hummed on the floor and sang my
latest creation: "I Guess I'll Just Sit Here until I'm a Old
Man." It had real possibilities.

A click at the door. The door, in fact, opened. I peered
through the Batlady glasses at their owner. There was
Gladys herself, and there I was, all belly-naked.

I was wearing her Batlady glasses and I felt around
the floor. None of my clothes volunteered. Wearing ap-
parel, come out, come out, wherever you are.

She spotted me and pulled back. "Oh—"

I looked up in the darkness and I pulled the glasses off
my eyes. "I believe these are what you're looking for." I
held the glasses out to her.

She didn't know what to do. What was she supposed to do? I waited. Softly I said to her, "Come on in." I smiled and made small quick gestures with my hands. "I'll put on my robe. Let's have a nightcap."

"I never knew you was up. I remembered putting them on the couch and I thought—"

I lowered my voice, going down slow. "Just make yourself comfortable, sweetheart. I'll put on my robe and be with you in a minute. Do you know 'Trane? *"Kulu Sé Mama?"* Let's put it on."

She stepped forward. "Maybe just one little drink. A nightcap."

So here we go. Bo swished on by the lady's eyes. Gladys is a hungry little piece of woman, and if you can't take her from there, Bo, you *better* keep on sittin' there till you're a old man.

In the bedroom Ruth's head came up from the pillow. "Sweetheart?"

"Who else?" I fumbled into the closet and got my red satin bull-robe.

"What time is it?"

"Late."

"You still mad at me?"

I bent over the bed and kissed her forehead. It was very hot, damp.

"That's nice," she said. "Coming to bed?"

"Shortly."

Something should be done. For the life of us. "It's okay, baby." There on the pillow, her head. I touched her hair with my hands.

"I didn't *mean* not to say good night to Henry."

"It's okay. I know you didn't mean not to."

"President—President—"

I moved my hand away from her hair. "Aren't you on a first-name basis *yet?*"

She was fumbling. If this keeps up, she's going to be wide awake. "Go to sleep, baby."

"Bo?"—a little panic.

"Sleep, baby."

And I went out. I returned in my scarlet robe—she bought it for me—and Gladys and I sat listening to 'Trane's "Vigil" and "Welcome," that painful and clearly intelligent emotion. We danced. Blow the tension and share the sweet. That music is this life. She was so sweet and innocently needing it, abandoned by some husband, not *that* good in white foreign languages. We glided into the Opium Den, and her clothes came off cleanly, like pieces of a simple mind, quickly. We were together there, naked, with the needle of the phonograph swishing lonely at the center. I rose for a moment, padded on out, and pressed a button. I spoke to the economy turntable, whispering: "Don't worry." Say this for me, I never tore *no*-body's hair out. My 'Trane—"Welcome" again. That sound is all hope, retrieving pain. I went back to her, quiet and open-eyed in the spare bed. It was so soft there, and she cleaved to me with quick little motion, there in soft hollows.

She wanted to mother me and I was not against it. Singing lullabys. Gladys kept my head cool upon her poignant chest. She sang and I dropped off. Her fingers touched my face. You can't say no.

In my dream the criminal-investigator had told President that Ruthie had turned state's evidence. He came charging over to the faculty quarters and ran his Cadillac skidding into the front of the house, the whole chromed nose of that huge dark vehicle in the front porch, and then he got out, lurching, and he pulled the gun out of his shoulder holster and he ran around the house and stuck the gun into my bedroom window and he fired and blew a head off a neck.

When I jerked up, awake, my heart was roaring and I sat, cold in the sheets, sweating; the plastic venetian blinds were beating against the open window. I looked out: pouring rain. Then another clap of thunder hit, dull and hard, a slug from President's gun.

When I leaned down to comfort Ruthie, it was Gladys. Hmmm. So I got up and went into the other bedroom, and in her sleep Ruthie's hand touched my skin. "Baby?"

"How's your head?" I said.

"Hunh?"

"Nothing." I got up and went out into the living room and sat for some time with a drink. I'll be gone in the morning, and Gladys and Ruth can awaken separately and separately discover each other and finally grow something over coffee. For the present, in the darkness, I listened to Texas rain. It's not rain. Hemorrhage. I turned off all the lights and sat, humming, hearing the blood blown into the windows.

They slept, and I was on my way to service. In the Sunday-morning sunlight the cows had arranged themselves in a wide circle near the fence; the middle was occupied by the body of an old horse. Dead. Lying motionless. Archie's black Cadillac, the chariot, turned in off the highway; he honked at me cheerfully, and I didn't much want to flag *him* down, but something had to be done with the horse. I waved my arms, and he stopped. I wandered around the hood and looked in: Unk's face was half smiling behind the gold-rimmed glasses, and he fiddled for a second with the hearing-aid. He looked as he had looked when Ruth and I had first come in from New York. Nothing visible. No hard feelings. That is what he has done, his contribution: he has kept the night out of the day. The night is the night.

His car window came down. "What's your problem, Beaunorus?"

As if answering his question, I pointed to the field.

He stared at it for a moment, the horse lying and the cows bleakly staring. "Well, I declare, that horse looks dead."

"He looked a little dead to me."

His hand turned his motor off. The Pres stepped out

of the Cadillac in his springy canvas shoes and left his blue
suit coat on the front seat by his academic robes. He circled around the car and gingerly stepped through the
barbed-wire fence into the pasture. He walked through
the cows toward the horse—and, Lord above me, he looked
so kindly, stopping at the scene of an accident. What's
all this nonsense about the Little One and pulling Charlesetta's hair out by the rut? I swear to you, I *swear* that man
was not at the Boston Tea Party. But now the criminal-
investigation is here, all systems go; I had seen the state
car, a brown Ford with government plates, when the CI
asked directions just down from our cellblock.

He bent down and spoke in a low voice and
touched the horse on the head; the long neck reared, the
mane flaring, and the horse struggled to its feet. The cows
did not move. Uncle Archie stood, supreme, looking up
at the horse, talking low to it, at home with it. For a moment, as they stood there together, frozen in the sun,
Achille T. Washington's life seemed like a series of desperate gasps. He burns to take the pasture in his arms.

He came back through the cows, crawled through the
fence, and we stood beside the car. He leaned back, his
dark blue suit against the black fender. "Those cows, my
Lord." He crossed his arms. "During the war I took my
basic near here, and I was heading my platoon one day"
—he pointed to all the dull cows ignoring the white horse
—"and we hit a dozen milk cows." He chuckled. "A dozen
milk cows on the axis of attack."

Sergeant Washington, leading his black troops, walks
quietly into the cows; he watches their bloated udders,
he listens to the gentle heifers touching awkwardly, the
unmilitary sound of their bells. You had a rifle, President. Now you got a pistol. Good soldier, you make your
prisoners talk. You served your country well.

"The kids still givin' you decent treatment, son?" He was moving back into the driver's seat.

"Abner gives me plenty of feedback." I looked at the road.

He nodded, slow. "He's a good boy."

Watching him think of his son, I turned in sunlight. "But too many of them keep sayin' what they think they're supposed to say."

He looked at me.

"Then we point out that what they're sayin' is pretty silly, and they laugh—like a big cat in the corner of the room has talked." Dixie fireballs between us, and Boss smiles slightly.

He was not altogether sure what to say and so he got into the Cadillac. "You keep at it, son, y'hear?" He looked out into the pasture, eying the horse.

There was a pause, and then he said, "Going to Sunday service, son?"

"I look forward to your words of wisdom."

"I'll give you a lift."

B. Green is not getting in that car. "No, go ahead. I'll stay a minute and check out the horse you raised from the dead."

So he drove on up to the administration building. I followed the car with my eyes. Nothing of that evening with her. Nothing of our old poker fiasco or last night's throwing the *Bundy Bee* into his teeth. And he's up to his neck in the investigation. One thing I know: you are not going to go quietly. I brushed the sweat off my forehead and turned around. The horse was still on its feet, but now one of the cows had gone down and turned dead. Nature is such a mystery.

And Achille T. Washington is not going to go quietly.

At three minutes after the hour they came out through the stage, behind the cyclorama, and entered from the left. Mrs. Strout struck up "Holy, Holy, Holy" on the piano and Reverend Flowers stepped forward to the podium; he raised his arms, and, standing, we broke heavily into song. The auditorium was half filled and in the front row sat Jim Marshall and Barbara, looking up, beaming, at Buddy on the stage. Buddy's white collar was much too big for him and his black jacket was much too small; he sat on a straight chair by Pres, with his hands folded dead in his lap. Archie had moved Barbara up from the registrar's office this week; now she was official secretary to the President.

After a short musical interlude, Mrs. Strout at the blond piano, Flowers leaned forward and gave the signal to Buddy. Our boy stepped up, his big white starched collar sticking out at his neck. The lectern was too high; he couldn't see over it. He turned, puzzled, and Boss held up a robed arm, smiling, and pointed to a spot beside the lectern. "Speak up, Buddy; you don't need that microphone." The boy turned around, tin soldier, and stood to the left of the lectern. He raised his voice, calling out, shrill, "HOLD FAST YOUR DREAMS. BY LOUISE DRISCOLL." He paused and then yelled it out, breathlessly, his little head snapping forward at the ends of the lines:

"HOLD FAST YOUR DREAMS!
WITHIN YOUR HEART
KEEP ONE, STILL, SECRET SPOT
WHERE DREAMS MAY GO,
AND SHELTERED SO,
MAY THRIVE AND GROW—
WHERE DOUBT AND FEAR ARE NOT."

I sat, my head bowed, listening to that earnest, piping voice in the empty space of the auditorium. I believe you, Buddy. Just keep her goin': one still, secret spot where dreams may go.

"O KEEP A PLACE APART
WITHIN YOUR HEART,
FOR LITTLE DREAMS TO GO!
THINK STILL OF LOVELY THINGS THAT ARE NOT SO."

Lord, Buddy. I stared at Presydent's black-robed figure up there. Buddy, say your piece so loud that it'll carry clear over to the quarters, where Ruth and Gladys are at this very moment discovering each other. The women are slowly female. Gladys laughs nervously. Ruth puts on the kettle.

"LET WISH AND MAGIC WORK AT WILL IN YOU.
BE SOMETIMES BLIND TO SORROW. MAKE BELIEVE!"

Buddy roared out that last great imperative, jerking his head forward, "MAKE BELIEVE!" and it cost him. It cost him dearly. The terrific force of the two words made him stop for a second. He stood in complete quiet and quickly ran through it from "Think still of lovely things that are not so," the words racing on his little lips, and then he hit that wall, that "Make Believe!" and it was no go. His mind was a complete blank. The verses had gone right out of his head. Perhaps he could leave it at that. Pause, don't hesitate. But no, it was obvious there was more—somewhere. Turn, pace. Think, honorable Washington—*think!* He stood on one foot and he was ready to make a run for it when a big, heavy golf-coach voice from down in row number one shouted out, "Forget the calm." Like a bullet Buddy was off again, speeding toward his target:

"FORGET THE CALM THAT LIES
IN DISILLUSIONED EYES.
THOUGH WE ALL KNOW THAT WE MUST DIE,
YET YOU AND I
MAY WALK LIKE GODS AND BE
EVEN NOW AT HOME IN IMMORTALITY!"

He stiffly bowed his head and returned to his seat like a flash. He sat beaming.

So the Big Guy walks to the podium. I stared up at his black robe hanging from his broad shoulders and the little wires of the hearing-aid sticking out from his ear. He spoke first of the upcoming Religious Emphasis Week, which we kick off this Sunday. Along with our Criminal Investigation Week, we suppose. He looked down, smiling at me, smiling at the thoughts I was having, and I lobbed a smile back up at him. He was looking forward to continued educational excellence, of which these Sunday services are an inextricable part. Presydent, you got a pair of brass balls.

He reached into the shelf of the lectern and pulled out

a Bible; he held it up high in his hands. He laid the Bible
on his big right hand and turned the pages with his left.
He was solid as a rock in his black robes. "I read from the
book of Matthew, chapter six, verses twenty-eight to
thirty-four:

> "And why take ye thought for raiment? Consider the
> lilies of the field, how they grow; they toil not, neither do
> they spin:
>
> "And yet I say unto you, that even Solomon in all his
> glory was not arrayed like one of these.
>
> "Wherefore, if God so clothe the grass of the field,
> which today is, and tomorrow is cast into the oven, shall
> he not much more clothe you, O ye of little faith?
>
> "Therefore take no thought, saying, What shall we
> eat? or, What shall we drink? or, Wherewith shall we be
> clothed? . . .
>
> "For your heavenly Father knoweth that ye have need
> of all these things."

I turned and glanced at the last row of the audience,
and Henry was sitting there, straight as an arrow, his bald
crown shining, an antique plate. That's something. Meanwhile, the lilies of the field, how they grow; they toil not,
neither do they spin. All criminal investigators, please
take note. And somewhere in Heaven, Presydent, an old
angel sings for you. Dew glitters like silver tears on the
clouds, and all heaven holds its breath while for you the
one old angel sings softly, his heart breaking in the leafy
woods of the sky:

> "But seek ye first the Kingdom of God, and his right-
> eousness; and all these things shall be added unto you.
>
> "Take therefore no thought for the morrow; for the
> morrow shall take thought for the things of itself. Suf-
> ficient unto the day is the evil thereof."

And, when we got out, I stumbled blindly through the heat down the road toward home, dripping incoherent smiles to folks dressed up. I almost missed them. They were sitting in sunsuits, profanely accustomed, on a brown blanket spread out at the edge of the frogpond. Sipping iced tea. Gladys and Ruth.

There, you see?

I went on over and we were a bit clumsy—Gladys, especially, not at all used to this sort of scene, but she held up. It was damn awkward as I joined them, and Ruthie was just very careful, slowly feeling her way through. I looked at her face, her way of touching the deepest points. We talked about nothing, and the sections of the Sunday paper lay off to one side.

He called the final faculty meeting of the summer. For Friday, a last act: Bossman pulls out the gun and opens fire. Who can grab him? Who, in this here colored establishment, can be trusted to be ready with muscle for the outgoin' President? At ten o'clock Thursday night I made my decision. Jim Marshall. Our manly golf coach. The previous afternoon he had sent a drive whistling 230 yards. I sighed. "Jim, why can't I do that?" He showed me his gold teeth. "Well, that's *power*, Bo. You can't *teach* power."

The fireflies scooted among the long grasses of the frogpond. At the edge of the auditorium I peered across the paved street. The White House stood in total darkness. I broke into a little trot; I did not like it, being alone in the moonlight—President is sitting up there, staring under his helmet, the scoop drapes pulled back, his pistol at his feet wrapped in a box of Charlesetta hair. We are tracking each other. Victor Charlie and USMC. Victor Charlie builds his zigzag tunnels and hangs snakes in them, poison ready to erupt on your neck as you crawl. I shivered and pushed on, shaking my head.

I started to ring at the Marshalls' porch, but then I heard a small chorus of laughter coming from out behind the house. They were sitting under the trees at the back, around a smoldering little brick barbecue. Jim and Barbara, Zip Luper and his wife. Jim, what say we disarm the tyrant?

One is entirely too direct. I went up. "Hey, Jim, could I speak t'you for a moment?"

A split-second silence. Barbara glanced quickly at her hubby. Jim looked at her, then at Zip, and he said, "Sure, Bo." He got up with me and started walking around the little house. We gathered the vast Texas starlight above us, shuffling in ankle-deep grass. It was beautiful soft, comforting grass. After we had strolled to the front, Jim seated himself on the porch steps; he absently, carefully dusted his hand along beside him here and there, gently stroking the concrete steps. "What's on your mind, Bo?"

I stood in front of him, glancing nervously up at the darkened White House. I think we know where we stand. "Just wondered if it were safe to go to this final faculty meeting tomorrow."

He looked out beside me. His eyes were playing dumb, trained to the right of my hips, gazing at the long lawns where we always drove our golf balls. "Not sure just what you mean, Bo."

"I have Presydent on my mind."

Jim was not looking at me. His left hand was still dusting his own mortgaged porch step and he was scanning the driving range. "Presydent?"

"One hears things and I saw what he did to his wife and—"

"The way I figure it," Jim said, "a man's private life is his own business. Archie got his problems just like you 'n' me."

"Now Jim, they don't send criminal-investigators to talk to *us* about our problems."

"I saw that man. The investigator." He crossed his arms on his knees again. "And I told him what I'm telling you now."

I stared up again at the darkened White House. I took my time. "So if anybody asked you, you'd say he is doing a good job?"

Jim nodded his head; finally, he had made his very important decision. "In nineteen-sixty-three we had three hundred students. You know how many we got now, in the regular year? Over nine hundred. He put this school back on its feet." Jim swept one arm out toward the campus. "Just look around. Our building program. We got four new buildings since Presydent took over, two more on the drawing board. In nineteen-sixty-three we had one Ph.D. on the faculty. One. Old Prudhomme. Now we got six."

"You like old man Henry? Do you like him, Jim?"

He looked up at me. "Some folks say he's a Communist."

I brushed my toe on a line in the cement. "Come on, man, don't give me that shit." Is it safe to go to faculty meeting? Put all your cards on the table right away. *Strategy,* Bo.

Jim sat forward again. "I mean what I say. I'm not kiddin' you. These Afro-American Studies, all the thing now, Archie Washington was way ahead of his time on that one. We had a course on the Negro in American Culture the year after he took over. Presydent himself had a seminar on the ghetto. Hell, he even let Henry teach a course on black heroes." Jim laughed.

"What's so funny?"

"Oh, they tell me the old man had been proposing that course for twenty years. Every spring in the curriculum committee he'd propose it and they'd ve-to it. But when Archie came in he let the old man do it." Jim leaned forward. "Look—Presydent brought *you* down here. And your Ruth. We got this new grant for Communications. And we got Operation Head Start for all the little kids. Top to bottom, Archie Washington has done a hell of a lot for this school."

"I see."

"Sure, sometimes he goes a little mean. But he's done a hell of a lot of good. I don't see no other man to help this school like he done."

I shrugged.

"Bo, he's one smart man. He's a strong man." Jim paused and then offered a smile. "You only been hearing gossip from Ophelia Jones. She had a crush on Presydent. They was goin' together once, fifteen years ago. She's just all frus-trated. That's her whole problem."

"They went together?"

"Sure they did. Sure. She wasn't always built like that. They was a passionate article."

I nodded. Jim's got himself a sweet set-up here, teaching health and coaching golf, and now Presydent's moved Barbara up into his secretary's chair, and Buddy's going to grow up to be a fullback on the Bundy varsity eleven.

Jim pretended that I had made an odd joke. Full of masculine tactics and old certainties he said, "Bo, it's nothin' you have to worry over."

He asked me to stay for a drink, but I headed back in the darkness toward the frogpond. Archie was behind every bush. I stopped and talked with him. He wasn't there. He was nude. He had a dull silver spear. He was hunting lions for the tribe. The African lion usually hunts at night. Archie too. I gathered and saw and smelled the power in him as we stayed downwind of the beast. He cas-

ually hefted the spear and there it was: the golden cat,
clean and silent, risen for its muscular night of life,
lapping at the frogpond. Archie went on ahead, naked,
crouched, his butt full of lean muscle. He means business
and he respects the beast.

Archie grunts, removing his spear. He turns and looks
at you, without emotion.

Downstairs Toast and the Soul Merchants were practicing. I had seen them on my way up to my office, crouched on stools in the choir room, half a dozen guys wearing derby hats and black glasses. Now the amplifiers on the two electric guitars were turned up to the breaking point. Toast began: he broke his voice like a cracker, and then they were off; the throbbing noises fumed up into my office, walls and my shoe soles gummy with sound. Just before dinner is the time to make all the noise. Immediately adjacent to my office I could hear the big yellow boy playing a broken piano and singing "Some Enchanted Evening." Across the hall a Mortuary Science major had *La Bohème* turned up on the hi-fi; I could see him through the open door, typing to it.

I stared out the window and tried not to get hypnotized by the cottonwood tree. *"Che gelida manina"* in duet with "Across a crowded room" and both backed down below by the electric guitars and drums and Toast, who sounded like he was screaming. "You gotta live. For yourself. For yourself and nobody else." Pounding, pounding: "You gotta live. For yourself. For yourself and nobody else." I looked as hard as I could at the cottonwood. In Basic Communication we had been reading Wordsworth; in the blistering noise I said, " 'The still, sad music of humanity.' " Archie. Archie Washington? I stared down at my flowery necktie, hanging, washed up, on my wet shirt. I peered again at the blur of leaves. Quickly I sat forward. I thought I had seen it. Yes: without breeze, in the dead heat, the bugs eating holes in the leaves were thinking. Below, a saxophone was added. I could feel the reed vibrating in the mouth. " 'Therefore let the moon shine on thee in thy solitary walk.' " I said the words aloud, but in the music I could not hear them. The White House garage had been empty for three days. Nothing. The campus drones on at half-speed. Where is our Presydent?

Brace yourself, Bo. The criminal-investigator was scheduled to drop in on me at four-thirty. When Henry had called to set up the appointment his voice was low and muffled, as if he were talking through cloth. He was in the French Underground. And now I tried to settle myself, ready with words for the Man from the State.

Earlier, Mr. Elmo Carlson had come in. He wanted a D, and I told him I was going to fail him. He'd only come once to class and never handed in a piece of work. Now how the hell am I gonna pass you, man? I asked him to sit down.

"I'd rather stand."

We glared at each other. He said he couldn't graduate unless I'd give him a D. I dropped my eyes back to my desk, but I could still feel his gaze ripping through me. I pretended to work. He just stood there. Finally his voice said quietly, "What your wife want to hang around black people for?"

I looked up.

He pulled out a cigarette and stamped it on his watch. "This is s'pose' to be a school for black people."

"You think she wants to steal it?"

He moved to the door. "No, I didn't think that."

Suddenly it came to me. "Carlson?"

He turned.

"One day last week my wife went to her office in the Training School and there was a tarantula in her center desk drawer."

His face didn't move.

"How do you suppose that hairy bugger got into a closed desk drawer?"

His long lacquered hair was like a cap. He stood his ground. "I am sure I don't know. Maybe he was lookin' for a white woman."

I stood up. "Get out of here."

"I'm goin', I'm goin'." But at the door he stopped, utterly still, metal; he turned. There was a moment when he sucked all the air out of the office and then he walked back in.

He planted his palms on my desktop and leaned over, staring at me. He said, "Do you have a sense of humor?" He was all on top of me. "It is extremely amusing, a fact. But I don't want to tell you if you don't have a sense of humor."

"What's the fact?"

"Namely, I am the most intelligent student in this school."

I stared, lost in his face. "Prove it."

He smiled, and little electric wires were skidding up his face. "No." And he left.

It was a bad little scene and I was still jumpy about it, frustrated and angry. I stood up and stretched and went to one of the parched windows. I rested my forehead on the pulled-up glass. The landscape was making waves. I felt the glass sticking to the wet skin above my eyes, and my heartbeat was throbbing with the music. Christ's blood streaming in the firmament. That Constance Daumier in the back row. Now who would ever guess she had come from Haiti? I saw by her term paper that when she was a little girl her feet swelled up and her granny the witch told her to go down to the beach and throw her shoes in the sea. Which she did. And her feet went back down to normal again. Can you give me Granny's address? What has become of Poppa Doc Archie? The criminal-investigator? It all comes from servin' Jesus. Archie just took the man from the state, took him and caressed him and led him to expensive bourbon on the patio. We are men of the world, surely we can talk this over reasonably. The round ice cubes clicking in the tall frosted glass, the Showdown cards fliping up off the bottom of the deck. Whoa, seems to me to be some burned hair here.

Don't pay it no nevermind.

But, why, I declare, Colonel Washington, that's your wife's hair.

No, it's the cat. Say, lad, you could use a refill.

He's got a million of 'em.

I stared at the tree, and the sound rolled over me; there was a woman down below, yes, I believed there was a woman added. Is that woman—is that a woman singing down below with Toast? Yes, I believe it is. I believe it is a woman singinging in the firmament. Yes, that's a woman all right. She's on to Toast's latest conception. Oh yes. "Stop and Go." They yelled it: "STOP," then five seconds of throbbing space-silence before, rush, "GO"—and we go with the organ. Man and woman, young and old, the thing
—STOP (dum-thum-a-dum-diddy-die-ditty-whaw) GO—

playing our bodies, some instruments—STOP (yes) GO (oh yes)—all the feeling of it, Toast and his home boys, all in it, STOPGO, electricity fumes, ears, those guys all in it with all their lives. . . .

And where the hell *is* that criminal-investigator? I got my pen ready for the affidavit.

I went back to my final exams. Why, look here, Mistress Daumier draws me a picture of a happy future.

I was sitting there grading when Mrs. Cravens arrived. It was ten after six. Freeman Hall was all still. Seventeen years ago Mrs. Cravens had finished two semesters at Bundy Colored Agricultural and Normal University; this summer she was back. She had five children. She stood, squat, in the doorway. She was smiling and pointing to her watch. "Professor Green," she said, "am I too late?"

You ain't just whistlin' Dixie.

She did not know what to do. She stood with the grin dying on her round face. Finally I turned my eyes all the way up to her. "I'm sorry, Mrs. Cravens."

The woman stood there. Her eyes fastened on my eyes. "What is troubling you?"

And I just sat. Poor Archie. You must finally get to hate folks you love and cannot help; it is a curse and the hot prairie air is raging with it, particles zipping and dust skidding into our skin like scientific laws. The criminal-investigator is a no-show. All I want to know is this: did Henry call it off or did Archie? Which man stepped in?

Mrs. Cravens tries to help. "I find that some days it just don't pay to get out of bed."

She came forward slowly, and the old woman in my office, she reached over my desk and patted her professor on the arm.

Oh, lady.

At last, my eyes rollin' into my brain, I said, "In the final exam you wrote on self-deception. You wrote that your husband drinks too much whisky."

Mrs. Cravens sighed and sat down. "He do."

I rummaged slowly in the paper pile on my desk. I pulled out hers and read the first paragraph: " 'My husband Mr. Cravens has self-deception. Mr. Cravens thinks that when he drink whisky he keep his body going. But he is wrong. His body is degraded.' "

Mrs. Cravens was sad in the chair. "That is the truth."

That is the truth. Stop and go. Mr. Cravens' body is degraded, and in here it is hot as all hell. "It's too hot."

She kept on sitting there. "Nobody can do nothing about the weather in Texas, especially me."

Toast, Ruthie, and Bo, all together in the front seat of that big green box, the Bundy wagon. Toast wanted to take us to a favorite spot, on a lake over beyond Big D, and we had ourselves a little picnic. We swam and had a cook-out, and the two of them were making real headway. We stayed late, talking in the dusk and watching the fire glow out. First stars and close wisdom. On the way home, as we passed around a tall can of Colt 45, it was warm and right. The radio up, and we were telling dirty jokes at sixty-five. Then, on an empty stretch of two-bit Texas road, the old red gumball flasher and the sireen. So we pulled over.

White fuzz-face took his time coming to the window, all boots and badge and rawhide, slicing into our warm front seat. He saw the One White Girl between the Two Black Boys. He made it clear. That's what we were stopped for. Them Texas Ranger pigs got great eyes.

Oh, shit, Mr. President. I thought for a minute that my man and I might have to get out and stand with our hands on the car roof and Depidy Pig would have give us a chorus of the cattle-prod blues. It was the way his eyes slowly touched all our bodies with disgust: 2 negr. mls., cauc. feml. A white woman and two black boys, oh, on with it; Sergeant Crud took Toast's license from his wallet and checked that out, he wasn't wanted for anything, and then he checked the vehicle license plate and we didn't steal the school car, and the four-eyes-SS-correspondence-school-pig-buddy back in the squad car radios in and out, and finally we get a ticket for having our brights on.

With our traffic ticket in the visor, driving on again into the night, we didn't say anything; Toast kept checking the lights of the squad car in the rear-view. He had his brights on. After a bit, the Law roared on past. Gumballs forever.

So now we swim in the frogpond.

And the pond water is cold. The slime of the bottom oozed up between my toes. Toast surfaced and swung a circle of silver water with his head; he waded to me, sniffing. In the sunlight. Almost to manhood. He held up his arms, stretched skyward in the heat of the noonday sun. We decided to race the length of the pond. Dead heat. We had pushed ourselves all the way out, and he gagged me and I pretended I was coughing and we splashed water against our chests. We laughed and then we floated. Summer school now over, the last day, and we had the pond to ourselves.

"I do believe maybe her play was even better than ours."

He went down up to his neck and thought. He is a Roman fountain detail; the centuries have slightly eroded that small stripe on his face.

"Did you know she was preparing it?"

He looked at me. "Yes. But I didn't tell you because she said it was a surprise for you."

"That it was." That it was. There I had been, all caught up in my skits, rehearsing with my folks, and when she came in that night—"Put on your green suit, I got something for you to see"—I did not know what was coming.

It was over at the Training School, and the curtains were bedsheets with flowers and birds and animals painted all over them by the kids themselves. Most all the parents were there. Ruthie sat with me in the back, and the kids did everything. They were ushers. They gave out programs. And they did the show. *Hunting the Dragon*. They all went out hunting the dragon—running through the audience too, and one little guy stopped to whisper to his mother—and when they finally found the dragon it was four of 'em inside, eight legs under the stitched-up, painted-up potato sacks. Turns out it was a dragon *because* it was hunted—actually, rather than breathe fire, wanted to sing. So the kids gathered around and decided what to do with it. They had a parliamentary debate. Great dialogue.

"Well, now, we got to check this dragon *out*."

"When you're dealing with a dragon, you need *patience*." (This opinion hooted down.)

"You mess with ol' dragon, you *die*, brother."

One six-year-old was playing an old man, with an elaborate white cotton wig, and he seemed to think all old people were drunk. He played the old man as a drunk, weaverin' around and periodically fallin' down. They finally voted: Give the dragon a chance. And with a coalition government adopting a wait-and-see attitude, the dragon fell all over itself—the four kids inside bangin' around against each other, giggledy-fart.

At the curtain call the dragon discharged its members, and the whole cast stood beaming, one little girl joining in the applause.

On the way home Ruth was flushed with the event. "Did you like it?"

I stared at her face.

And now here she comes, barefoot through the afternoon heat. She had left her jumper in Toast's battered old Fairline 500 and now she was wearing the purple bikini, darling as hell. It was like nothing on her.

I swam over to the edge of the pond, near her, and her blue eyes were sunlight, she was so beautiful, her lively skin hard and soft and lean. Now that school is over, why don't we mosey on down to the Gulf Coast? There, runnin' along the beach naked, laughing, your bright ass swinging behind you, and in we go; she is terribly pleased with her old hub, Bo, and we fall into each other, her sides against these arms, and we stand thigh deep in the crystal blue water, her eyes, and we laugh and gasp, the salt water is radiant, sharp, streaming on her little Chosen People breasts, the pink nipples teased and sharp from the shocking cold of the first plunge. I went down under water and closed my eyes. I am setting a breath-holding record. The water rushed into my ears, stopping them up. If there *is* a breath-holding record, I guarantee you a black man holds it. When I surfaced, Toast had her in his arms and he was swishing along in the water, abducting her into the pond grasses.

"Hey!"

He turned; without a thought about anything he dropped her, splash.

"Marco Polo," he said.

"What?" I rubbed the water out of my eyes.

He was laughing. "Marco Polo, Bo."

Whoever was It had to close his eyes and stumble around, and when he yelled, "Marco," the other two had to

respond, "Polo," and It tried to nab you. Ruth played in
bikini dead earnest; her mouth and eyes were all closed
up tight. When I was It, I tried to get Toast; I kept lung-
ing and scratching the air for him. I was frightened in the
dark when I couldn't seem to get him, and they were
splashing me, the water sharp and hot against my face.
"Marco." "Polo." "*Marco.*" "*Polo.*" Toast and Ruth were
yelling, the two of them ganging up on me in the frogpond,
and I stopped and stood hip-deep, dripping in the water,
coughing and rubbing my face.

"Calm down, boys and girls. This is *me* talkin' to you."
Toast was slapping sharp water against my face, and I
yelped again, "Calm *down,*" and in the darkness behind
my lids I lost it—the bullets of water hit and opened up
red holes in the dark. I turned my back to them, crouching, and my eyes are open but there is nothing, only the
heat of the darkness and the pond water burning. Archie
Washington outside the palace window bursts in, ugly
with gun, and the window is water and as he bursts the
hearing-aid shorts out sparking, the whole pond is electro-
cuted—

Toast's voice: "Parco Molo. Bo-lo."

I lunged forward. My hand, raging down, got fabric,
and when I opened my eyes Toast had used Ruthie as a
shield and I had yanked purple cloth away—her breasts
were free. Girl, you appeal to me. Toastie was riotously
nervous with the white bare tits. The three of us for three
reasons instantly submerged ourselves into the waters of
the pond, whee-shaaa, dig?

Late that same night Ruthie and I went out, down the hundred yards of dirt road to talk to Henry. The red porch light was on, and a lamp put a low yellow light in the living-room window. I knocked on the screen door. There was a long time, and then he came, teeth out. He was dressed in back-to-Africa pajamas: the short-sleeved shirt was dark jungle green, and the pants were long streaks of red and white and brown, veldt grass on fire. The pajamas hung there, clean and cool and loose on his little black frame. Henry has not an extra inch of flesh. The abdomen sticks out under the green shirt, but the skin on the hairless shins, the skin of the bare arms, the skin on the crown, that is military. I had started to back away when I saw him dressed so, but he pulled us in.

The old man put the bottoms of his bare feet together and sank back into the chair. The little fan whirred lazily at his feet, and we stared at the lighted fishbowl, the black bullet bodies, still.

I let out a little laugh and shook my head. "Should have seen me, Henry." I giggled again, and he stared at me with empty eyes. "Got a bit nervous about President and his *gun*. Figured somebody with muscle ought to be ready to disarm him."

His empty eyes blinked again, and he pulled on his jazzy pajama leg.

"Jim Marshall is the man I asked."

Henry sat forward and rubbed his hand over his bald head. "Good Lord and Pappy O'Daniel. Jim Marshall's just bought himself a new car, boy. Who do you think is makin' the payments on that ve*hic*le?"

"Let me guess."

"Why, Archie just moved Barbara Marshall up into the front office. Jim is one of Archie's *boys*. And you go down there and ask him to take Archie's *gun* away?"

"I'm not a intellectual for nothin', Henry."

He got up, stood above me with his thin arms outspread. He called, *"A intellectual?"*

"Sorry about that."

"Intellectual?" He squatted over, like a quarterback in a huddle, and barked the signals. "You know what an intellectual is? An intellectual is a man who'll run out in the middle of a field, shouting, 'There's a tiger loose.' " Henry erected himself again and shouted the phrase, with eyes wild and bald head swinging. " 'There's a tiger loose.' " He hopped over to one corner of the room and growled. "An intellectual will stand out there screaming, 'Beware of the man-eater,' and he'll keep on screaming it until the tiger comes and eats him up."

He came back and sat down, breathing. Then: "Oh, you parlor pinks and drawing-room radicals."

"Yes, I know strategy—"

He butted in. *"Strategy.* Now that word's a trouble. On the one hand, you intellectuals in-voke that word for in-action. Don't stick your neck out." He played Uncle Tom. "Don't forget your stragedy, boy. You stroked the tiger on the *left* whisker when you should have stroked him on the right." He swished forward on his red slippers, jabbing his finger out, a debating point, at my face. "But I'll tell you what strategy is, boy. Don't look a gift horse in the mouth, but know when to *kick* the ass you *kiss*."

We sat quietly for a moment, in the night stillness of his front room. Ruthie moved on her chair and said, "So what's the latest about—him?"

I turned and looked at her face, at the echo of the words in the air. I looked at her knowledge of him.

Henry's face softly widened into a smile. "No, Archie just couldn't make that faculty meeting." He rocked back in the chair and pulled his bare feet up onto the seat, just in front of his buttocks. "The board had him on the carpet for *five* hours."

"And?" I said.

He stared up at the ceiling. "I don't think the ax has fallen *yet*. But she's on her way down." He sighed. "Oh, that Archie Washington. He belongs in the Smith-son-i-an Institute." He kicked the fan, whirring. If Henry doesn't like that fan whirring at his ankles, why does he always put it there and kick it?

We sat in silence. Ruthie made we-should-be-getting-home motions. Henry's eyes are aged. Then, as I was thinking how old he looked, the dark little face lighted up and he sent one of his full-throated giggles bouncing up again into the low lamplight.

Ruthie said, "What, Henry?"

"All my life I have specialized in getting rid of troublemakers."

I looked at him. I considered it as a career.

"All my life. Back in the depression I was in West Texas, and we were trying to unionize a plant. Somebody kept leaking to the bosses all we said in the union meet-

ings. I was comin' on about Crispus Attucks and Niger Cli-
tus and all those great old boys. But it was leaking out.
Somebody was spillin' the goods. So the boys came over
to my house one night. They asked Prof what to do. They
figured it was one old Uncle Tom leaking on them to the
bosses." Henry laughed again, and his body was spry and
young and curling into a ball. "I got me a pair of black
boys. And I told those two: 'Late at night, you go to that
old Uncle Tom's shack. Black Boy Number One, you
break down Uncle Tom's door. You run right over it. And
you have yourself a flashlight. A *big* flashlight. And you
roar right into the bedroom and shine your flashlight into
the eyes of old Uncle Tom and his wife.'" Henry got to
laughing too hard and he gulped for air. "'And Black Boy
Number Two, you go right behind him. And I want you
to curse. Curse—every foul ob-scen-ity in your Texas vo-
cabulary. And you take a Dallas Special—'"

Ruthie said, "A Dallas Special?"

"One of those *switch*blades. 'And you grab old Uncle
Tom by his pajama shirt. Rough him up. Rough him up
good. Get that Dallas Special out and get the blade to glit-
ter in the flashlight, and you tell him if he ever leaks another detail of the union, you'll cut his throat. Ear to ear.
And the old woman's too.'" Henry kicked his bare feet,
pale soles flashing in the air. He laughed too hard and began to cough, the cough and the laugh getting all mixed
up together. His feet came down. He gasped. "No news
went out upstairs after that. They got their *union*."

I stared at his living face. Henry, we can't leave. Tell
you what, you let Ruthie and me shack up here. Under
the couch. Nobody needs to know. Feed us when you feed
the fish.

The old man lay sprawled in the chair. One of his thin
fingers was in his mouth, and he was nibbling on it, his

lower teeth and his upper gum, nibbling on that finger. He was looking out through the front window to the little red porch light gleaming. To himself: "It's the system. The *sys*tem. During Reconstruction the South averaged a lynch-ing every three *days*. The white folks would have an ex-*cur*-sion—lynch a nigger and have a *bar*-be-cue. That's how, after a hundred years"—his voice went down into a little whisper—"we got Sweet Archie T."

Ruthie was shaking her head, little quick twitchy nods. To the silence, to him, to his knowledge, to everything, she said, "I know."

Henry looked at her for a moment and then stood up in front of his chair. "You *know?*" He scowled, walking to the center of the room. "How does a little white girl from up North know what it *was?* How does she *know?*" He turned his finger, sweeping over to a dilapidated book-case beside the air-conditioner. "In there I got copies of advertisements for fugitive slaves in the Southern press. Good God, they had as many as five thousand a year." He stared at nothing in the center of the room. His hands roamed on his little body. " 'Stamped N.E. on the breast and having both small toes cut off.' " He raised his left leg, the red and white slashes of the pajama pants, and he stuck out his bare foot. " 'Wears large neck iron and large band of iron on left leg.' " He spun around and presented his face. " 'Branded on her left cheek, thus, *R.*' " Henry made an R on his cheek, his fingers slashing. " 'A piece is taken off her left ear, and the same letter is branded on the inside of her thighs.' "

Ruth stood up, and her voice was sharp. "Cut it out, Henry. Don't—Don't do that."

He stopped for a second in the low lamplight, and he was staring at Ruthie and at me. He drew back. He shook his head. A soft word was forming in his mouth. His old hand went out onto Ruthie's shoulder; he was steadying himself, against her from a distance of years that was all closeness—their eyes on each other, her blues, his blacks —he dropped it for a minute, and in the silence from outside the house, out front, there came a masculine shout.

"Henry!"

It was our President.

"Henry!"

The old man's head snapped around and he went to the window, bending down; his little butt bobbed up back into the room. "Archie," he said to himself.

I stood behind him.

"He's drunk. Oh, Lord, look at that man stagger."

"Henry, get away from that window," I said.

The voice from the front lawn boomed again. *"Henry!"*

"Come on," Ruthie said, "get away from there."

Henry turned around and he seemed to be holding something very heavy in his hands, his hands held out, palms up, under something in the air. He sighed and came to us and turned his hands over and then folded all the fingers together. "You go out the back way."

"I'm not going out," I said.

His old eyes came up, sharp. "Go out down the back stairs. Out through the Zulu Club. You know the way."

"No."

His voice was low, and his eyes did not leave mine. "I told you to go. Now you get yourself and your wife out of my house, boy."

My eyes twitched down, falling, and focused on his

huge abdomen, bowled, under the jungle-green shirt, and on down to his bare, small feet.

"Go on, children," he said.

I turned and pushed Ruthie in front of me back through the semidarkness into the dining room. Behind us I heard the front door open and close again.

We felt our way, whispering. I tripped on the stairs down into the Zulu Club. Mamma? Mamma Prudhomme, you asleep? I was frantic, dazed, and I ran smack into the low ceiling at the doorway into the Zulu Club. Didn't stop. Shook my head, and I could see through the little windows out into the night, and we blundered into the screen door.

"You wait," I said to her.

I got down in the grass beside the old dried-up hedge. I crawled forward on my knees, scuttling in the sharp grass and dust, and I made my way toward the drooping tree, its limbs hanging out over the hedge in Henry's front yard. I made a break, ten feet, and hid myself there, crouched behind the treetrunk.

Up on the porch, under the hot red bulb of light, Henry stood in his pajamas. Down on the walk, ten yards away, Archie Washington, Presydent, was rolling forward on his toes and back onto his heels. His black summer suit was hanging loosely around him, and the left sleeve was all torn at the elbow. Only a T-shirt under the coat. No hearing-aid. The suitcoat was floppy, drifting away from him, and his big chest bulged out against the T-shirt. There was dirt on the T-shirt, dusty splotches where he had pawed his chest with his hands. He had stumbled and fallen on the way over, fallen on his hands skidding, cutting.

He stopped rocking. His eyes, behind the glasses, were glazed, roving, threatening to turn back and look at his brain. He tottered forward.

Henry said softly, "Keep your distance, Archie."

He stopped and shook his head. "Henry, this is your doing."

"What do you want, Archie?"

"Your doing."

Henry was silent in his pajamas. His eyes were burning, deeply burning, holding Archie, trying to hypnotize him. Then the old man bared his upper gum and closed his mouth again. He turned around and started back in.

"*Henry.*"

The old man stopped and walked back to the front of the porch. "You go to bed."

Archie recoiled a step and fumbled in his right coat pocket. He pulled it out, his pistol. And he held it out at arm's length.

Ruthie came frantically to me, on top of me. I clutched her there, beside me behind the tree, and the two of us were children beside the tree.

Now is the time to run for him. While the Little One sees me spurt. On his blind side, his deaf side. Now is the time I have been waiting for. She's gonna see me lay you low. I'll come screaming up, out from under the tree, both arms flapping, wings, and I'll tackle him, rip his legs right out from under him. A ten-yard loss. Before I'm halfway there, I'm gonna have bullets in my lungs. Henry, you can talk him out of it. *Talk,* old man. I grabbed her to me, crushed her against my side.

Henry's eyes, smoldering—they began to kindle under the red porch light.

The snub-nosed pistol, black in his hand, lurching, pointing up to the porch. The black finger, the gun, wavered with cramped power.

"Archie, you know you can't shoot me." Henry said it very quietly, casually, with a dignity, a fatal softness. He was absolutely there, in all his years, full on the porch. The edges of his little body burned crisp in the small red light.

Bossman slumped. "You think I'm *wrong?*"

Henry's silence was there, the inescapable answer.

"I'm not *wrong.*" President looked like he was going to faint, collapse on the walk. He jerked back on his heel and he started to sit down, then caught himself on a post in the air. He staggered up again, standing. "And you keep away from my *boy.*"

The mouth opened and the top gum glistened. Henry would not be moved. He would not be afraid. He sighed, and his composure was deafening.

The President let out a little cry. The mind clicked off, imploding, walls falling in. "Keep away from my *boy.*" He gathered himself and in the brain-raging coils, fire-sparks, a waste of blood—

He fired.

The sharp crack of the shot blistered through my body, and I jerked, lurched forward on the ground, and a scream started out of Ruthie's mouth—a scream, but no sound—and I caught it, slapped my hand over her mouth. I rolled on my side with her, and I could have stopped it —I could have stopped it—and up on the porch, under the red light, Henry had not moved.

He had not lurched back with the slug. He stood quietly. His eyes were still trained, gleaming down at Archie, Archie and the echo of the shot. The old man chose to ignore it.

Archie stepped back, fell back a step, and he turned; I thought he was looking for me and Ruthie, maybe he heard the first gasp of her throttled scream. But he was staring only into the darkness and the heat. For an explanation. Henry's face was living and unmoved. Then the old man did the most extraordinary thing.

He smiled.

It was the smile a man gives late at night when he adds a long column of figures for the second time and gets the same answer. A private smile over the integrity of his calculations.

Archie turned back, aimed, and fired again, and Henry again did not move. There is no blood on his face, no blood on his crisp pajamas, his person.

Henry reached to his neck and he slowly wrapped ten fingers around the pajama shirt and—the noise crackling, low like a brush fire—he began to rip. He ripped the pajama shirt open, and it slid from his little shoulders, down off his arms, down onto his porch. The bronze abdomen jutted out. "Put a bullet in the cancer. Archie, put a bullet"—and for the first time he raised his voice, obscene —"in the CAN-cer."

Archie fired again. And again. At each shot the bloated stomach of the little man reached out closer—*Presydent is not missing*. Henry, the old man, is immovable. His nostrils flared, bullet holes, moon craters, and he stuck out his arms, the fingers jagged, metal shards, and the blasting of the snub gun accumulated in the yard, drawing the earth and trees and houseboards to it. Henry had opened up his arms and made of his body a corral for bullets; as they pump in, the sound is weight. Henry is alive. Death, like nausea, a dirty word. But he lives. Henry cannot die. He lives on the earth.

Ruthie's mouth was burning against my hand like blood, burning in smothered cries on my palm, and that old man has got to be full of lead but no holes, no nothing, he just *stands* there.

Archie fell back, and his eyes were rolling, numbers rolling on a slithery sleek new cash register, and two more shots rang out, helpless, and then the gun clicked, spent, clicking. Henry's face did not change, he did not move, his eyes molten, ready to spill. The President fell backward, caving in, and he sat down on the walk. He stared at the pistol in his hand and it changed into a spider, biting down in his palm, rooting itself, its hairy legs scratching on his fingers. We'll have to cut it off him. And he shook his hand and the gun wouldn't let go—get it off me, get it off me—and finally the pistol did let go and came flying over, in my direction, in the air. It landed in front of the tree, skidding on grassy know-nothing dirt.

Henry opened his mouth. His voice was stinging low and quiet, something growing under snow. "You're through, Archie." He turned on his bare heel. "Go home and cut your throat." And he walked back into the house, a final man.

The red porch light blinked off.

Archie lay on the walk, moaning. He was moaning some vague, huge mass of sound to himself. In the darkness I could hardly see him, wrapped up in his black suit, and Texas was only his voice. We cannot move, the Little One and I. He will hear us. The black mass, a bear, huddled, licking its wounds, moaning. He stopped. Nothing.

He vomited.

Lying on the cement, he turned and spat. I was waiting for him to die; now he had a huge cough, gagging, and then silence. He shook, and his head went down, banging. He was utterly pitiful and insane. Ruthie and I watched him, bowed down, the man licking cement with his forehead. My hand was all gone from her mouth, and she was quiet. Across the street, in the small board house, a light came on.

Slowly, with the light, Archie pulled himself up. He stood and fell to one knee, and then started lumbering forward, mechanical in the darkness. He was still moaning. He kept his feet and came by us, and the moans began to form themselves into a word. As he went past, ten yards away, I heard the word, caught in his throat, something that would not come up. "Abner." He chanted the name to himself as he wove free of Henry's yard—holding on to the "b": "*Ab*-ner." He went to the roadway leading back up toward school.

I looked at her. She was free from my hand, there in the moonlight of the yard. She sat there so separately. She whimpered, and I reached for her.

"Bo?" She said my name as a close little part of her body. *"Bo?"*

"Easy, now."

She was quietly losing her mind. *"Bo?"*

Across the road a tall black man appeared, wearing only a pair of faded blue jeans. He came stealthily, picking up his bare feet. When he got on the Prudhomme front walk I could see an old revolver in his hand, the barrel half a foot long. He stood in his farm pants, sniffing the air, a skinny middle-aged black man; he did not know what the trouble was, but he knew it was there somewhere. He was smart and quiet, a high-school vocational-arts teacher, prairie auto shop, and he looked up at the porch with the gun sticking out in his hand. The old revolver was brown and it looked like it was made of wood.

I stared at the empty pistol on the grass in front of me, cruel, useless, shining in the moonlight. It was a photograph of itself. The man started to walk in my direction.

I said, "Don't shoot."

He stopped and held his own bizarre gun out.

"Don't shoot," I said again.

His voice cracked, stiff. "Who're you?"

"Nobody."

He kept on holding that ridiculous gun out; he couldn't place me—a voice behind the tree.

"I'm comin' out now. Brother, don't shoot. I don't have nothin' to do harm." I stepped out to where he could see me. I looked at his long bare chest.

He pointed the gun at the ground. He came slowly up to me. He stared. "Oh, you're the teacher from school."

"Yes." I looked down at the grass. "There's a gun down there." I leaned over. "It's empty."

"That man runnin' away—that man Archie Washington?"

I picked up the gun. "Yes."

He inspected me. His high cheekbones moved. "Did he shoot Henry?"

"Henry's all right."

We stood in the yard. He was quiet. I watched his ribs and I said, "I'm a friend of Henry's." I cradled the pistol in my hand. "Blanks."

He didn't catch on.

"Blank cartridges. That's what it had to be. Somebody must have put blanks in this gun. So he'd think it was loaded."

The man stepped away. "I say to my Mrs., I say somebody killed for sure."

"It was blank cartridges. That's what it was." I sighed and regarded the pistol. I held it out and then tucked it in against my leg. "I'm going to take it to Henry."

He looked at his own pistol. "I got to be goin' back now."

"Good night."

I watched him pick his way back across the street and I waited until he was all the way into his house and the light clicked off. I turned and walked back, and Henry's emaciated, healthy hounds were up and walking around—what's all this noise?—and I played with their old heads. Ruthie came up silently beside me. We stood there in the darkness, patting the dogs and looking up at the moon bent and placed in the sky. The moon is made by hand. Set in the sky by hand.

I opened the screen door to the Zulu Club very quietly, and we crept in, walking on tiptoe. Just as we reached the stairs we could hear her voice, Mrs. Prudhomme's.

"You *sure*, Poppa? It certainly give me a *start*." The voice was quite weak, muffled, as if she were talking through cloth.

Henry's voice, too, was low. "Just the boys. Those big cars of theirs, backfirin'."

"It certainly give me a start."

"You go back to sleep now, darlin'."

We sat on the bottom step. I rested on the stair and held the gun loosely between my hands. Ruthie's hand groped and was flat on my thigh.

"Let's go back, Poppa. There's lots of people I used to know."

"Yes, darlin'."

"Poppa, do you suppose Lester is still alive?"

"Lester?"

Upstairs, Henry sat down beside her; the old bedsprings squeaked.

"He was a gravedigger, Poppa. I was a little thing, and I use t'walk by the buryin' ground and see him dig. He was courtin' a one-eye widow. 'Oh,' I'd say, 'Mr. Lester, why you courtin' that old one-eye widow when you know so many of us young girls have no beaus?'" The old woman laughed. "Come next day, at the post office, there was a letter for me. He say if I ever need him, he would be at my service." Again, a little sleepy laugh, like a sigh. "I was so embarrassed, Poppa. I never let on I got that letter." Silence for a moment. "Let's go back."

"Surely, darlin'."

Gently I put the gun down on the step and put my head in my hands. I stared at the darkness. I could see Ruthie's hand flat on my leg.

"Poppa?"

"Yes, darlin'."

"You not wearin' your shirt."

Silence in the house.

Her voice: "You positive, Poppa, you don't want us to be down, safe? In the ground?"

"We want to be inside where it's dry. Darlin', in the ground the rain comes down."

"But the breeze, Poppa. I love the *air*. And all the trees blowin' overhead."

No answer.

Then she said quietly, "You paid Mr. Stiles?"

Henry's voice, gently: "We don't have a worry."

They were quiet again. After a time he asked her if she wanted to go to the toilet. She said she thought maybe, yes, she did. He turned on a light.

Quietly I picked up the gun. The little light filtering down the stairs into the Zulu Club was enough. I could see the Voodoo god in the corner. I put the gun in front of it. He'll find it in the morning. Upstairs, they were trudging into the bathroom. I went out and held the screen door for a minute in my hands, and then let it click shut.

Ruthie and I walked up the path toward school, toward quarters. I stopped momentarily on the path and looked at the grass. Blank cartridges. That's what they were. Blank. Six—all six. Blank. Empty cartridges in the gun. And he thought it was loaded, ready to kill. I was thinking about the gun, walking without looking, and then her hand was quick, scratching on my arm. I looked at her, and she pointed.

He was sitting just off the path on a big rock. His black suitcoat was folded on his lap, his arms over it, and he was staring straight ahead. Three more steps and we would have been on top of him. His head nodded, all alone on the emptiness of the prairie-field. He looked completely sober. The heavy head nodded and he had not heard us.

From his mouth came out two sounds: "Uh-huh." The head stopped nodding and the whole body gathered tight, leaning forward. "Uh-*huh*," he said again into the midnight.

I was sitting out on the grass, fifty yards from quarters, when I saw her. She was wearing her robe and as she came forward, with the light behind her, she didn't have anything on under the robe.

She stepped forward, into my slave hut. I am dying of worms, and Massa's daughter in a gown has come down bravely to watch ol' Uncle Bo pass to the great beyond. I heah de Angel voices callin', Ol' Black Bo.

We ain't goin' nowhere, no.

I put my hand on her arm. She's absolutely nothing, a blown-up white cloth. Now when you kill her, Bo, you go on up to Uncle. He'll take care of everything. We'll have a charcoal barbecue. Fricassee of Ruth. Sink your teeth into white meat. A drumstick. Uncle Archie, I see she eats as good as she fucks. Finger-lickin' good.

When Stanislavski's father died, Stanislavski stood over the deathbed and said to himself, "I must remember how the muscles in my cheeks are pulling at this moment. Someday on the stage I will play a part where this memory will come in handy."

Now, kill her, strangle with a kiss, and remember your body.

Note the odor of pig-shit.

I looked out again at the land. White folks got him—but the land too. Just the land and the sky, star-spangled and like the sound of wind, hollow and huge.

I am black.

A dirty black nigger under a willow tree, crouched lookin' above a hairball to the moon, and witches screaming with cunt-hair in the swamp. I hate it that they slept together. I hate it so much.

Her white hand on my shoulder. Keep *away* from me. Cut her in little pieces and strew her in the pond like cut-bait. The Little One. The black wind roaring in my ears, roaring so hollow I can't breathe, going . . . going . . .

She stood there.

"Oh, man," I whispered.

She stood there. Just like that.

I looked up at her through my fingers.

She waited for what I was going to say; she waited some time. She sat down.

I reached for my cigarettes, but I didn't have them with me. We just sat there. One minute, two minutes, five minutes. And then her fingers reached over to me, trembling. She was touching my face. Oh, my clothes coming off, slow debris, and her gown soft and loose on the ground.

When we reached to explode inside our one body and the body moving, I felt rippling electric water shooting as high as my cheeks; I imagined that there was a sign, and in that splitting second light could be seen—the feeling on my cheeks, our startled need. My body ached and I rolled and heaved softly with her and we were there. At first I thought it was her nails digging into my back, but then I realized that those piercing points—they were the ends of her fingers and into the finger-ends, pads, she had packed the bite of the nails. Gradually, with a low sound in our throat, we made it all the way home. Home.

Soon I was able to lower myself, a fluid inch at a time, beside her on the hard hardness of the ground. I stared into the dark across the frogpond. No limit. No limit now. I was staring into a black funnel and it was a mile long. I could see anything. I turned my face back to her face, and the darkness was burning around her as if she were in lamplight. There was not a straight line on the Little One. I searched everywhere but I could not find a straight line: each feature disappeared into the curve and lift of the next feature, and especially around her mouth there was a constellation and ease of flesh that I could not bear to look at. I felt that if I looked at her lips for one moment more I would go out of my mind.

We stood up, groped together, helping with our clothes, on our way inside, back into the faculty quarters. Our crazy, unkempt bed. She sighed and put her head over in the hollow between my chin and shoulder. I blew at her hair in front of my mouth. We started into sleep. I smiled in the darkness: I remembered that first night we had made it together. In Bayonne. Christmas. It was a little cottage, *Clair Coteau,* and the old couple in charge had never seen a black man before.

I leaned into her sleeping-place and kissed her.

With the relevance of sleep she said, "Dancing is ridiculous in the morning."

Pondering helpfully, my brain tumbling into sleep, I said, "We engender ourselves at night?"

She rolled, threw out her arm. And she was in a dream with the word: "Engender."

Her smile, the open secret of our sleep.

Terrified cry ringing out, and in my dream I saw that she was being attacked; he was a stealthy Texas fiend. I shouted out, *"Ruth, Ruth"*—her name twice, only her name twice. The sound of my voice, my groaning scream, and terror raised sheets of heavy ice needles running my shoulders. Out of the bed feet first, and I was with her in the slight breaking light of the morning.

What had happened was that she had awakened at the first hint of light and she had to take a morning pee and stumbling sleepily back from the bath she was frightened by her image in the hallway mirror. She thought someone had come up to our place, an attacker. It was the night, the blasting of the gun, death to life. I stood patting her and staring at our childish images in the mirror, and she was panting in my ear. "I'm sorry, oh, Bo, I'm so sorry." Her breathy lips clinging to my ear: "Oh, your voice—awful sound. Terror, trying to comfort me, grief."

"Easy, baby." But I was trembling too.

———————————

Last Texas morning. Bolo Green sits in Zip's folding chair on the porch and, dressed only in Bermuda shorts, goes on sweating. Air visible, a slight reddish haze everywhere, thick light in the air. The faded T-Bird sits crouched, musclebound metal, poking its grill at me. A large dark bird scoops across the frogpond, vast wings flapping twice, then gliding, just above the surface, looking for Victor Charlie. Somewhere over there, out of my sight in the Texas sunrise, Achille T. Washington sits up on his roof swing, staring at the blue incandescent metal of the sky.

A little figure came up the beat highway, surrounded by two tall dogs and a short one. The man was talking to the dogs, and they danced and played.

Henry.

I stood up. When he got to me he called out gruffly, "You leavin' these premis-ees today?"

"I guess we are."

"Well, put on your shirt. Get your Snow White and come on down to our place for breakfast."

"Really? I—"

He turned. "Twenty minutes." And, conversing with dogs, he went back the way he came. I watched him go. The dogs were rooting for him.

I went in, awakened Ruthie, we showered together. I think it was our best shower, everything considered.

On the way over to the Prudhomme place, in the crawling morning heat, I kept muttering on the road: "Henry, Henry, Henry." I did one of my little old soft-shoe routines, shufflin' off to Buffalo on the depraved Texas road. Put your arms around me, Henry, ho-ho-ho-hold me tight, chung-katcha, chung-katcha, cuddle up and s-s-snuggle up and sque-e-eze me tight, oh, o-o-oh, won't you roll them e-e-eyes, chunga-katcha, chunga-katcha, boom-lay-boom, Henry—oh, H-e-e-enry, Henry Prudhomme, King of the wild frontier, Born on a cotton farm in Tex-ee-ass, Loudest state in the land hardly free, Henry, He-e-enry Prudhomme, king of the wild frontier.

My God, Bo.

But she was pleased. She said, smiling, "Henry is courtly."

Courtly.

When we arrived at their house we stopped at the screen door and peered in: he was standing over by the TV fish, turning through a huge book. He was dressed in his old floppy brown suitpants, a white shirt. His *feet*, his *feet*. Let's hear it for the red carpet slippers! Henry, remember us, we were in jail together?

I clawed on the rickety screen.

He turned. He didn't have his uppers in, and he came forward, laughing like an old darky. "Well, the Greens." Saying it like we was of the turnip family.

"How's it go?"

"Well, next week back to Dallas and they'll fool around some more in my bile duct."

We stood in the living room. I could hear the lady of the house in the kitchen, and I feasted my eyes: the bronze head, sharpest round-thing-in-creation, those bullet-wise eyes. His fingers are so thin. "Another operation?"

"Well," he said, "I'm taking these shots, you know. Every month. For that old devil cancer."

I nodded.

"But the doc gave me a double dose last time, and I got the running hot and cold *chills*." He put his arms around his chest, clutching. "Hot and cold, oh, for a couple of days there."

Ruthie said, "You push yourself too hard."

He was silent for a second. "If I can only keep my *health*."

"Tell us," I said, "what's gonna become of Abner?"

The old man brightened. "I may get through to that boy. He's got a bug in his ear. Wants to join some new outfit out of Houston, the Black Rangers." He smiled. "Lord, the boy was telling me, down in the Zulu Club last night. About the theory and practice of counter-in-tim-i-da-tion."

"Archie will love that."

"Oh, Archie—" He was silent for a moment, and I was waiting for him to fill me in on the decline and fall of Presydent, but then he sighed and said, "Wish I'd had something like the Black Rangers when I was coming up. I had a terrible temper as a boy, you know. My mamma used to say to me, 'Henry, you is going to end up hanged by the neck.' " He looked at me. "Now, when you're hanged by the neck your utility is diminished."

I smiled. "No, you can't lose your temper. Like that Career Day, when you went on a rampage in Washington's office?"

"On the ram-page?" Henry heaved himself up. "Storming about all his cri-i-imes." The old man was beginning to hoot, furious in his living room, and then as suddenly as it had started he fell back down in his chair, giggling. "I was no more upset than I am now."

"Fooled me."

"You see, boy, sometimes you have to be a Thes-pi-an." He smiled. "On the ram-page, *hell*. Throwin' open windows and doors." His giggle began to double him up. "Archie runnin' around, lookin' out at those folks on the lawn, pullin' down the windows and shuttin' the doors." Henry's laugh climbed up, peaked, and descended; his voice, then, was low. "Poor Archie. He sat down on top of his desk and crossed his arms and put his head down and said, 'Old man, why do you persecute me so?' " Henry was solemn for a moment, then roared.

Mrs. Prudhomme was up and around now, in her housecoat with pink rosebuds. She had fixed up a vast breakfast—potatoes and eggs and ham and toast. We sat. After Henry mumbled a sharp little grace I said, drawing a napkin over my knees, "So, the old black Marxist thanks the Lord God for his victuals."

Mrs. Prudhomme, pouring Ruth's coffee, said, "Oh, my Henry don't believe in God. He just has a real nice affection for him."

We ate. The talk came around, often enough, to Presydent. I said, "Lord, I keep thinking of him, that Sunday. There he was, the criminal-investigator breathing down his neck, and he just stood up there givin' us Holy Word."

Mrs. Prudhomme ran her long fingers through her frizzy white thin hair. She said, "My dear old mamma used to say to us when we were bad and then we'd say something pretty—old Mamma would say, 'How can I hear what you *say* when what you *are* keeps ringing in my ears?' " She smiled at Ruth and drank her coffee.

We were silent for a minute over our plates. Henry looked at Ruth, and his head was nodding, nodding, but then his eyes roved away. He was not looking at me, and his head kept nodding, jaw hanging slightly open. Then he came together and turned around to click on the little decrepit radio on the sideboard. Race trouble in the news. Henry sat himself bent to the newscast, and the head nodded again. The troops were really having a time of it. Henry listened for a minute and then clicked the radio off again. He sat silently, then began to giggle, the old man chewing on his finger like a schoolboy. The giggle was running all through him, and he bent protectively. Mrs. Prudhomme didn't like riots. She looked at him. He looked at her. Then he broke out giggling again. Oh, if I was twenty years younger. Hand me a brick, world, and *stand* back.

I said, "Is the final word in? On the investigation?"

He touched his napkin to his lips. "Well, the investigation is closed. Archie came out of her un-sca-a-thed."

The word broke over the table and fell in little pieces around us.

Ruthie said, "It's not possible."

Henry shook his head. "I don't know how many *strings* that man pulled, but he came out with a clean bill of *health*."

He has stopped it. The dominos were all falling down, and then—Archie Washington stood up in his academic gown, and he stopped it. This, he said, shall not take place. It was already crashing down around him, and he stopped it. The cornered animal, frantic with his wounds—he stopped thrashing and he found a weak spot in the net and he is at large.

Henry sighed at his place. "Poor Ophelia. She's goin' now. Homer, already gone. Ophelia thinks she's got a place at Lincoln. Homer's got something lined up in Hawaii."

"Hawaii?" Ruth said.

"He just slipped out. Nobody's seen him since Sunday. Vanished. Never even came to say good-by to his old purr-fessor." Henry shook his head. "The Hawaiian Islands."

"But," I said, "I thought you had enough support to—"

"Oh, hell, boy, I knew all along it was a long shot. Archie's got too much dope on too many of his enemies. He deals with 'em and he promises them—and if that don't work he bru-ta-lizes them so they got to run."

"I know one man," I said, "who didn't run." And as I looked at the old man, thinking of him on the porch that night, he now seemed so old, old as you ever get. He didn't look at all weak; he just looked so fragile.

"Archie, Archie," he said, talking low, talking to himself, "too many men up top want him in there. Archie's been wheelin' and dealin' for too long in East Texas—and it just didn't matter what kind of case we had. The *case* was there, but the *court* was not in session. All our letters, all our complaints, all our evidence. We cry it out, as *loud* as we can, 'NO, get this devil *off* us.' But the Man says YES, and Archie stays on."

I sat there, waiting. "I thought something was wrong when that criminal-investigator didn't show up to interview me."

Henry looked up absently, and he was so far into his own thoughts that it took him a time to register mine. "Oh, that," he said at last, "hell, the state man had packed his bags and already left that morning."

"Archie bought him off?"

"Oh, *no*, boy. When are you going to learn? Archie got to Anderson and company on the Board of Regents. *They* stopped the show." He slowly, slowly shook his head. "I still thought we had a chance, that old Thaler or Titus might push for us. But I got the verdict yesterday. As far as the state board is concerned, Archie's got another chance." And then he said it, the sentence that made me turn from the table. Henry said in a low whisper, "I wanted to get that man before I died."

I excused myself and walked out into the living room; I stared through the window at the empty front porch. Ruthie and I, we're never going to see the old man again. Devil cancer is eating him alive, and this investigation was keeping up his will to live. But now . . . I have to keep this porch in my mind, this little porch in East Texas, Henry's last stand. That is what I have to remember: he lost the war, but god*dam* that night was one beautiful battle.

"Now come on, Greens, you got to catch that *plane*."

I turned, and here he is, alive, the old man coming into the living room with his arms around his wife and mine. I looked down so's he wouldn't see my eyes, and all I could see was his old red carpet slippers.

I took all the last trash out and stood for a moment staring into the barrel. Straightening up again, turning back to the house, I saw Toast leaning against the corner of the building. He stood in a red short-sleeved shirt and black pants tight on his legs.

He pointed to the Bundy station wagon pulled up in the gravel of the driveway. "You ready to go?"

"You're going to drive us to the airport?"

He nodded.

"But I thought Homer—" I trailed off and stared at him. "I guess by now Homer is strumming his uke on Waikiki."

He looked at me, and then we went in for suitcases. We dumped them into the back, and Ruthie and I got in the front seat with him. Toast said, "He told me to bring you up to the office." He gunned the car by the frogpond, and we zipped on up to the administration building. He parked under the trees. "I'll wait out here."

Barbara Marshall, in the outer office, was erasing on the electric typewriter. For just a second she did not know what to do. She stared at me, at Ruth, and then she said, "You want to see Presydent?"

"Doesn't everyone?"

She smiled at me. "Well, he's on the phone right now."

"He said he wanted us to come on up."

"I think he'll be through shortly." She went back to her erasing.

I stepped to the pigeonholes and cleared out my box. There was a note from Betty McKay—a request for a recommendation—and a blue-mimeo notice about turning in materials. Gladys. I haven't said good-by to Gladys. I left her a little note. Just as I was pushing it into the back of her mailbox, the voice boomed out from behind me.

"Well, you two, come right on in."

He stood in his presidential doorway, and he was radiant. In a white linen suit. Ka-*pow!* The suit made his skin look sanded and stained and polished by hand. Under the fluorescent light and backed by the gold scoop drapes, he stood there in that white suit—the Best Negro in America, the cover of *Time,* Man of the Year.

Before we got settled his phone rang again, and he said, "Oh, *hell,*" and went for it. Someone named Harvey. "Right. Right. Good enough." He is saying words into the phone. His lips move and he is thinking, working, big and packed at his desk. "Okay, now it's real fine, I appreciate your support. And say, boy, don't let it be so long the next time, y'hear?"

He put the phone down on its cradle and then took off his gold-rimmed glasses and rubbed his eyes. Briskly the glasses went back on and he leaned over the desk, smiling. "Abner's got the car to take you into Dallas?"

"Yes."

"I trust you'll have a pleasant flight."

"I trust so."

He crossed his hands on the desktop. Those hands, jutting out from the white cuffs. He said, "I still haven't given up hope you're going to write me a report on your visit here."

"Sorry about that. We meant to get it done before we left. We'll mail it to you."

"Good. Good." He stared at Ruthie for a moment. Goddam, he's going to say something. Then he sat back and put his arms out, stretching the white suit, and he clasped his hands behind his head. "I suspect you two have learned a good deal in these short weeks."

Jesus, man, those balls of yours are made out of something harder than brass.

"You're going straight on back to New York?"

I nodded.

"And you'll be back at Columbia Dramatic Arts in the fall?"

"I expect so." I looked at my hands. "I'll be a teaching assistant."

Ruthie put in, "You should see him in front of a class. I sat in a couple of times."

Archie smiled, looking from her to me. "Oh, son, she's really praised you to the skies this summer. You got yourself a *staunch* supporter."

I started to say, Well, she's told me some kinda interestin' things about you. He said deeply, "How much do they pay, if I may ask, for an instructor at Columbia University?"

I told him.

His eyes went around the ceiling. "We really could just about match that figure."

I do believe he's feelin' me up for a job. Wants to keep the family close. And it'll be nice to have the little lady in callin' distance.

He sighed and patted his palms on his chest.

Ruthie said, "We don't want to keep Abner waiting in the car."

He turned to a pile of paper on his desk. "Take a couple of these. A little reading matter for the trip." He chuckled and handed us each half a dozen papers stapled together.

I read the title: "Bundy University's Sixth-Grade Day."

"I'd like to claim it as my own brainwave. But I just do my readin' in the professional journals—and when I come across something good I see what I can do to bring it to Bundy." He loved those words "bring it to Bundy" and sighed, smiling.

"Yes?"

"My program is in its third year now. Every spring we herd up all the sixth-graders for miles around and bring them here for a day. Just so they can see a college campus. You got to get 'em young."

"I guess you do."

"Oh, the choir sings for them and the band plays. They're free to poke around and go into the gym and the labs, and then we give them a big luncheon in the cafeteria. In the afternoon we show them a movie over in the auditorium. Some Walt Disney movie about Natureland, y'know."

"Yes, I know."

Ruthie looked straight across. "It's a good idea."

"And, my, they write letters back to us about their visit. One little fellow took a shine to me. He wrote that when he grows up he wants to be a college president."

"Well," Ruth said, leafing absently in the report, "we better keep our eyes on him."

Archie glanced up at her sharply, and then at me.

"Where do you suppose would be the best place to send this piece? *Life* or *Look?* Mainly, I want to get attention, And they can send a photographer down."

"Yes, I think you should get attention." I smiled at him. "They definitely should send a photographer down."

He looked at me, straight on, and then he stood, gleaming. "Well, good-by, folks." He shook Ruthie's hand —been nice knowing you—and then he extended his hand to me. "You keep in touch now, y'hear?"

In the clasp, warmth, he had slightly pulled us toward him, and he said, "Yes, something tells me you two are going to make it." It was odd, his saying it like that, and we all looked at each other. An awkward silence of surprise. We were on the edge—on the very edge of something. . . .

I said, "Well, you, anyway, have made it *now*."

I drove it straight into him, that little line, and suddenly all the pressures and torments of these weeks—all the energies of his lifetime, it seemed—clotted in his face, thick blood. His eyes did not blink; his whole head was complete with his victory and its price. In the depths of his will, all the way down in the heart of fire, Archie Washington had salvaged his life. It was an agony of dissonant music, and he listened with ears almost deafened by the roaring of what he had done.

"Yes, son, I always take care of me and mine." The farewell joviality was there, but he couldn't quite make it cover what had just rushed into his face.

A little silence. And Ruthie spoke to Pres. "I suppose, then, the smart people around here are yours."

Archie pretended not to have caught her meaning, and he touched his hearing-aid.

I said, "You heard her."

He turned to me. "Now, boy—"

"I'm not your boy."

All he did was open his office door.

Barbara Marshall looked up from her electric type-writer, erasing again. She smiled without really seeing us, a secretarial reflex.

Archie pulled himself together and said to her, almost easily, "We're going to miss these two round here, aren't we?"

The green box of metal and glass, our station wagon, sped along with us inside. The trees by the side of the road stood out shadowless in the noon. "Uh, I gave you an A in the stupid course."

Toast winked at me. "Well, if you didn't, he'd have knocked her up to A." Then something must have been in my face, for his grin vanished and he turned back, staring at the road. He hunched his shoulders over the wheel.

Bare-chested neighbor, carrying the old woodlike revolver. He stood on the lawn, and I called out and then he said, yes, he said, "Who're you?"

Immanuel Kant asks, Who're you, Beaunorus Green? None of the Above.

As we drove, every once in a while we would break into little fits of speech. It was like everybody was trying not to mention it. I pulled our red pot-light out of my coat pocket and played with it a while and then deposited it on top of the dash, where it rolled and bounced. We heaved down to rock-bottom silence, came up once in a while for vague talky patches, and then at long last, off to the left, I could see the buildings of the Dallas airport, wavy in the heat. I glanced at my watch: two o'clock. We had three-quarters of an hour before our plane. Toast slowed at the speed-limit sign, and we turned into the airport parking lot. He pulled into a space and clicked off the ignition.

Ruth said, "Could we just sit here for a while?"

He turned the key again, and the air-conditioner came back on.

Nothing to say. Everything to say. We sat quietly in the cold machine breath. Finally Toast said, "Flip open that old glove compartment."

I did. A pint of whisky, two-thirds full.

"Help yourself," he said.

I unscrewed the cap, took a jolt, and handed the bottle to Ruth. She drank, coughed, and passed it on. After he drank, Toast said, "You got to see one thing. He—well, he just hates himself when he goes crazy. It means they got him. Every time he goes crazy it just means they got him. I know."

I waited, and then to the air-conditioner I said, low, "I saw what happened, man. He tried to kill Henry."

"I heard about it." Toast jerkily turned and looked out the window at a trio of businessmen, white and dapper, crossing through the parking lot.

"Give me another belt," I said. "I better tell you that little story."

Toast kept looking at the businessmen as he handed the bottle, turning, holding it out. "Let's not talk about it."

"Loyal to him. Loyal to the end. I saw him try to *kill* Henry. Toast, look at me."

His head turned, and his eyes were quick.

"Look, man, I tell you the truth. They were standing there, a yard apart. Henry carries on all the time. A big talker. Right? But I saw him on the porch. In his pajamas. Barefoot." My hand reached up to my forehead. My fingers prowled and pressed, above my eyes. "I saw it all—there."

Toast stammered, "He—he—Poppa—"

"Don't you see? They *did* get him. Every time the Man says, 'Yes, this is the way you will do it,' Archie has to go along. And he pays for that. He *pays*. He just can't keep his head together any more." I was firmly repeating Henry's lesson for the black man, but I suddenly had to stop, stop cold, because Toast's eyes were all over me. That look of his, total distrust.

Do not look at me that way, brother.

I dropped my hands to my lap. "I guess you're thinking the Man says yes to Beaunorus Green."

"Oh—well, I don't say that."

"Toast, don't fool with me."

He waited a moment before hunching himself slowly forward over the wheel. "I must admit, when I heard that 'Stanford, Phi Beta Kappa,' well, that is quite a different thing." He paused again to measure his words. "Hell, I would like to be a success. Sure. I got to be honest with myself and say I know I want a lot of the Man's things. I know that." He shook his head. "But I know there is something else, and it is very beautiful, and I have to be ready to die to protect it."

We were very close, very far. He pulled in a little breath, and I thought he was going to go on. He was not. So we just sat with it there, the intimacy and the distance.

The silence is an unheard buzz.

Into it I said, "You asked me one night why I came down here."

He nodded.

"I guess I know now." I took another drink. "Jesus, though, we really ought to turn around and drive back there. We ought to face him together. Get him *out* of there."

Now Toast went back into his sharp little half-embarrassed smile. "Oh, come on."

"Well, I'm cutting out, but you are stuck here and you are up to your neck. You are up to your hair in it." I glanced up sharply, and his eyes darted away from mine. "Toast, don't you see?"

At last he shrugged. "You're not tellin' me anything. I put those blank bullets in his gun."

I looked all over his face.

He took my eyes, nodding, then glanced away again.

At length Ruthie said, "Why didn't you just take the bullets out?"

"Take them out?" Toast sighed into his helpless little laugh. "Shit, if he looked in there and saw somebody emptied his gun, he'd kill with his bare hands. He'd kill *her*—he'd think she emptied it." He looked, explaining, to us. "I had to make him think it was loaded."

"So," I said, "Henry knew those bullets were blanks."

A little smile groped its way onto his face. "No, Henry did not exactly know. I told him that I was thinking about putting in the blanks. But he didn't know for *positive* they was there. He told me yesterday—he said that at the time, on his porch that night, he surely did *hope* they was blanks."

I shook my head. "You know that. You had to put blank cartridges in his gun, to keep him from killing somebody. You know that—"

He twisted in his seat. "Oh, sometimes I don't know what I think."

I sat back and I could feel the whisky.

He gently touched his face. "I wonder if you ever noticed the back of the house?" He smiled sadly. "We had a little fire one night. Three winters ago. Father, he had this can of kerosene and he was going after some crazy old nightmare and—" The fingers groped on his chin and dropped onto the wheel. "I could've died." He looked at me blankly. "He loves me."

We sat in silence.

"And that is one remarkable thing. He got me once this summer—it was when she was returning his call from the hospital. I went up on the roof in the morning, that's where he sits. And we came on down together from the roof and she was on the line. Poppa and I was goin' in by the hall coat closet. And he stop and the hospital was waitin' but he put his hands on my head. I didn't know what he was up to, but when we were standing there I saw what it was. He was blessing me." Toast felt around with little irrelevant motions on top of his head. He was feeling for his father's hands.

I felt for them. "Oh, Toast."

"Hell, that's another thing. I don't mind bein' called Toast. That 'Abner' isn't a beautiful name itself."

"No."

"And I was always called '*Thumb*suckin' Abner.' " He looked over at Ruth. "Would you believe it—I sucked my thumb until I was thirteen."

The Little One smiled faintly, her eyes on his face. Her soft little guessing smile.

"I have just had one hell of a time comin' up." He took the bottle and he drank.

And so we just sat there again. When after a time he passed the bottle back to me I said, "I don't want to get drunk. I mean, I do, but I guess I'd better not."

"Well, sometimes it's necessary."

"We got to take the plane."

He shifted in his seat. "Now, there's a time when it's

not exactly necessary. But it's surely amusing." He smiled. "You must of flew a lot of times, across the Atlantic Ocean and all. Me, I've been on a plane three times—and I was blind twice and stoned once."

I took the bottle. There was only one shot left. I looked at him. He has to drive this school car back. I handed the bottle over to Ruthie, and my girl finished it. She'd sleep on the plane. I shook myself. "Well, it's that way." I said it again, mumbling to myself. "Whatever it is." I blurted, "Toast, man, I can't tell you how I feel."

He let out the little pocket of air in his mouth.

"Next summer," I said, "we want you up with us. Promise us that."

He smiled, eyes down. "Okay."

"You've never been to New York?"

"No."

"It's something."

We sat for several minutes in the car, watching people moving through the parking lot, coming happily off planes, going onto them. Finally I looked at my watch. "It's about that time."

"Okay." He drummed a little beat on the wheel. "New York City. Man, I would like to check that out."

"So come with us now."

"Now?" He looked at me. Then, softly: "No, I can't come now."

"The crisis is over."

"Oh man," he said, "the crisis is never over down here." He looked from me to Ruth and then out the front window. "But I do plan on comin' to visit you." He smiled. "Yeah, I can see it." He played with it a bit in his mind, then caught himself. "Hey, let's get going. I can think about all that while I'm drivin' home."